The
Water
and
The Flame

Books by Cheryl Lafferty Eckl

Personal Growth & Transformation

A Beautiful Death:
Keeping the Promise of Love

A Beautiful Grief:
Reflections on Letting Go

The LIGHT Process:
Living on the Razor's Edge of Change

Wise Inner Counselor Books
Reflections on Being Your True Self in Any Situation
Reflections on Doing Your Great Work in Any Occupation
Reflections on Ineffable Love: from loss through grief to joy

Poetry for Inspiration & Beauty

Poetics of Soul & Fire

Bridge to the Otherworld

Idylls from the Garden of Spiritual Delights & Healing

Sparks of Celtic Mystery:
soul poems from Éire

A Beautiful Joy: Reunion with the Beloved
Through Transfiguring Love

Twin Flames Romance Novels

The Weaving:
A Novel of Twin Flames Through Time

Twin Flames of Éire Trilogy
The Ancients and The Call
The Water and The Flame
The Mystics and The Mystery

The Water and The Flame

Twin Flames of Éire Trilogy - Book Two

Cheryl Lafferty Eckl

FLYING CRANE PRESS

THE WATER AND THE FLAME:
TWIN FLAMES OF ÉIRE TRILOGY - BOOK TWO
© 2020, 2021, 2022 by Cheryl J. Eckl, LLC
Excerpt from *The Mystics and The Mystery* © 2020, 2022 by Cheryl J. Eckl, LLC

Published by Flying Crane Press, Livingston, Montana 59047
Cheryl@CherylEckl.com | www.CherylEckl.com

Cover photo - Philip Thurston, thurstonphoto.com, used with permission.

This is a work of fiction. Names, characters, places, and incidents either are the product of the author's imagination or are used fictitiously, and any resemblance to actual persons, living or dead, business establishments, events, or locales is entirely coincidental.

Library of Congress Control Number: 2020907204
ISBN: 978-1-7346450-2-6 (paperback)
ISBN: 978-1-7346450-7-1 (e-book)

Printed in the United States of America

Dear Reader,

When my thoughts turn to Ireland, the first image that comes to mind is of water—of wild, dramatic waves hurling themselves against primordial cliffs. Or thousands of peaceful wells—all reputed to be openings into the body of the Goddess Ériu, who gave her name and spirit to the Emerald Island.

Then I think of flames, like the cozy turf fires that have warmed me body and soul on cold Irish days and nights. Or the double bonfires of *Bealtaine*, which the Celts have lit for centuries on May Day Eve to purge winter's gloom and welcome summer's season of good fortune, courtship, and fertility.

Fire is essential in this land where North Atlantic summers can feel very short. And where, regardless of season, the flame of freedom burns bright in Celtic hearts who know in the core of their being they are free.

Now, in *The Water and The Flame*, twin souls Sarah and Kevin have merged with their past-life druid selves, Alana and Ah-Lahn. As a result, one of the Ancients, the powerful Ascended Master Saint Germain, has assigned them a commission to help other pairs of twin flames—those created in the beginning as a single, scintillating ovoid of light—who must balance their own karma and permanently unite in Divine Love.

But when and how that challenge will unfold, they do not know. Not yet. Perhaps Glenna Morrissey, the fiery young Broadway actress whose story this is will prove to be one of those twin flames.

As Sarah's memories turn to this woman she met several years ago, she cannot know how intricately their pasts are intertwined or how important they and their beloveds will become to each other in a future that is fast approaching.

Won't you to stoke your own inner fires now, and join me as we discover how the water and flame of Éire transform Glenna and her soul's twin, Rory, on the adventure of love and passion that has been lifetimes in the making for them and their Friends of Ancient Wisdom.

Le gach dea-ghuí (With all good wishes), Cheryl Lafferty Eckl

P. S. You will find a Glossary and Irish language Pronunciation Guide at the back of the book, plus a few notes about the Ancients.

Prologue

A driving rain battered Sarah's bedroom window. Thunder crashed and lightning illumined the trees bending precipitously outside the spacious town home she shared with her husband, Kevin.

The twin babies in her womb stirred. Their movements were still only tiny flutters and bubbles in her belly, but tonight she sensed they were as uneasy as she, shuddering alone in the house.

Kevin was stuck in Manhattan. He had taken the train into the city to pick up a rare book for Fibonacci's Esoteric Bookstore, where he worked. A sudden delay on the Long Island Railroad had stranded thousands of commuters, so he had stayed at his buddy Mark's downtown apartment.

This was the first night in almost a year that Sarah and Kevin had been apart. Ever since taking the courageous step of merging their present consciousness with their past attainment as the first-century Irish druids Alana and Ah-Lahn, they had spent nearly every minute together.

And when they were not physically in each other's company, they each had the clear awareness of the other as a tangible presence in their heart. The silver cord that linked them soul to soul was stronger than ever. The unity of love they shared was a miracle that still amazed them.

In reality, they did not need phone calls or texts to communicate. Their spiritual teacher, F. M. Bellamarre, who often appeared to them in his ascended-master presence as Saint Germain, had encouraged them to practice the telepathy they had perfected as priest and priestess in the Temple of the One Light on Atlantis.

The more they practiced, the more proficient they became. So that now, when they wanted to connect, one of them simply beamed, "I am here," and the other answered, "And I."

Tonight, however, they had opted for a phone call because Kevin was staying with a friend.

"Are you sure you're okay, Hon?" Kevin wanted to know. "I don't like being away from you when it's storming."

"I'll be fine," said Sarah with a lilt in her voice that lightened her husband's heart. "And if I need you, I'll send you a signal."

She stroked the silky black mini-panther cat and adolescent wire-haired wolfhound who were keeping her company. "Sprite and Hero are here and I feel strong. You keep yourself safe and don't worry."

Kevin was determined not to be anxious about the safety of his family. Instead, he affirmed in his heart and soul that Sarah would carry her babies to term. Neither husband nor wife dared imagine the consequences of a third miscarriage.

Besides, Saint Germain had assured them that this pregnancy was under his protection. If an ascended master said they were safe, that was the truth. They must simply take precautions to ensure the family's health and safety.

So far, all signs were positive. Sarah had passed the pivotal four-month mark of her pregnancy. She was resting as directed and was generally more at peace than Kevin had ever known her to be. And she was writing. The creative flow of new life growing in her womb seemed to stimulate inspiration. As the babies quickened, so did her imagination.

Kevin hoped she would sleep tonight, though he knew that when the muse kindled a creative spark she would lose all sense of time, often writing far into the night.

His pal Mark had already gone to bed, so he stretched out on his buddy's none-too-comfortable sofa, said a prayer for his wife and unborn children, and drifted off to sleep.

Sarah couldn't relax, but the storm wasn't the problem. The front was moving through, lessening into a pleasant April shower, perfectly in time to welcome tomorrow's first day of May. Rather than disturbing her, this gentler rain created a soothing atmosphere that reminded her of the misty, soft days of Ireland.

She eased out of bed, trying not to wake her pets who were curled up on Kevin's side of the bed. However, instantly sensing the possibility of a nighttime snack, Hero and Sprite woke up and eagerly accompanied Sarah to the kitchen. She made herself some chamomile tea to go with the scones she'd been craving all evening and found treats for the fur kids.

Once they were all fed, she returned to her bedroom where inspiration often emerged. The babies were quiet in her womb. The dog and cat settled themselves on the bed and went peacefully back to sleep.

Sarah propped herself up on a half-dozen pillows, her journal on her lap. Allowing her imagination to glide into the rain's steady sound, she suddenly felt it—that wonderful surge of inspiration she longed for, but could not force. Her muse was stirring. The spirit of Éire was calling.

She ran her hand over the fine linens she had brought from Ireland and cast her mind back to winter solstice of last year. The day her babies were conceived.

In a gesture that had become second nature, she rested her hands over her belly where her twins were resting quietly and remembered those days of new life. She had known almost immediately that she was pregnant. In her previous pregnancies, she had felt a swirling, spiraling energy in her womb and breasts, though never so powerfully as this.

As her meditation intensified, she was now acutely aware of the spiraling energy building within her, becoming more dynamic, as if the energy were also outside of her, swirling around her body.

She felt herself being enveloped in a sensation of such intense love that she knew was more than affection for her unborn children. Here was the passion of souls united in a work that must be accomplished by twin flames on behalf of other soul pairs.

Exactly as Saint Germain had promised.

He had explained that she and Kevin would be instruments of soul liberation for many other souls who were being primed to discover the True Self each one must become to support their reunion as twin flames.

Basking in the vibration of this commission, Sarah snuggled deeper under the covers and let her imagination flow freely. She was surprised that her thoughts turned to Glenna, the young woman she had begun writing about nearly eight years earlier.

While Sarah was still working as a marketing writer for powerful New York politician A. B. Ryan, her co-worker Debbie had introduced her to an actress friend named Glenna Morrissey.

The two young women had felt an immediate connection, and being introduced to Glenna had sparked Sarah's imagination. She wrote a brief sketch about her new acquaintance, which she shared with Kevin when they first met years ago. For some reason, a full story had never gelled.

Now she found herself wondering about Glenna. What was she doing these days? Was she still acting or had life sent her in a different direction? Had she ever visited Ireland as she had wanted?

The voice of Sarah's inner wisdom answered:

Pay attention. There is alchemy afoot on behalf of twin flames.
Your next commission from Saint Germain begins tonight.

Enfolded in the aura of inspiration, Sarah was certain that she and Glenna had known each other in ancient Ireland, though she wasn't sure of their relationship. Perhaps they had both known Debbie, who had been embodied as Alana's aunt, the seer and healer Dearbhla.

"Should I pursue the connection with Glenna?" Sarah wondered aloud to her soundly snoozing pets.

Unseen spirit helpers agreed and set the stage for that connection. Although the storm had picked up again, the sound Sarah heard as she drifted off to sleep was no longer rain drumming on her roof.

Instead, she was hearing the thunderous applause of a standing ovation. For tonight was the closing performance of a smash Broadway musical revival where Glenna Morrissey was taking another curtain call with the cast that had been her theatre family for the past twelve months.

One

The sold-out audience clapped and cheered, hooted, stomped and whistled in the loudest, longest standing ovation Glenna Morrissey and her company had ever received. Closing nights were always exciting. This one was spectacular.

Tonight's performance had been one of those shows that every actor lives for. When you can do no wrong. When every member of the cast has brought their A-game to the stage. When every joke gets a laugh, every sad song evokes tears, and every big chorus number is a show-stopper.

The glory of success whooshed up Glenna's spine and out the top of her head like fireworks. Looking left and right at her fellow actors as they stood hand-in-hand across the stage receiving the applause they had earned, she knew her blue eyes flashed with the same joy, her face registered the same wide grin as theirs.

However fleeting those emotions might be when the applause stopped and they all transformed back into every-day mortals, this was a great night.

The year-long run had been a blessing of steady work. Glenna had even received a Tony Award nomination for her role as the leading lady's best friend.

Winning would have been the cherry on top of this sundae of a show. She almost didn't mind losing to her friend Cassie, who had always been favored to win for Supporting Actress in her own musical that was still playing across the street in Manhattan's theatre district.

Almost.

Glenna had tried to be gracious, but even now, as the magnificent, gold velvet stage curtain descended and the house lights came up, she had to admit she was bitter about the loss. And more than a little worried about her future.

What if tonight is as good at it gets? she thought as she changed into street clothes and brushed her dark blonde hair into long, casual waves. Had she already peaked at the age of twenty-six? Would she ever get such a terrific part again?

Competition was fierce in New York, and hopeful ingenues were moving to the city from every corner of the world. Being cast was more difficult than ever, in part because so many Hollywood celebrities were now taking their turn on the stage. That didn't seem fair to Glenna, but there was nothing she could do about it.

Worse still, an actor with principles was likely to be overlooked in favor of one who would do anything to land a part. To a certain extent, show business had always been that way. But Glenna and her friends agreed that, these days, they had to be more wary of the unscrupulous.

Fortunately, her hard work at regular dance classes, acting work-shops, and voice lessons had payed off. Her notices were the best of her career, and her agent, Mel, was busy lining up a score of auditions for the coming season. Only last week he had looked her straight in the eye and made her promise to stay positive.

"Mel says I should be encouraged, so I will be," she declared to her image in the dressing room mirror.

"C'mon, Glenna, the party's starting!" called her co-star, Patsy, urging her to the bar down the street where actors had gathered for decades to celebrate their successes and commiserate over their status as newly unemployed.

Patsy had been Tony-nominated for her sparkling portrayal of their show's leading lady. She had lost out to Lenore, Cassie's co-star, who won her second Tony in as many years. Glenna was astounded that Patsy seemed honestly not to care.

"I don't do this for the awards," she had answered Glenna's undis-guised amazement at her nonchalance. "Just being on that stage night after night is reward enough for me, don't you agree?"

Glenna didn't agree, though she wouldn't say so.

She'd been aiming for a Tony since she was five years old. She remembered the day well. She'd been tap dancing on the tile floor in her parents' kitchen. "I'm going to be a famous actress!" she had declared to her mother—and she had never given up on that dream.

But was that dream giving up on her? She dared not consider the possibility. Not when a cast party beckoned.

For a few hours she would celebrate with her fellow players. After tonight they would all be going their separate ways.

The laughter and the tears would be genuine, as they always were. Impermanence was simply part of the deal of living the actor's life. Many of her friends thrived on the uncertainty.

She could only wish that she did.

Libations were flowing freely by the time Glenna walked through the bar's heavy oak doors. At least for tonight, all the cast and crew were friends again, and the inevitable backstage squabbles that made a company operate like a typically human family were forgotten.

She sang heartfelt songs of farewell with her pals. As more than a few of them were Irish, "The Parting Glass" rang out from full throats and teary eyes. You had to have a heart of stone not to feel the emotional tug of that melody and those words, thought Glenna as she joined in.

> But since it falls unto my lot
> That I should rise and you should not,
> I'll gently rise and I'll softly call
> Good night and joy be to you all,
> Good night and joy be to you all.

The singers were gearing up for another round of boisterous tunes when who should stride in, but the famous theatrical producer, Roland Newhouse. Heads turned and conversation hushed.

Excitement and speculation about who might be getting good news rippled through the company. However, when Newhouse approached

Glenna, her pals turned back with a shrug, and conversation resumed. Tonight the luck was hers, not theirs.

Newhouse was dressed in a thousand-dollar cashmere overcoat. Nothing unusual there. What was different (he was notoriously wary of being upstaged) was that he was accompanied by an even more expensively dressed man whose tall stature and full head of silver hair gave him an air of powerful self-importance.

Glenna did not know this second person, although there was something oddly familiar and troubling about his expression. His dark, cobalt eyes seemed to flash at her with a jolt of surprise. However, he quickly changed his demeanor to one of intense interest, as if he knew something about her that he would exploit if given a chance.

Newhouse spoke first. "Good evening, Ms. Morrissey. May we have a word?"

"Of course. How nice to see you, Mr. Newhouse. I didn't think you frequented noisy cast parties."

"I usually don't, but I was told you would be here. I wanted to be the first in what I'm sure will be a long line of producers and directors vying for your considerable talents in their next shows. Right, A. B.?"

The man only raised his eyebrows and nodded.

"Let me present A. B. Ryan, my partner in an exciting new theatrical venture. I've told him that securing you as our leading lady guarantees the show's success."

In the space of an in-breath Glenna felt herself start to extend her hand to A. B. and then draw back from touching him. Instead, she returned his nod and addressed Newhouse, "You flatter me, sir."

"No, indeed," he enthused. "Not after reading reviews like this." He pulled a clipping from his coat pocket, puffed out his chest, and read aloud with stentorian emphasis:

Ms. Morrissey's performance is no mere revival. There is a freshness to her talent we have not seen in the parade of ingenues that have graced our Broadway stages of late. She sings like a nightingale and dances like a fiery gypsy. *Brava!* Ms. Morrissey.

With the assertiveness of a skilled salesman, Newhouse carried on. "I have it on good authority that your agent is already fielding a number of inquiries about your availability. I want to be your first consideration. Our new show is a guaranteed Tony for you, my girl. It's got everything. Great songs, dancing, drama, comedy. Hollywood people are already asking about the rights to produce the movie."

Gesturing to A. B., whose face was enigmatic, he declared, "My colleague is ready to fund the production. Are you interested?"

"Obviously, yes," answered Glenna. Any wariness about A. B. Ryan evaporated in Newhouse's enthusiasm. "To tell you the truth, after not winning the Tony I wasn't sure that my career hadn't already peaked."

"Nonsense, my girl. You're just getting started. Stick with us and we'll make you a star the likes of which you've never imagined. I'm off to Boston tomorrow, but I'd like to see you in my office next Friday. Shall we say 11:00 a.m.?"

"Thank you, yes, that will be wonderful." Glenna tried not to gush. "I look forward to our discussion, Mr. Newhouse."

He ostentatiously kissed her hand and breezed out, obsequiously ushering A. B. Ryan through the doorway before him. That imposing personage had not said a word to Glenna, only nodding once more as if his acknowledgment were sufficient to seal the deal.

Her friend Patsy thought Roland Newhouse looked like the cat who'd just swallowed the canary. But who, she wondered, was the bird?

"What did they want?" she demanded of Glenna, whose clear blue eyes followed the producers out the door.

"To make me a star," she said dreamily.

"Well, be careful what that stardom might cost you," Patsy warned. "You know what they say about the Newhouse casting couch."

"I'm not worried," said Glenna. "I know he's got a reputation, but isn't that with the newbies? I'm an established actress, and Mel will look out for me."

"I hope so," said Patsy. "I'd hate for you to be taken advantage of by him or his partner. Are you sure his show is the real deal?"

Suddenly feeling annoyed that her friend would question her good luck, Glenna shrugged and answered brusquely. "Guess we'll find out, won't we? Anyway, I'm going home now. See you later."

Gathering up her coat and bag, she quickly made the rounds of good-bye hugs and air kisses with her fellow actors and hurried across the street to catch the subway to her tiny apartment in Brooklyn.

Once Glenna got home, she fell quickly into bed where she dreamed of glowing reviews from all the New York papers, bouquets of scarlet roses, multiple curtain calls, and the well-deserved Tony Award, which, of course, she would graciously accept with all due humility and poise.

She watched as her image was projected onto enormous movie screens around the world in the film version of the role that, naturally, would be hers. Surely an Oscar would follow.

The dream's only puzzling image, which she completely forgot upon waking, was of A. B. Ryan standing like a spectre with his face obscured in an odd sort of fog or mist.

Two

Morning brought a radically different dream from visions of awards and accolades. Glenna awoke with hornets buzzing around her head, annoying her with their persistent noise. Abruptly, the buzzing ceased, but now the hornets were pounding on her apartment door.

"Go away, you stupid bugs!" she moaned. Waving her hands at imaginary insects, she propelled herself out of bed, only marginally aware that her clock read 11:30 a.m.

"Hold on, I'm coming!" she shouted at the source of the noise and groaned as a wave of nausea greeted her too-vigorous arising.

She threw on a cardigan over the sweatpants and T-shirt she had worn to bed the night before, and opened the door to a wiry teenager dressed as a uniformed courier. His eyes bugged out at her bedraggled appearance.

"Glenna Morrissey?"

"Yes."

"Sign here." He pointed to an electronic pad, handed her a registered letter, and hurriedly made his escape down the hallway.

"What in the world?" said Glenna aloud, carefully closing the door to minimize the pain of a dozen tiny Rockettes who were emphatically executing a precision kick-line in her head.

Dragging her hand through her hair, she squinted at the name on the return address. "I don't know anybody named Breathnach in Galway, Ireland. This must be a mistake."

The room began to sway around her.

"Ooph," she groaned through the fog of too many glasses of last night's celebratory champagne. She needed strong black tea and she needed it now. Putting on the kettle, she pulled up a bar stool at her kitchen counter and carefully opened the letter. The message inside nearly knocked her off her precarious perch.

Dear Ms. Glenna Morrissey,

I am authorized by my late client, Mrs. Caroline Rooney, to send you the enclosed check for three thousand euros and a one-way plane ticket to Shannon Airport in County Clare, Ireland.

Mrs. Rooney was the wife of your father's third cousin, Seamus. The Rooneys had no children of their own and died owning few possessions. However, they had accumulated considerable savings which they willed should be divided amongst their distant relations, of whom you are the last to be contacted.

The only requirement is that you use the one-way plane ticket as-is within two weeks of your receipt, which date will have been duly noted by the courier service.

Once in Ireland, you may spend some of the euros to purchase a return ticket, or you may use them all for an extended stay in our fair country. Whether you choose to remain or return is up to you.

The Rooneys lived in Dingle and would have been delighted to welcome you to their home. Perhaps you will visit the area.

Feel free to contact my office if you have any questions about this gift.

Congratulations and best wishes,
(signed) Gerald H. Breathnach, Esq.

"This can't be happening!" Glenna exclaimed as the kettle whistled for her attention. After mechanically making her pot of tea and being careful not to move her head abruptly, she shuffled over to her tiny, two-person dining table and eased onto a cushioned chair to read the letter again.

"I don't believe this!" she repeated to her empty apartment. Here in her hand was a near exact copy of the letter that a friend's friend, that novelist, Sarah-something, had invented about her years ago.

At least she'd assumed that Sarah had invented it when the two had laughed together over lunch at the restaurant in Grand Central Station at the impossibility of such a thing happening.

That was the last time they had seen each other. Now she wondered—did Sarah have a crystal ball or merely a fertile imagination? Whatever the source, she'd better track down this woman and get to the bottom of the coincidence that had worsened her headache.

With her eyes partially shut against the glare of the stubbornly cheerful morning sun that streamed into her apartment, Glenna scrolled through the contacts on her phone, found what she hoped was still Sarah's number, and hit CALL.

After what seemed like endless rings, a woman answered. She sounded tired.

"Hello?"

"Is this Sarah Callahan?"

"MacCauley, now—but, yes. Who's this?"

"This is Glenna Morrissey. I don't know if you remember me . . . "

"Oh, my God, Glenna! You've been on my mind since last night. I wanted to call you today, but I couldn't find your number. I'm so glad you found me. I had such a strong prompting to connect with you. I hope nothing's wrong."

"I'm not sure," answered Glenna with a silent command to her stomach to stop lurching. "I can hardly believe what's just happened. I hope you can explain it. I think I'm going crazy."

"Tell me," said Sarah. She moved to her sofa and plugged in her headset. She'd been hoping to hear from Kevin saying that he was coming home. If he communicated now, she hoped he would tune in that she was on an important call.

Last night her voice of inner wisdom had said to pay attention— that their next commission was beginning. Was this the first step?

Glenna's voice brought Sarah out of her reverie. "Do you remember that imaginary letter you wrote years ago about me inheriting money and a plane ticket to Ireland?" she asked.

"Yes, why?"

"Where did you get that information? Was there something about me on the Internet? Did you talk to my family?"

"No. I compose from inspiration. I can only write what my muse tells me or shows me as an image. That's where that letter came from. Why?"

"You may not believe this. I'm not sure I do. But I'm sitting here with that exact letter in my hand. It arrived this morning by special courier from an attorney named Breathnach in Galway, Ireland."

"The exact wording? From the same person?"

"Yes!" Glenna was on the verge of tears. "Sarah, how is this possible? Did you give that little story to anybody? What about your husband? Would he have told a theatre-goer who decided to send me a copy as a joke?"

"No. Kevin doesn't repeat anything that's not his to share. I read him the letter when we first met, but I kept the only copy. When I was at a writer's retreat in Ireland last year I did read the letter to a few other participants when we were exchanging samples of our work, but nobody was taking notes and I didn't use your name. At the time I wondered why. Now I'm glad."

"Me, too!" Glenna blew out a breath. "Somehow I know this is not a mistake or a prank. The letterhead appears official. The return address looks authentic. A real courier delivered the envelope.

"I remember thinking when you showed me the bits of story you were working on that you had an uncanny ability to make fiction feel very real. It wasn't until later that I remembered my father having mentioned a distant cousin named Seamus, but I knew nothing about him. I suspect my father didn't either. Otherwise, he might have contacted the Rooneys to ask if I could visit them.

"My parents knew I longed to go to Ireland. They wanted to send me, but couldn't afford the expense. Then my acting career made foreign travel impractical."

Sarah swallowed hard, suddenly remembering a couple of similar situations. Was her muse able to see into the future? She knew that Alana had developed considerable skill as a seer. Perhaps she had already been exhibiting glimmers of that ability years ago, long before she took off to Ireland for the writer's retreat where she had dreamed about her remarkable past life as a druidess.

"You know, I think my muse may, indeed, have a crystal ball and, occasionally, her prophecies just pop into something I'm writing. I had a similar experience last summer."

"Really?"

"Yes. Before I went to Ireland, I had been journaling about what it would be like to write there. A few days later, I got an email announcing a writer's retreat in County Wicklow. At the same time, Kevin and I weren't getting along, so I took a chance and flew to Dublin."

"That's amazing," said Glenna.

"I know," agreed Sarah. "Even more amazing is that I recently found a journal entry I made over a year ago about getting pregnant at winter solstice. And I did!"

"You're pregnant?"

"Yes, with twins, if you can believe that."

"I can't imagine," said Glenna. Nor did she want to. Not with her acting career about to take off. "So, were you tuning into future events about my life or did your muse make them happen?" Glenna's strong black tea had cleared her head enough to ask the key question.

"I'm sure it's only occasional attunement with a future possibility," said Sarah. "I cannot imagine having the power to make my imagination come to life, nor would I want to. That is not something the Universe would condone—no matter how prescient my muse might be."

"I'm relieved to hear that," said Glenna.

Sarah continued, "It is odd, though, that you would get this letter so many years after I wrote the same words in a bit of story that I never finished."

"Well, do me a favor, and don't write anything else about me unless I ask you to, okay?" Glenna laughed, though from the edge in her voice, they both knew she wasn't joking.

"Oh, don't worry," answered Sarah. "In fact, I'm going to be very careful about what I write in my journal. I don't want my muse giving the Universe any big ideas. I'm already getting two babies . . ." She nearly added, "to replace the ones I lost," but decided Glenna didn't need to know that part of her personal story.

Both women laughed, more congenially this time. And Sarah was curious.

"Tell me—and I promise not to write a word about this—what are you going to do? Will you accept the offer and go to Ireland? Are you free to do that?"

"Amazingly, I am," said Glenna. "And I can't help feeling the Universe is being totally unfair to send me this letter. The Broadway musical revival I was in closed last night . . . "

"Oh, you're still acting!" Sarah enthused. "I'm happy to hear that. I could tell when we first met that you were passionate about your career. I hope it's going well for you."

"So far I feel like I've been making progress, although now that my show just closed, I'm out of a job again."

"I guess that's the way it works for professional actors, isn't it?" inquired Sarah.

"It is. Some people get used to it. I never have. I always worry that I'll never work again, and I can't help feeling bitter this time that I didn't receive the notice I should have."

Having grown up with a mother whom her father called his "Celtic Warrior Wife" and a brother who shared their mother's temperament, Sarah recognized an Irish temper when it was about to flare. In such cases, the less said, the better.

She was grateful to feel Glenna pause before she spoke again.

"Anyway, at last night's cast party I got an incredible offer from Roland Newhouse, a famous Broadway producer. He wants me to star in a new show he's developing. He's got the funding for it and everything. I'm supposed to meet with him this coming week."

"That's great," said Sarah, pleased to respond supportively. "Seems like the Universe is on your side after all."

"It would appear so," said Glenna. "But, frankly, I'm suspicious. I thought I was going to win a Tony, then I didn't. I'd been wondering if my career had peaked, then I get this offer for a starring role. I've always wanted to go to Ireland, and now both money and a plane ticket have landed in my lap.

"Here I am on the threshold of enormous success, and out of the blue I'm sent an opportunity to travel, but with a timeline. It seems so unfair! Maybe you could pull out your muse's crystal ball and write me a decision. What do you think I should do?"

"I haven't a clue," answered Sarah firmly, "and I certainly won't be poking around in the ethers for one. It does occur to me, however, that perhaps some unseen helpers are actually looking out for you. Making a decision may not be that difficult. Tell me, where do you do your best thinking?"

"In museums and art galleries," Glenna answered without hesitation.

"That's where I think you should go," said Sarah. "Give yourself the afternoon. Go look at beautiful images. Take your notebook and jot down any inspirations that come to you. I wouldn't dare write anything for you, but I'm quite sure you can make notes for yourself."

"That's a great idea!" agreed Glenna. "I can't tell you how relieved I am. I don't feel crazy now. I have no idea how things are going to work out, but I have a feeling maybe they will."

"So do I," said Sarah. "And please let me know what happens. I'll be eager to hear about your adventures, wherever they take you." And were those adventures of Glenna's going to take her back in time? Sarah wondered as a glimmer of their past associations twinkled in her own recollections. She decided to encourage their contact further.

"When you get back, if you don't mind taking a little jaunt out to Long Island, you and I could meet at this delightful coffee shop called Fibonacci's. I've connected with some wonderful people there whom I think you'd enjoy. In fact, if you come out, I'll ask Debbie to join us. Now that neither of us works for A. B. Ryan, we . . . "

"My God, I forgot you both worked for him," Glenna interrupted. "This whole saga gets stranger and stranger."

"How so?" Sarah could hear anxiety building again in her voice.

"A. B. Ryan was with that producer, Newhouse, last night. I'd never met the man, but for a second he looked at me as if he'd seen a ghost. You know him. Any idea why he would react that way?"

"I couldn't say." Sarah paused. Actually, she had a very strong sense of why A. B. Ryan would be surprised to see Glenna. She dared not voice her suspicion, but felt she should warn her friend of old—as she was becoming quite sure they were to each other.

"Let me caution you about getting involved in any scheme he's a part of. I have my reasons for believing he is not to be trusted. Newhouse may be okay, but I think you should be very careful of A. B. Ryan. I can't tell you exactly why right now, but I can say that the man is not what he purports to be."

Sarah heard Glenna go silent on the other end of the line. "Do you have a good agent?" she ventured.

"I do, one of the best." Glenna bristled at the question. She could trust Mel with her life. He'd never steered her wrong. In fact, he looked out for her as he would his own daughter.

Sarah continued carefully. "You might want to have him do some checking for you—just to make sure you're not being led into a venture that is not in your best interest—personally or professionally."

She felt another flash of resistance shiver across the phone line.

"Huh!" said Glenna, remembering how Patsy had also warned her. "You're the second person to say that." She was quiet for a moment.

Sarah waited, silently beaming light and love to this friend of ages past. She was relieved when Glenna took another deep breath.

"Since I seem to be getting messages from the Universe through people I want to trust, I suppose I should listen." Then she chuckled at herself. "But I don't want to. I like the idea of being a star."

"I understand," said Sarah gently. "I still dream of being a famous novelist. These babies may have other plans. I have no idea. That's a future that has to make itself known in its own time."

"Isn't that the way?" agreed Glenna—amazed that she would find herself opening up to a woman she barely knew. Except, right now, she felt a flicker of some deeper recognition between them.

"Well, I'd better let you go. Thanks a lot, Sarah. You've really helped me. I'll be in touch."

"You're welcome, Glenna. I'm glad you found me today. I know our reconnecting is important. I look forward to learning why."

Three

Forty minutes later, after another cup of tea, a piece of avocado toast, and a hurried shower, Glenna was out the door and on the subway to the Guggenheim Museum—one place where she knew she could clear her mind. Something about the building's spiral design had an almost magical affect on her entire being.

She never tired of the Impressionist and Post-Impressionist works that were part of the museum's permanent collection. Today Édouard Manet's *Devant le Glace* and Claude Monet's *Le Palais Ducal vu de Saint-Georges Majeur* caught her particular attention.

She could easily imagine herself as the young courtesan gazing at her reflection in the mirror in Manet's painting. Was she about to sell herself to Roland Newhouse and A. B. Ryan for a dubious chance at fame?

And what if their offer was legitimate? Should she relinquish a promise of real stardom—her lifelong goal—just because other people worried about the risk? "Nothing ventured, nothing gained." Wasn't that the old adage? Her future was as shrouded in mystery as Monet's misty view of Venice.

"Do you find truth in Monet's art?" She heard a man address her in the smoothly modulated tones of classically trained film and stage actors from a bygone era.

She was surprised that she had not heard him approach. As a long-time resident of New York City, she always made a point of being aware of her surroundings. When she turned to see who had spoken to her in such a refined accent, her heart leapt as if greeting an old friend, though she observed only a well-dressed stranger.

He was a bit taller than her five feet, six inches, but he did not tower over her. There was nothing looming in his presence. Rather he bore himself with a combination of quiet dignity and kindness that immediately put her at ease.

His very fine wool and silk herringbone jacket and coordinating navy trousers looked like an expensive men's ensemble Glenna had noticed in the window of Bergdorf Goodman only last week. The large gold ring on his left hand—an amethyst set with diamonds and rubies—was his only ornament.

Here is a man who knows how to look his understated best, she thought. His bearing indicated a person of mature years, yet his light brown hair and beard were flecked with reddish gold, not grey. His face and hands were as smooth as a man in his early thirties. As he commented further on Monet's work, he smiled with the vitality of youth.

"Painting the truth of a scene is what the critics of the time praised Monet for, you know. He was said to have desired to strip Venice of its mythical status and depict only exactly what he observed through the air, the haze, and the mist.

"I have always thought he had an exceptional gift for depicting the air. I admire his masterful combination of subtle colors and refined technique that perfectly portray the misty days found in many places around the world, not only Venice. Take Ireland, for example. Finest soft days of any country I know."

"Do you know Ireland well?" Glenna asked eagerly.

"Fairly well. It is certainly one of my favorite places on this lovely blue planet of ours. Over the years my other responsibilities have prevented me from visiting as often as I would have liked. However, several of my closest friends are deeply attached to Ireland. Through them I hold the land of Éire in great affection. Its music, myth, and poetry never fail to inspire me. Have you been?"

"No, but I may be going—in less than two weeks, as it turns out."

"Good for you. What is the occasion, if I may ask?"

Later Glenna would reflect with amazement on how, without forethought or restraint, she had unburdened her heart to this witty, though moderately grave man of undetermined age whose business card introduced him as F. M. Bellamarre, A., M. C.

"I'm not familiar with the letters after your name. Are they a type of degree?" Glenna rubbed her thumb along the *fleur-de-lys* design embossed in deep purple on the front of expensive ivory card stock. There was an email address written on the back.

"You might say that. I am Alchemist, Master of Ceremonies," replied the man with a twinkle in his unusual, violet-colored eyes.

"So, you're in the theatre? Do you act, write, direct?"

"Over the years I have done a bit of this and that. I am probably best known for my plays. Nowadays I am more of a producer."

"Anything I might have seen?"

"Perhaps, although I believe your tastes run more to musical theatre and dance, am I right?"

"Yes, how did you know?"

"You stand like a dancer, my dear."

She looked down at her feet. Her toes were turned out at a forty-five degree angle. Glenna laughed. "You're right, I do. Years of childhood ballet classes. By the way, my name is Glenna Morrissey. I am very happy to meet a fellow thespian, Mr. Bellamarre."

"Please, call me F. M. That is how my friends address me. I shall be very pleased for us to be friends."

"So shall I."

With that brief introduction, Glenna and F. M. Bellamarre talked as if they had been trusted confidantes for many years. She spoke excitedly about the offer from Newhouse to star in his musical and did not hide from F. M. her disappointment at not winning a Tony Award.

He showed sincere interest in her story, though he did raise an eyebrow when she complained, "I know my show was a bit of fluff, but my reviews were better than Cassie's. So why didn't I win? Politics, probably."

Although he made no comment, she immediately felt embarrassed that she should say something so petty to a person who emitted an aura of such dignity. She was grateful when F. M.'s expression quickly changed back to one of empathetic understanding. "Yes, I can see why you might be challenged in your choices."

As their conversation progressed, he demonstrated extensive knowledge of art, music, theatre, opera—every aspect of culture Glenna happened to mention. His attention was particularly peaked when she commented that she had always wanted to do Shakespeare.

"I love his roles for women," she enthused. "They are so decisive in the actions they pursue—like Lady Macbeth bullying her husband to commit murder. Even the romantic ones, like Juliet, take bold steps to get what they want."

"And what do you want, Glenna?" F. M. inquired. "Are you willing to take bold steps to achieve your goals?" Then he added, as if he were speaking a sort of prophecy, "The Universe sets a challenging road for those who are entrusted with exceptional talent."

"I want to be great!" answered Glenna with a passion that surprised her. "I know I have the potential to be a really accomplished actress, yet I feel that I'm missing something—a part of me that I used to have at my fingertips, but that disappeared ages ago."

F. M.'s amethyst ring flashed in the display light that illumined Monet's painting. His bright violet eyes deepened.

"Ah, yes," he replied with a note of compassion that touched Glenna. "So many souls are sensing that absence these days—almost as if having lived many lives they have lost pieces of their original essence. Rather than gaining mastery over time, they have slid into superficiality. Is that what you are feeling?"

"Exactly! Thank you for understanding. Most people don't. I feel like I'm stuck in one of Monet's mists."

"Well, if you would be open to an alternate possibility, I have an opportunity that may interest you."

"Yes, I am interested," said Glenna without hesitation.

"As I mentioned, on occasion I am a theatrical producer. In five weeks' time some of my friends are beginning rehearsals for our production of Shakespeare's *The Merchant of Venice* at a charming replica of the original Abbey Theatre in Dublin. They have christened it Aeon Repertory—a nod to one of the Abbey's first supporters. Only yesterday I learned that our Portia is not available. You would make a splendid replacement."

"Really? How can you be sure? You haven't heard me read. You don't know if I can produce an acceptable accent."

Glenna studied his face. She could tell he was serious.

"Oh, I am a very good judge of character and natural ability. Here is what I propose: Accept the trip to the Dingle area and remain until *Merchant* rehearsals begin. The journey from West Kerry to Dublin is much shorter than flying from New York. You can satisfy your dream of portraying one of Shakespeare's most beloved heroines, earn a bit of money, and then decide on your next step."

F. M. answered the unspoken question he saw cross Glenna's brow. "If the musical that Misters Newhouse and Ryan are producing is only now in development, you will have plenty of time to take advantage of all three opportunities."

Glenna's hand went to her heart. "I could never have imagined such a possibility."

F. M. nodded knowingly. "May I recommend that you sleep on the idea and let me know your decision in the morning. I feel certain you will have a very clear picture of the future you wish to pursue after a good night's rest. You can send a message to my friends at the email address on my card. They will inform me of your decision.

"As fortune would have it, I have planned a short holiday in Ireland. I expect to be in Dingle during the time you are there. I am acquainted with many artists, actors, and musicians in the area—all uniquely creative individuals whom I am certain you will enjoy. I know they will be as delighted to meet you as I have been this afternoon."

"Thank you so much," Glenna beamed as an image quickened in her mind's eye. "You've given me lots to consider. I can almost see how everything might fall into place."

"Until tomorrow, then," said her new friend.

She was tempted to hug this extraordinary person who had appeared in her life at the very moment she needed him. Instead, she extended her hand.

With the grace of a dancer, F. M. took Glenna's offered hand and held it for a moment in both of his. He smiled at her with the most profound kindness she had ever experienced.

In that moment she felt a gentle tingle of energy radiate throughout her body, leaving her with a sense of peace and confidence that was far beyond the mental clarity she had originally hoped to find at the Guggenheim.

F. M. released her hand, bowed slightly, and walked away. As he disappeared around the arc of the museum's grand interior helix, Glenna couldn't help thinking that perhaps the Universe was being kind to her after all.

Four

That night Glenna slept as she had not done in weeks. And she dreamed a dream so vivid—and so different from the dream of worldly fame and stardom—she could have sworn it was a memory, not a creation of her imagination.

She was a young woman living in first-century Ireland. She held a position of authority in her community and was graced with a refined sense of self-confidence and poise.

For today's special occasion, she was wearing a long blue dress made of handmade linen. Around her neck she wore her finest torc, a circlet created from delicate interwoven strands of solid gold. Her long, dark blonde hair was pulled back from her face and flowed down her back, nearly reaching her waist.

She was participating in a wedding ceremony being conducted by a man she thought looked like a god. His own light blond hair blew in the soft breeze, creating a halo effect around his head.

He smiled adoringly at her as she sang a song about true love to the couple being married. She loved this man with all her heart and hoped they, too, would soon be wed.

When Glenna awoke the next morning, the glow of the couple's mutual affection held her in a tender embrace. Whether or not that sensation was real, she now had no doubt that she must go to Ireland. The dream was so real, she could almost feel herself being called to reunite with this person, with a love she had not felt for any man in this life.

She made her decision. Roland Newhouse's promise of fame and fortune slid to the background of her priorities. She would accept the gift from the Rooneys and the offer from F. M. Bellamarre to portray Portia in *The Merchant of Venice.* Almost immediately upon emailing his friends, she received a reply.

> Greetings Glenna,
>
> You have made a wise decision in accepting F. M.'s proposal. As soon as you are settled in Dingle, you may send him a message at this address. He will contact you during his holiday.
>
> By the way, our producer said he cannot promise that playing Portia will make you famous, but he ventures to predict it will make you happy.
>
> We look forward to working with you,
> Your friends at Aeon Repertory

Less than two weeks later, Glenna was at the Newark Airport, waiting for her red-eye flight to Shannon, Ireland.

She had arrived hours earlier than necessary. Not because she was concerned about missing her flight. Nor because she was escaping opposition from her family or friends. Her parents had been almost giddy over her good fortune.

When Glenna had met with Roland Newhouse, he had admitted that his musical was actually several months away from rehearsals, which made her agent, Mel, and her friends even more supportive of her going to Ireland than they might have been.

"What a lucky break!" Patsy had exclaimed. "Maybe I'll come see you play Portia. I've always wanted to visit Ireland."

"Be sure to send me all your notices," Mel had reminded her. "Doing Shakespeare in Dublin—even if it's only at the Aeon—is a terrific addition to any actress's resumé."

Glenna was grateful for their encouragement. That should have been enough to keep her from hesitating. However, she knew she was hunkered down hours early at Newark's international terminal because she didn't entirely trust herself not to back out at the last minute.

Now that she had checked her luggage, cleared security, and found a seat in her gate's waiting area, she was much less likely to decide this whole thing was a dream. Her head was still spinning in amazement at how quickly all the details for her departure from New York and arrival on the other side of the Atlantic had fallen into place.

Her parents had been all too happy to store her few belongings in their basement. Glenna suspected they secretly hoped she would one day settle near them in New Jersey and live a normal life—"normal" meaning almost anything other than her present choice of career.

A former boyfriend, who confessed that he continued dating her only because he lusted after her apartment, had jumped at the chance to sublet her cozy corner of Brooklyn—if even for a little while.

After speaking by phone with Gerald H. Breathnach, Esq. (who, thankfully, was an actual attorney in Galway), Glenna had decided to deposit her three thousand euros in a Bank of Ireland branch as soon as she arrived in Dingle.

She had located a room with a family that took in a few guests in a large home they had converted to an inn. They provided most meals and offered a discount if Glenna occasionally helped with the cooking and washing up. Here was an option she hadn't thought possible.

She was a bit nervous about the idea of being part of an unfamiliar family, but decided to give it a try. She would save money on food and she wouldn't need a car in town because the inn was within walking distance of all the important attractions in Dingle's town center.

There were plenty of tours available for longer excursions, and she looked forward to reconnecting with F. M. and meeting members of his artistic community. She hoped they would be willing to show her some sights that most tourists never get to visit.

Mr. Breathnach has assured her that Dingle townspeople were very welcoming to newcomers. To make certain she arrived safely, he had arranged for a car service to pick her up at the airport.

At last, Glenna was on board her flight and settled into a window seat where she could contemplate the midnight sky and catch her first glimpse of Ireland in the morning.

She knew she should try to sleep like her frequent flyer seatmates who were already wrapped up in pillows and blankets after declining the dinner meal. At the moment, Glenna was wide awake with anticipation.

For now, everything was set—at least all the details she could control. What kept her awake were the unknown, uncontrollable details of leaving behind her personal life (not very active), her Broadway career (on temporary hold), and the close friends she knew she could always depend upon.

This adventure meant stepping off into a greater unknown than Glenna had ever considered. She had always thought of herself as a courageous person, but right now her insides were quaking like her thirteen-year-old self standing in the wings of her first lead role in a musical.

She was playing Angelina in Gilbert & Sullivan's *Trial by Jury*. All the other players were on stage with no one left to push her out from the wings. She had to make the entrance by herself.

She could still remember how her heart had beat wildly and how she'd felt as if she would expire on the spot. She hadn't, of course, though after years of experience, she still got butterflies before going on stage, especially in a leading role.

This trip to Ireland was like that.

Glenna felt as if something truly significant was waiting for her and it scared her more than seemed reasonable. However, the die was cast. She was crossing her own personal Rubicon to the future, and she was determined to embrace the journey, no matter what.

Five

Despite Glenna's excitement, she did manage to sleep a couple of hours, though morning had not yet dawned when she awoke. Most other passengers were still snoozing when she raised the window shade to spy Orion's Belt, visible despite the wing's blinking lights.

She decided to make some notes in her journal—something she hadn't done in months. It had been so long since she'd put pen to paper that she'd forgotten how pleasurable writing could be and what a poetical turn her thoughts could take when she stopped sorting and planning and trying to control every aspect of her life.

When ancient Egyptians died they called it 'Westing.' Today I am very much alive and 'Easting.' Heading for rebirth in the Emerald Isle. The land of my heart.

How amazing that a mere six-and-a-half hours separate this voyage's frantic origin from what I hope will be a sublime destination.

Venus rises before the sun that now begins rouging the horizon in the golden-pink glow of illumination's affection.

A three-quarter moon hangs lantern-like above the veil between worlds.

A fluffy cloud-carpet masks the deep blue ocean that lies beneath.

Cloud cliffs mark a boundary of air, and cirrus islands float below, mimicking the mythical land of Atlantis that once was here, now fallen beneath the waves of antiquity.

Three thousand miles across the sea, my soul's home waits for me with promises of magic and insights that cannot come unless I pay attention to the sights and sounds that exist only outside of ambition.

Ninety minutes remain till I'm home. A strange idea, considering I've never been to Ireland. Or have I ever been away? Certainly not in my dreams.

The patchwork fields, broad valleys, precipitous cliffs, and pounding waves have haunted my sleeping and my waking since I was a child.

I am nearly home. Saying so makes my heart so glad I can hardly contain the joy that would probably make my seatmates chuckle at my naiveté. Aren't we all a bit jaded by the place we know so well that we do not even see it?

As Glenna gazed hopefully out of the airplane's tiny window, the clouds parted and the greenest green she had ever seen or felt flowed into her being as a river of presence, of healing, of insight, of mystery beyond speaking. All in one ineffable instant of recognition.

She truly was coming home. Her soul was no longer abandoned on a foreign landscape. She was returning to her point of origin. She felt Éire's welcoming embrace rise up to meet her from ten thousand feet below. She returned the embrace with her whole heart, barely noticing how her eyes filled with the tears that had been held in abeyance since she took embodiment in this life.

She came to ground and was greeted with signs declaring *céad míle fáilte*—a hundred thousand welcomes. Home at last! No other words could capture the thrill that surged through every cell of her body.

Glenna was relieved to meet the cheerful, slightly balding driver named Declan who was waiting for her when she cleared customs. As Shannon International sported a cafe with well-prepared local fare, he suggested that she enjoy her first full Irish breakfast before they headed off to the Dingle Peninsula—a two-and-a-half hour journey.

"I have a daughter about your age," Declan commented. His clear blue-grey eyes smiled as he watched Glenna dig into her meal of scrambled eggs, sautéed mushrooms, broiled tomatoes, sausage, brown bread, and tea with milk. "She always eats here when she comes to visit from the States. She lives in Boston with most of our family."

His voice softened as he gazed off toward America. "There aren't so many of us left in the old country. We try to keep our youngsters here, but it's hard. My girl says that Ireland feels too small to hold her."

"How interesting," said Glenna. "Sometimes I feel that America is too big for me to handle."

"How long will you be with us in Dingle?" asked Declan.

"Three weeks at least. Then I'm going to Dublin for a couple of months. I've been invited to perform in a Shakespearean play at the Aeon Theatre."

"Oh, now that's grand!"

"Yes, it is." The idea of just how grand was beginning to sink into Glenna's awareness. "After that, we'll see."

"Oh, sure, and your future will unfold, won't it?"

"One way or another," she murmured, more to herself than to her new friend. "One way or another."

Glenna finished her meal with an eye on Declan's last bite of the fresh scone he had ordered with his coffee. He caught her meaning and said reassuringly, "We'll take a break along the way for tea and scones. No Irish journey is complete without at least one stop for refreshment. We're not in a hurry here in the West. We'll still have you in Dingle in plenty of time for a late lunch and a good rest after your journey."

"I'm not sure I'll ever sleep again, I'm so excited to be here," exclaimed Glenna. "May I ride up front with you? I'm hoping you'll explain to me what I'm seeing. I don't want to miss a thing. And please call me Glenna."

"Of course, though once we reach the motorways—courtesy of our old Celtic Tiger technology boom—you can feel free to rest your eyes. The highways are very convenient, but rather less like Ireland than visitors expect. Don't worry. I'll wake you when we're approaching the peninsula."

True to his word, his lyrical brogue adding a magical touch to the descriptions, Declan told Glenna stories about the scenes they passed.

Limerick. "One of our old Viking towns."

The picturesque village of Adare. "Former home of the FitzGeralds, Earls of Desmond, and now an elite golf club at Adare Manor."

And countless villages whose names Glenna knew she would need a guidebook to remember.

After the promised stop for tea and scones and lulled by the rhythm of the town car gliding along well-paved motorways, she did fall asleep.

An hour later, Declan spoke gently to rouse her. "Wake up, lass. We're approaching Tralee, gateway to the Dingle Peninsula. We've not quite fifty minutes yet, but coming up soon is a grand view of Inch Beach and sights you'll want to visit while you're here. Shall I tell you more stories?"

"Oh, no, thank you, Declan," said Glenna, blinking in surprise that she was seeing rather than imagining the island of her dreams. "I just want to let my heart rest in this glorious landscape. I know I live by the Atlantic Ocean in New York, but I've never seen anything like this!"

"Sure, it's the Wild Atlantic Way. Some marketer decided to promote the phrase, but it's apt, wouldn't you say?"

"Wild, indeed. I simply can't contain it all! Perhaps if I stay long enough."

"Oh, I think a lifetime is not time enough, *a chara*. I've lived in West Kerry all my life and I'm still surprised by the land and the sea and how they speak to each other."

"Then I'll just listen for the conversation and relish the sights," smiled Glenna, fixing her gaze on the dramatic landscape as they made their way to the harbor town of Dingle.

"Here we are, then," said Declan as he pulled up to a charming, two-story stucco home. The building was painted a restful golden-ivory color with terracotta trim around the paned windows and upstairs dormers.

A cheerful front garden blooming with multi-colored petunias, daisies, and flowering shrubs completed the picture.

The entry was faced in the dark, grey-brown stone that Glenna had already noticed was a common touch on many of the newer homes—which this one was. The contrasting, ivory-painted sign hanging over the terracotta front door announced: *Teach na beannachta.*

"That means 'house of blessing,' " Declan answered Glenna's curious gaze as he knocked on the front door and set her luggage on the stoop. She offered him a gratuity, which he gently refused.

A matronly woman with light red hair and soft green eyes opened the door and greeted them both with a dazzling smile.

"Good day to you, Declan," she said warmly. "And who have you brought us now?"

"This is Glenna from New York City," he said, matching her friendly tone, the light of good humor sparkling in his eyes. "You take good care of her, Fiona. We're in the way of being fast friends now."

He turned to Glenna. "You'll be very comfortable with Fiona and her family. And we're neighbors, you see. My wife and I are just up the hill. The house with the blue door."

"Will you come in for some lunch, Declan?" offered Fiona. "Or will Máire be feeding you when you get home?"

"She will, *a chara*, and then I'll take a bit of a rest. 'Twas an early morning, coming to meet you, Glenna, but I enjoyed introducing you to our fair land. Walk up sometime for a visit, why don't you? I only make the Shannon runs for Mr. Breathnach now and again. Otherwise, I'm around the peninsula. You take care and enjoy your stay."

"Thank you, I will," said Glenna, spontaneously hugging her new friend. "Maybe I'll book your car for a tour."

"I'd like that," said Declan, tipping his cap and driving away with a grin that spoke volumes of the familiarity he had noticed about this latest seabird flown home to nest in her soul's sanctuary.

Six

Brother Rory sat straight up in his narrow monk's bed, his heart pounding, mind racing. He clutched his aching head, feeling his light blond hair matted to his skull.

He was burning up, his nightshirt soaked with sweat and clinging to his fit, thirty-year-old body. His bedclothes were flung about in disarray as if he'd been fighting for his life.

He was shaking in the desperate knowledge that he would not live to see another day in the medieval religious community of Clonmacnoise.

He could still feel the sword in his right hand and the wound in his left leg that prevented him from standing.

He was certain that blood poured down his cheek from a gash where the Viking's battle axe had skimmed his forehead—before the invader had fled, carrying off the beautiful young woman he loved more than life itself, and had failed to save.

He thought his heart could not be in greater agony, but then he lifted his eyes to survey the scene before him.

Thatched roofs and wooden structures were all aflame. Through the acrid smoke of enormous fires into which the marauders were tossing precious treasures of sacred art and learning they neither understood nor valued, he could see the bodies of his comrades strewn around him.

Not only defenders of the rich monastic community had fallen in the melée.

Turning his head where he lay slumped against a tilting grave stone, he groaned at the sight of still-armed corpses mixed with those of dead women, children, monks, priests, and the elderly who had not been hauled off to the frightful dragon ships that would carry them away to be sold or kept as slaves.

Now fully awake, the smell of blood still clinging to his nostrils, Rory stumbled into his bathroom and wretched away the ghastly sensations that had terrified him back to consciousness.

Wiping the sick from his mouth, he heard the bell toll for Matins and Lauds. He had to get to the chapel. He hurriedly donned his black habit and sturdy shoes that Irish monks wore as protection against the cold and damp, and joined his brother religious in morning prayers.

Although his faithful recitation of Vespers and Compline the night before had not stopped the nightmares, he hoped that sooner or later his devotions would settle his mind and peace would come again.

As he took his place in the choir with his black-robed companions, he breathed a sigh of relief. Singing parts of the Office in Latin grounded him in a tradition that went back nearly fifteen hundred years. The simple chants rarely failed to connect him with the spirits of Benedictines, Cistercians, Franciscans, and others long since departed from this world. He prayed that this morning he would feel them join in the giving of his devotions.

Even as a child, Rory had loved morning prayers the best. He had always been an early riser, up before the sun, no matter the time of year. Repeating the rosary (which, he regretted, his order no longer said) had given him a feeling of security and confidence to face whatever the day presented.

When he'd decided to take Holy Orders after completing college and working for a couple of years as a history teacher, he had felt certain that praying the Liturgy of the Hours would be the highlight of his service and would ease the pain in his soul that he had dared not confess to anyone—not even the Father Abbot.

He had been right—until recently.

Unfortunately, this morning's prayers had only marginally eased Rory's troubled mind. He had little appetite for his usual breakfast of porridge, brown bread, and black tea, so he left the refectory early to change into his Wellington boots and work clothes.

Glad to be out in the morning's fresh air, he walked briskly to the dairy barn where the cows he helped tend were being gathered and prepped for their morning milking.

Most of the local farmers milked closer to dawn, but the monastery dairymen scheduled this task to accommodate morning and evening prayers. The cows didn't seem to mind, as long as they were regularly relieved of their liquid burden.

Rory worked here as a part-time assistant to the dairy manager. The young monk found great satisfaction in the position. He loved working with the animals who had very distinct personalities and preferences for their position in the milking line, which he did his best to accommodate.

For him, the earth and the earthiness of the dairy cows was a particular manifestation of the Divine Mother. "Hail, Mary, full of grace!" he often said under his breath to the bovine ladies whose precious milk had nourished the monastery and surrounding villages for decades. A Celt to the core, Rory loved his cattle and felt himself the wealthiest of men during calving season.

He relished the organic nature of his work. Yet, standing in the pristine milking plant, he could not help feeling that *An Síoraí*, the Eternal One, was calling him to a purpose that his soul had chosen in that mystical realm between embodiments where a lifetime's profoundest decisions are made—a purpose very different from his current occupation.

This morning, as he walked the milking line, making sure that no cow was in distress and that the machines were working properly, his mind drifted back to the dream that had awakened him so violently.

This wasn't the first nightmare of past confrontations with dangerous foes he had experienced of late, but it was certainly the most vivid. Other dreams had contained some positive images, but they were still troubling.

Last week he had seen himself walking across a grassy clearing on a wide hilltop. He was accompanied by a man he recognized as his best friend. They were druids preparing for the man's wedding, which was about to take place. The clearing had been decorated with masses of wildflowers, and hundreds of people from surrounding villages called *túath* were gathering for the ceremony.

As the dream progressed, it skipped ahead in time to a terrible scene in which that same man—his dearest friend with whom he had studied in their mentor's sacred grove—was dying in his arms. Again, Rory had been jolted awake, this time by the heart-wrenching sobs that erupted from his own throat.

"This can't continue," he said firmly to himself as he helped turn out the cows into their lush, green pasture where they would graze happily until evening milking time.

His mind was made up. If he experienced one more nightmare, he was going to see Father Crispin. Although he hoped the abbot wouldn't ask him too many questions, he realized he was coming to a crossroads and he couldn't make the correct turn by himself.

That very night, another dream disturbed Rory's slumber. This one was different from the others and, considering his vow of celibacy, the most discomfiting of all.

Unbidden came a beautiful woman dressed in a blue linen gown, a golden torc glistening like yellow fire on the smooth, milk-white skin of her slender neck.

Fair of face and form, a shower of dark blonde hair flowing down her back, she walked toward him with the grace of a fairy queen. Instantly he knew that he loved her as the true mate of his soul. Here was his partner of many lifetimes, a lover of word and song, as devoted as he to the spiritual mysteries known to the ancients.

Scenes of different lifetimes flashed before him. He observed them serving together on behalf of their people in eras of peace and enlightenment, and in times of great calamity and loss. Sometimes they lived as siblings. In other scenes they were unknown to each other.

Often they worked in the service of freedom and justice for their Celtic people. Particularly were they concerned for the liberation of those same folk from superstition, fear, and the dark arts that held many in rapturous sway.

Yet as the vision returned of the beautiful woman dressed in blue linen and radiant as the gold she wore, he knew that he had disappointed her love and broken her heart. He had failed her many times. And had he, by his failure, caused her to eventually choose ambition and glory over a more spiritual path?

Though some might argue that we are not to blame when our actions cause others to take a detour on their life path, Rory believed that we are—and that in his beloved's case, he was, indeed, responsible. These were situations for which he had never forgiven himself.

When he awoke before dawn the next morning, he remembered that the inability to forgive himself was a more current emotion than he cared to admit. He also knew that the dream scenes he had witnessed were true recollections. Whether enticing or frightening, the dreams were real. He recognized the eras and locations. He had seen visions of past lives, not vain imaginings.

Since childhood he had been an avid student of his homeland's past. Nowadays, in addition to his work at the dairy, he taught that history at the boys' boarding school connected with the monastery.

He was aware that his students considered him an excellent, though somewhat obsessed instructor who often seemed to be reliving the events they were studying as he lectured about ancient tribal rivalries, betrayals, foreign invasions, and the unrelenting determination of Éire's enemies to wipe her people from the face of the earth.

When he related the fact of thousands of Irish women and children, as well as men, being sold into slavery in the West Indies and the Americas in the seventeenth and eighteenth centuries, the class had sat in stunned silence.

They'd always thought that only the potato famine in the nineteenth century was responsible for depleting Ireland's population. Now they had more reason to understand the scars upon their national psyche that were rarely spoken of, even in their own homes.

"The lads are correct about my obsession," he admitted, speaking aloud as he entered the milking plant for his morning shift with the cows. Even more than his vocation as a monk, his homeland was his passion. God and country were inextricably linked in his being.

Some days, as he stood before a room full of eager faces, he could feel his very soul cry out, searching for the reason why his island's foes were bent on obliterating a language and a culture that yet, century after century, managed to absorb those foes back into itself—even resurrecting its culture in the current fascination with all things Celtic.

Perhaps that passion was the impetus for these dreams to surface so violently. Rory considered the possibility and hoped it was true.

At the end of his shift at the dairy, he would seek out the abbot so he might discuss his turmoil—at least the portion to which he was willing to confess. If anyone could offer him a respite from his current difficulties, it would be Father Crispin.

Seven

Father Crispin had been abbot longer than most of the other monks could remember, although he had about him an air of agelessness that defied explanation.

Not a tall man, he stood straight as a rod and walked with an easy, flowing gait. His shock of unruly white hair still fell boyishly across his brow, and his soulful brown eyes twinkled with a sort of enigmatic mischief whenever he lectured about the origins of Celtic spirituality and myth and their confluence with Christianity.

The abbot had his own strong interest in Irish history—particularly in the druidic beliefs and rituals that he asserted were nothing less than the fertile soil into which St. Patrick and other European missionaries had planted the rich seeds of Christianity.

Father Crispin and Brother Rory shared a belief that the druids were seers who maintained vivid connection with magi astrologers and other mystics around the world. They had known all about Jesus well before the Europeans arrived two or three hundred years after the dramatic events in Jerusalem.

Many had known of the Master's coming long before his birth. In addition, they were aware that some of his original followers had traveled to Britain as early as the years between 40-50 AD, bringing his mystical teachings with them.

These druids could have easily convinced Patrick that the trifolium shamrock was the perfect symbol for Father, Son, and Holy Spirit—although they would have insisted on a fourth petal to include the Divine Mother, who was everywhere present, animating the holy wells of the goddesses whose mysteries had always nurtured the Irish soul.

The abbot's office was the stuff of legend among students and monks alike. It carried the subtle aroma of old leather and frankincense, as if the man had absorbed the incense of the mass he said daily.

His chamber had once been a library with massive oak bookshelves nestled between tall, thin windows that looked out from the main monastery building's Norman architecture onto its expansive gardens, now coming lushly alive in the welcome warmth of May.

When a much larger library had been built a decade earlier, Father Crispin had appropriated this space and filled it with his own collection of cherished texts—works of all the world's religious and mystical traditions, which he had studied at length and which no librarian had ever been allowed to organize.

Visitors to the office were frequently amazed at the abbot's uncanny ability to pull the exact volume he wanted from what appeared to others as a mind-boggling disarray.

Father Crispin had been expecting Brother Rory, but he was not prepared for the monk's disheveled appearance. Normally fastidious in his grooming, the young man's hair and habit were askew as if he had dressed hastily.

The abbot stifled an exclamation at the wildness in Brother Rory's countenance. "Would you prefer the confessional, my son? You appear unusually distressed."

"Thank you, Father, no. I do not wish the anonymity of confession. I have a great need for us to see each other face-to-face. I feel like I'm at a turning point, but I do not know from what I am turning or to what I am going."

"Do you have questions about your vocation? Are you unhappy in your work?"

"On the contrary, I have been very content here. Yet I feel as if I'm being drawn elsewhere, to another field of service that I would not willingly choose."

"How so? Tell me."

"It's these dreams . . ."

Rory's eyes, normally the color of a robin's egg, went dark and his gaze seemed to penetrate far beyond the veil between worlds as the young monk told of vivid recollections of historical scenes that Crispin himself knew to be accurate.

The abbot was well aware that many souls who were treading the path of ancient wisdom were often initiated by the Masters of Light through dreams (whether or not the seekers were consciously aware of being on that inner journey).

He proceeded carefully, believing that now was not the time to share with this anxious brother his own experiences in similarly altered states of consciousness.

"Is it possible that these dreams are merely conflagrations of your reading of history? We know that Viking raiding parties attacked Clonmacnoise multiple times in the ninth and tenth centuries."

"That is what I thought," agreed Rory, "until last night."

"Why then?"

"I dreamed of a woman—and I assure you I have not been hiding erotica in my cell."

"I am certain of that, my son. Can you describe her?"

"She was about the age I am now. Very beautiful with an inner fire that spoke of a strong sense of self and her accomplishments. I believe she was a bard, although I'd thought only men held that position. Still, she seemed to be in charge and wore her authority lightly."

Rory fell silent, remembering how his heart had burned at the sight of this young female bard.

"How did you feel about her?" asked Father Crispin.

"I knew that I loved her and had always loved her with a devotion that was beyond my understanding. I would lay down my life for her, yet I understood that my willingness to do so had not saved her in the past. I loved her, but I had disappointed her. Yet, looking at her was like seeing a female version of myself, so close were we in the essence of our souls."

Crispin nodded. He was very aware of such relationships.

"Father, what I am do to?"

"What do you want to do, Rory?"

"I cannot say. I don't feel that I can leave the monastery, yet I fear my work is beginning to suffer. I don't sleep well. My appetite is gone. My concentration on the Divine Office is erratic.

"I almost feel like my soul is scarred from some terrible experience of long ago." (He dared not say, or recently.) Perhaps I need a holiday. Is it possible that I could take a short sabbatical—to spend some time by the sea?"

Father Crispin folded his hands under his chin and closed his eyes. Rory waited for his comment.

"I believe you may be right, my son—about your soul being scarred," said the abbot after several minutes. "Such things do occur, more often than we might think.

"The Hindus call the phenomena *samskaras*, meaning mental and emotional impressions, recollections, or patterns that have been imprinted on our souls by the events of many lifetimes. These soul patterns have much to do with our current behaviors, tendencies, and dispositions. They may even draw similar situations to us for forgiveness, resolution, or transcendence."

Almost against his outer will, Rory could feel his soul leaning into a past that was shrouded in memories he wished would remain in forgetfulness. He forced himself to pay attention to what Father Crispin was saying.

"If a past event has been especially traumatic—as your dream recollections indicate—those patterns can cause repeated suffering, doubts, and fears of similar events until they can be transmuted and the soul liberated from entrapment or from the fragmentation that can cause a portion of the soul to break off and remain separate for centuries."

From the expression on Brother Rory's face, the abbot could see that his words had struck a chord of truth.

"Indeed, I believe you do require some time to deeply consider if your pursuing a monastic vocation is right for you. You must listen to your True Self, my son. Pay heed to your voice of inner wisdom, and I am confident the right future will make itself known to you.

"You are still a novice, not an officially ordained brother. The die of your vocation is not entirely cast. Before taking final vows, you must be one hundred percent certain of your decision."

Rory's shoulders relaxed and he chuckled slightly. "My brother, Craig, is always saying the same thing. He even accused me of hiding from life in a black robe with a book of Psalms."

"Well, we can't have that, can we?" Father Crispin returned Rory's smile, though his brows were knit and he spoke more seriously.

"Being a monk is meant to be a profound calling to a spiritual life, not an escape from the material world. We must consider what future your soul truly needs in order to dissolve this *samskara*, even if you do not fully desire that future at this time.

"Take your holiday, my son, and discover what your soul would run toward, not away from." Saying nothing more, Father Crispin rose to conclude their interview.

"Give me two days and I will have arranged a sabbatical for you. In the meantime, I will ask Brother James to take over your history classes. Spend more time at the dairy. Walk in the gardens. Let Nature work on you a bit. And do not worry, Rory. If these dreams are mere flights of fancy, they will disappear. Have faith in that."

"Thank you, Father. I appreciate your understanding."

"I understand much more than you might think, my son," said Crispin, his hand on Rory's shoulder as he walked him to the door.

"Today is Wednesday. Come see me Friday afternoon and we will have you sorted out. Now go back to your room and take some rest. You are excused from work this afternoon, but I expect to see you at dinner and evening prayers."

"Yes, Father, I'll be there."

Rory turned and with a lighter step walked outside to where May's warming breezes rustled newly leafed-out trees and carried the rich scent of cows up from the farm.

Late Friday morning, Rory had finished with morning chores at the dairy and was seeing to one of the younger cows who had not quite settled into the routine of the milking plant. She had been especially distraught when her first calf was taken from her, as must be done for the cows to continue giving milk.

Rory found himself deeply moved by this cow's loss and so did his best to offer her extra care and reassurance that she was a splendid animal with an important purpose. She seemed to be responding, although the dairy manager warned him not to let her become overly attached to his affections.

As he turned the cow out to pasture with the rest of the herd, he noticed a man of medium height and build dressed in Wellington boots worn over dark green woolen trousers. His pristine waxed linen jacket and tweed flat cap identified him as a visitor, yet he was walking through the damp grass with the assurance of one who had a clear destination in mind.

Rory hurried to intercept the man before he approached any further. "My apologies, sir, but visitors are not allowed on the farm to prevent outside disease from affecting the herd or their feed. May I escort you back to the reception center?"

"Oh, the apologies are mine. Brother Rory, I believe?" said the man extending his hand in a warm greeting. "Please do not be concerned about my footwear. I borrowed these boots from your dairy manager. And I see I have arrived too early. I had expected that Father Crispin would have told you about me by now.

"Allow me to introduce myself: F. M. Bellamarre, at your service."

They shook hands and Rory felt a surprising surge of energy ripple up his arm and lodge in his heart. At the two men briefly studied each other, he could not help but feel warmly open to this man who emanated a certain refinement that he had previously observed only in some of the elderly monks who were his brother religious.

He found himself speaking deferentially to this visitor, who seemed more familiar than one might expect of a stranger.

"I regret, sir, I have not been told of your arrival. I am scheduled to meet with Father Crispin this afternoon. I assume, then, that you know our abbot?"

"I have that honor, yes," answered the man with the ease of a fellow monk. "Father Crispin and I have been acquainted for many years. You could say we are birds of a feather.

"He has asked me to be your host on a three-weeks' sabbatical that I am told you are to begin right away. Can you be ready to depart following breakfast tomorrow morning?"

The man's quiet authority encouraged Rory to immediately accept his proposal. "I can, yes. But may I ask where we are going?"

"Oh, I am sorry, my son. I see we are moving rather too quickly. Your destination is the Dingle Peninsula."

Rory's expression brightened. "That is one of my favorite parts of Ireland. My family used to holiday there on occasion when I was a lad."

"I am glad to hear it," replied F. M. "As my guest, you will have your own well-stocked, self-catering cottage at a local lodge near Ventry Beach. This location will afford you daily access to the sea, which I understand from Father Crispin is your particular desire."

"It is, yes." Rory was relieved, though slightly taken aback that this friend of the abbot's should know so much about him.

"On Saturday you will travel at a leisurely pace through Limerick, the lovely village of Adare, with an overnight near Lough Gur—a site I have always found of particular interest and where I will rendezvous with you. You will arrive in Dingle by midday on Sunday.

"I suggest you pack clothing suitable for moderate-to-challenging hiking, outdoor sports of your choice, dining at a variety of pubs and restaurants. You will have ample time to wander the Dingle Peninsula.

"I will see you now and again, as this trip is for me both business and pleasure. Some of my friends have offered to show you around, so you will not need to hire a car unless you desire to explore Éire's beautiful countryside on your own."

"Thank you. I will be ready," agreed Rory. Renewed hope for his future brought more color to his cheeks than had been apparent for the past week.

"Excellent. Phelan, a friend of mine who is a very pleasant traveling companion, will pick you up at eight o'clock at the reception center. When you meet with Father Crispin this afternoon, please inform him that we have met and that all is arranged. I am otherwise engaged for the remainder of the day and have no need to contact him further."

With a slight bow, F. M. Bellamarre turned and walked quickly from the pasture. Rory peered over his shoulder to determine why the cows were mooing, but could ascertain no reason. When he looked back he saw no sign of the mysterious man who seemed to appear and disappear with uncannily quiet steps and speed.

Rory's Friday afternoon conversation with Father Crispin was brief and to the point.

"You will find F. M. Bellamarre to be a stimulating acquaintance," explained the abbot, though he offered few details.

"He is a man of considerable depth and someone from whom you can learn much. I council you to take every opportunity to be in his company. I have found his friends to be of the highest quality and his generosity of spirit to be unparalleled.

"Go with God, my son. I look forward to your full report when you return."

"Thank you, Father. I am profoundly grateful."

"You are welcome, Rory. Listen well and you will find your way."

Considerably lighter of heart and mind, Rory made his way back to his room to pack his few belongings. To his surprise, he discovered that a journal bound in soft brown leather was lying on his desk.

"To facilitate self-discovery" said a note written in a fine hand on the back of an ivory business card with F. M. Bellamarre's name and a deep purple *fleur-de-lys* symbol embossed on the front.

Eight

Exactly at eight o'clock the following morning, Rory walked over to the monastery's reception center in time to see Phelan pull up in his roomy SUV. The young man hailed him with the warmth of a friend returning from a long journey. Without hesitation, Rory responded in kind and, together, they loaded his gear into the vehicle.

Why do I feel like all of this has happened before? he thought to himself as he secured his seat belt. His life was taking on the atmosphere of a *déja vu*.

Phelan didn't waste any time with small talk. "So, tell me Rory. What's it like being a monk? Once upon a time I was an altar boy but, much to my sainted granny's disappointment, I never felt the call to the priesthood."

"I'm not sure what I felt was as much a call as a shove," laughed Rory. He liked this fellow already. "I suppose you could say that life circumstances sort of propelled me onto this path." He stopped there.

Not to be dissuaded from learning more about his passenger, Phelan asked another question. "Are life circumstances holding you to the same road?"

"I'm not really sure," said Rory thoughtfully and then fell silent.

"And you don't want to talk about it," laughed Phelan. "Fair play to that. Forgive my curiosity. I like people and I enjoy hearing their stories. But you're under no obligation to tell yours to someone you've just met." He smiled broadly.

"I'm wondering about the 'just met' aspect of our journey," said Rory with a chuckle. "However, I also like people and their stories and am not ashamed to admit to a powerful curiosity about my host. What can you tell me about F. M. Bellamarre? Have you worked for him long?"

Phelan was about to answer, but Rory continued. This man clearly has a lot on his mind, thought his traveling companion with an inner smile. This was not the first time one of F. M.'s friends had peppered Phelan with questions.

"I assumed that my abbot, Father Crispin, had told F. M. about me. Yet I could almost feel him gazing into my soul. Not in a bad way. More like a loving and enigmatic father seeking ways to help his son.

"The man appeared out of nowhere, set a major change in my life in motion, then disappeared with a promise of joining you and me at a mysterious rendezvous."

"He does that," agreed Phelan with a knowing grin when Rory paused at last. "I might say I'm used to his ways, except that the times and places of his appearances and vanishings are nearly always unique and unexpected."

"That eases my mind," said Rory. "And, truth be told, his presence yesterday immediately put me at ease. Something about him told me I could trust him—even with my life, which is a bit shocking."

"You can definitely trust F. M.," said Phelan as he maneuvered the SUV onto the motorway that would carry them to their destination.

"It will be my pleasure to tell you some of what I know about the man. And, just so you are aware, such information as I'm about to share with you is given only with F. M.'s permission—which he granted before you asked."

Simultaneously amazed and comforted, Rory leaned back in his seat and prepared to receive whatever confidential insights Phelan was permitted to impart to him. Clearly, this revelation was a privilege.

There's not a mean bone in F. M.'s body. One might say he is generous to a fault, but I can't imagine finding fault with his sort of generosity.

His is a giving nature, though he never bestows his largess on any but the well-deserving. Which can be a puzzle when you observe whom he considers deserving of his time, attention, and material gifts.

Once, I questioned his discernment about the character of a

person I considered to be somewhat peculiar, but he just smiled and said, 'Look deeper, my son. Observe the soul behind the mask and you will understand.' I don't always remember that advice, but when I do, I see what he means.

He possesses an inner reservoir of such abundance and good cheer that he appears to benefit as least as much from his giving as does the receiver.

He delights in his many close acquaintances, calling us his Friends of Ancient Wisdom. He claims to have known us in past incarnations and says that we have important work to accomplish for the planet. He says we must each play our part and that, even in our most mundane tasks, we are performing vital service.

'Every deed done well with heartfelt engagement and positive intention moves the world forward,' he says. And I have to believe him.

Since I left the follies of university studies to work for him as his assistant, my life has never been better. To help him be who he is by removing obstacles from his mission on behalf of his friends is my greatest honor.

"What were you studying at uni?" asked Rory when Phelan paused his story to negotiate one of the more complex roundabouts that connected the motorway with a rural road that would lead to their meeting place.

"Philosophy. And you may or may not be surprised to hear that I've learned more true philosophy in my year with F. M. than I did in the two years at university. In fact, that's where I met him."

The dean had invited him to present a lecture on 'Nature's Philosophy of Cooperation.' Being steeped in a world view that divides nature into manageable parts that can be subdued, I'd never heard such an idea.

He began by demonstrating how the good old Greeks had saddled us moderns with a philosophy of dualism that was the antithesis of the wisdom of universal unity known to many pre-Christian cultures like the druids.

That brought a few derisive hoots from the audience. But he only smiled and continued by claiming that many ancient mystical traditions understood this principle, which has been lost.

He didn't elaborate on the reasons for that loss, but I could see from the faraway look in his eyes that he had probably witnessed the destruction of that wisdom many times in the past.

He said a lot more, but the real core of his message was that the soul seeks wholeness and the freedom to live life in a spiral that is always moving into higher levels of consciousness. He pointed to nature's ability to adapt and to increase in a network of cooperation between species.

'If you would realize positive outcomes in your life,' he said, 'observe your world view. Does your philosophy espouse collaboration with your surroundings and your fellows? Do your beliefs bring you joy and abundance? Do your practices open your heart to all of life, even the difficult patches?

'If not, consider altering how you think. For as we think, so do we feel, and so do we live. The mind determines the direction our feet take and the outcome of our life's journey.'

"That's brilliant," said Rory.

"Absolutely," agreed Phelan. "As you can imagine, I was hocked. I asked to speak with him afterwards—which wasn't that hard because most of the students and instructors had exited the auditorium with considerable haste.

"F. M. gave me his card and offered me employment, should I ever need a job. I slept on the idea, contacted him the next morning, and withdrew from my studies immediately. I've never looked back."

"That's quite a story," said Rory in amazement. "So does F. M. conduct a study group or something like that?"

"Not really, although his conversations are extremely educational. In fact, some of us have taken to recording what he says. Pearls of wisdom have a habit of dropping from his lips at the most unexpected of times."

"Such as?"

"Such as the idea that the study of alchemy leads one to the unification of masculine and feminine so that opposites in your consciousness and in your relationships become complements."

"That's a big subject," said Rory.

"It is," agreed Phelan, "and as we're nearly at our destination, we'll table it for another time. What I will say now is that I know there is much about himself that F. M. does not reveal directly. I get the feeling that he wants us to discover the enigma of what he stands for—which is the freedom of the soul, among other things.

"Sometimes I get the feeling that he holds the truth of my being in his hand, with an open palm. 'Look closer,' he seems to say, 'and you will know who you are. Discover your True Self and you will know who I am.' "

"Brilliant," was all Rory could say. He looked over at Phelan and noticed that the young man's soft grey eyes were glistening.

"One last thing," said Phelan, "F. M.'s affection has a quality of eternality about it, as if he has loved each of us forever. It's an amazing experience to be on the receiving end of such unconditional love. That is one reason, though hardly the only reason, why we who know him adore him as our soul's greatest friend and champion."

Rory thought for a minute. "You know, my brother, Craig, mentioned something about an interesting group he calls 'The Friends' that he's become part of in New York City. Coincidence, do you suppose? Or a cosmic set-up?"

"I couldn't say," answered Phelan. "I do know that what you are seeking is seeking you. And here's the man with the road map."

As Phelan finished speaking, he pulled off the two-lane road and parked by a ruined church. F. M. was waiting for them. After greeting them warmly, he asked Phelan to remain with the car. Addressing Rory he said, "Come with me, my son. I have something to show you."

They stepped off to the right of the road and walked up a gentle rise into a stand of trees that sheltered a clearing. A collection of large stones that showed the ravages of time and human activity were tumbled together in the center.

As they approached the stones, Rory felt tears prickle behind his eyes and he exclaimed, "This looks just like Uncle Óengus's wisdom grove." With an astonished look at his companion, he shook his head and asked, "What did I just say?"

"If I may elaborate," said F. M. looking intently at the young man as if he desired to convey much more than a simple explanation, "you said this place looks like the wisdom grove where you studied with the great druid Óengus in the first century AD in the part of Ireland known as the Ancient East."

"How can that be?"

"The soul knows these things and looks straight through time when cycles are right for the past to be revealed."

"But why this scene and why now?"

"This site is but a simile of a location you knew well many centuries ago. Here is a reminder meant to ignite in you a spark of recollection of work that remains unfinished—work that you vowed to complete in a coming age. That age is now."

"I feel the familiarity, but I don't remember what I did here, or in some other grove."

"Let me assist you. On occasion, we must give the memories a boost. Come, sit down. We will not be disturbed here." He motioned to a sheltered place in the shade.

Rory sat on a large log while F. M. kindled a fire (seemingly out of nowhere) in the center of a small circle of stones. He took a seat next to his companion and invited him to gaze into the flames.

"Breathe into the images you see, my son. There is nothing to fear. These are scenes of a powerful and positive event you shared with those much beloved by you in the past."

A feeling of peace and safety immediately came over Rory. His eye caught the glint of light on golden torcs that graced the throats of three men dressed in the long white robes of druids. They were standing in a grove, where enormous, lozenge-shaped stones now brimmed with vital energy.

One of the men appeared to be very old, though his stature was youthful, his blue eyes clear and bright, his white hair and beard abundant with good health. The second was the same man Rory had recognized from his nightmare, his great friend who had died tragically. The third druid was none other than himself, the youngest of the three, though he was by no means immature.

The elder, whom he recognized now as his mentor, Master Druid Óengus, was speaking to him and his great friend. Rory could not understand what was being said, but he could tell by the intensity with which they listened that instruction was being delivered. It appeared that some ritual was about to take place.

As he watched, the three men arranged themselves in a triangle and began a chant that seemed remarkably familiar. He could almost feel the words vibrating on his own tongue.

The energetic vibrations in the grove increased as the volume and speed of their chant accelerated. Gradually, though steadily, a mist began to form around them, thickening until it became a radiant cloud of shimmering, milky white light substance.

He knew the three men were still in the grove. He could feel their presence. Yet their figures became less and less distinct until, with a flash of light that came from inside the cloud, they vanished.

Rory and F. M. were once more alone, sitting on a log, gazing at the fire which had gone to ashes.

"Where did they go?" he asked unsteadily.

"Wherever they were needed at the moment," explained the man whom he was now fully convinced was an adept—a rare appearance of a high spiritual master.

"What you have seen is one of many instances in which these three druids worked together for the betterment of their people. The cloud they generated is called the *féath fíadh* mist—a manifestation known by druids and alchemists in many generations. Remember it well, my son. You will know why when the time comes."

"What does all this mean? I feel the memory, but not the purpose." Rory rubbed his hands over his face and looked into his companion's violet eyes, which gazed back at him with an expression of profound compassion.

"The exact meaning remains to be seen and depends upon your response to events which await you on your sabbatical. Now I must send you on your way. *Slán abhaile.* May you go safely home. I will see you again soon."

Rory assumed that F. M. was behind him as he walked back to where Phelan was waiting with the car. But when he turned to express his gratitude and wonderment at the experience he had shared with this extraordinary man, he was alone with his traveling companion.

Nine

Even for a Friday morning, business was brisk at Fibonacci's Tea Merchants & Coffee Roasters. Most of the tables were filled and a steady stream of customers flowed in and out of the newly painted front door.

Lucky, the owner and Kevin's employer, had been meaning to give the entrance a face-lift. The two men had accomplished that task last weekend, refreshing the royal blue trim that graced the coffee shop and the bookstore next door where Sarah now was working a few hours a week until her pregnancy became too advanced.

"When I can't bend over to tie my shoes, I'll stay home," she had laughed when Kevin inquired exactly how long she thought she could continue. At nearly five months along in her pregnancy, she was beginning to see that time might come sooner rather than later.

With twins, she would be huge before they would separate themselves from the blissful unity she experienced more each day as they grew inside her—a presence she still considered miraculous.

She had walked over to the coffee shop from the bookstore for her mid-morning break and to visit with Debbie, who was supplying her with extra herbal supplements to support her body and the babies'. The two friends were sitting at the far end of the coffee bar, away from the commotion of other customers and conversations.

"You look like you've got a story to tell," said Debbie.

"I have," agreed Sarah, "but I want to share it with you and Róisín at the same time. Before she comes back from the kitchen, I'm wondering if you'll tell me more about her. I can see that you two have a very special relationship."

"We do," agreed Debbie. "She's changed my life—and not for the first time. What would you like to know?"

"F. M. said I should spend more time with her. What with finishing up work on my book with my editor, two months of morning sickness and bed rest, and now my few hours a week in the bookstore—beyond short conversations, I haven't really had an opportunity to speak with Róisín since last Christmas. What can you tell me, if I'm not asking too much, Aunt Dearbhla?" Sarah added with a wink.

"Oh, you're not, niece Alana," said Debbie with equal humor. Both young women cherished their past-life connection as seer and druidess who were also family to each other.

"The subject of Róisín is one of my favorites. You probably don't know this because Alana wouldn't have met her, but she was Dearbhla's grandmother and mentor. She was a druidess, a seer, and an herbalist. In this life we're picking up where we left off with her as teacher and me as student. Definitely an accelerated course, I can assure you."

A faraway look settled over Sarah. She smiled wistfully. "Róisín would have been Alana's great-grandmother. Our female lineage is truly ancient, isn't it?"

"It is. So you can understand why F. M. wants you to learn from this exceptional woman. I haven't shared these thoughts with many, but you need to hear them." Debbie could feel her heart expanding as she offered Sarah a window into her most precious human relationship.

"Her name has been Róisín—little rose—for lifetimes, and at this point in her soul's evolution, she is highly integrated with her True Self. She makes a point of appearing quite ordinary to the outside world, but to those who are among the Friends of Ancient Wisdom (even if they don't know it yet), her light and beauty simply radiate."

"That is so true," agreed Sarah. "Every time I see Róisín she appears more beautiful to me."

"Which is a testament to the acceleration of your own conscious-ness." Debbie beamed at her friend. Her voice grew melodious as she described her beloved teacher.

I believe that Róisín is incapable of ugliness or mediocrity. Her mind is like a cool laser, piercing illusion with such quiet precision you don't even notice when a situation has been clarified until, perhaps, you realize that chaos has vanished.

She says very little about what she perceives. However, if you observe her, you will occasionally catch her being very still for a moment, possibly lowering her eyes or looking off into the distance. My impression is that she focuses her full attention on what she's meant to see or hear, and then goes about her business in a perfectly ordinary manner.

I know that F. M. loves her deeply and relies on her to work closely with his friends, helping them accelerate their consciousness so he can eventually interact with them in his ascended-master presence as Saint Germain. I think he may also offer her a glimpse of souls he is gathering who need her special prayers to get here and her particular care when they do.

If it's true that you can know a master by his disciples, which I'd say describes all of us, then Róisín is Saint Germain's perfect ambassador.

Sarah leaned her elbow on the bar, her eyes wide in rapt attention. "What about Lucky? He has about him a presence of profound strength, and his humor is infectious."

"I've heard the Master say that Lucky is the philosopher and Róisín is the intuitive. He's the head and she's the heart. And on any given day you'll see them switch roles. She is very wise and he has a heart of gold."

"They're a remarkable pair, aren't they? They both treat others with such deference, it's impossible not to love them," said Sarah. "But they're not twin flames, is that right?"

Debbie nodded. "It is. Róisín once told me that her twin flame abides in what she calls 'The Great Silence.' The concept is quite unfathomable. He must be a cosmic being who doesn't interact with earth. I'm wondering if part of her test in this life is to win her soul's liberation by being totally reliant on her connection with *An Síoraí*, the Eternal One—that is, her own inner divinity."

"But with Lucky's help, surely?"

"Absolutely. They are the dearest of soul mates. They've been together for most of their embodiments in the last millennia. I think that's why they're in such complete attunement with each other. The love between them is profound—deeper than they show outwardly—with a loyalty that brooks no interference or inharmony."

"I am so grateful that you told me," said Sarah. "I hope you don't mind. I have another question."

"Go ahead."

"Do you ever wonder who or where your twin flame is?"

"I do. I've tried contacting my soul's other half on the inner, but a veil always comes down, so I've stopped. In fact, Róisín says I mustn't probe where *An Síoraí* has not revealed."

"Makes sense," said Sarah. "Does that make you sad?"

"Not really. Craig is becoming a good friend. He's not my idea of a romantic partner, but we do have some shared memories of our time together in first-century Ireland. And I love that he's one-hundred percent Irish. He's a great storyteller and emanates a sense of soul freedom that I admire. Having a pal is a gift."

Sarah reached over and put her hand on Debbie's. "And you know you can spend as much time with Kevin and me as you want. We're all family. Don't forget that."

The two women sat in silence, basking in the heartfelt communion they had shared. They were finishing their cups of tea when Róisín returned from the kitchen, carrying an enormous tray of baked goods which she handed off to the two baristas who were minding the busy coffee bar.

"Are you making each other cry, then?" Róisín inquired, seeing that the young women whom F. M. had given into her special care both had teary eyes.

"We've been talking about family and how important we are to each other," said Sarah, wiping the dampness from her cheeks.

"And I was telling Sarah how much I love and admire you and Lucky. F. M. told her to spend time with you and I'm encouraging her to do so."

"Ah, darlin', you'll make me weepy, too," said Róisín. She turned to Sarah. "Are you sure you don't want to sit at a table, *a chara*?" she asked with a chuckle. "We don't want you wobbling off that stool."

"I'm fine. Besides, if I start to sway, Debbie will catch me, won't you?" Sarah said with a grin.

"Don't you put that on me, girl. Kevin will have my head—and yours, Róisín—if anything happens to his precious family."

Debbie looked over her shoulder at Sarah's husband who was also her good friend. "He's doing well, isn't he?"

All three women turned to observe Kevin, who was seated at the back table with his philosophy students: Noah, Jenny, Valerie, Finn, and Rudy. At the moment they were vigorously debating the age of the Great Pyramid at Giza. The discussion was lively and Kevin was beaming.

"It has to be older than 2500 BC," declared Valerie. "Look at the side and angle measurements. They relate exactly to the British foot, biblical cubit, and French meter—all of which were identified in later centuries, and not by Egyptologists.

"These are constants that predate all of these discoveries, more like 25,000 BC. I think the builders, whoever they were, meant to preserve occult knowledge in the structure itself. We're just now figuring out what that might be."

"Plato knew something about the pyramid's significance," said Rudy, holding up a diagram of the philosopher's solids. "Look at the shape of his octahedron. Two perfect pyramids connecting at the base. Seems to me like 'as above, so below'."

"Is the pyramid above or below?" asked Noah, his brow wrinkled at Valerie's insistence on bringing math into their discussions.

"Or above, here below," quipped Jenny, reinforcing her self-assigned role as tension tamer. Valerie winked at her and Finn hugged Valerie.

"The students appear to be having a good time," observed Debbie.

"They do," agreed Sarah, "and I'm glad that Rudy's continuing with them. After our confrontation last winter, I wasn't sure he would be comfortable spending time at Fibonacci's in any capacity. But, so far, he hasn't had any episodes that I'm aware of. And he appears to be keeping his promise to Lucky and Kevin to be a harmonious member of the Friends of Ancient Wisdom.

"He's helping out at the bookstore, too—mostly when I'm not there. Kevin doesn't want me taking any chances. He's working really hard to show Rudy that we appreciate his gifts and interest in ancient philosophy, myth, and druidic lore. I'm not in a position to do that, but Kevin is. I'm proud of him."

Sarah was beaming at her husband, so she didn't see the cloud that passed over Róisín's brow. But Debbie did.

"What is it?" she mouthed silently. "Did you see something?"

"Just a flicker. Nothing I can identify. But I'll be watching, "Róisín said under her breath. Then she said aloud to Sarah, "It is grand to see your man so happy, these days."

"Yes, it is," said Sarah, turning and gazing into Róisín's bright green eyes. "And he wouldn't be here if you hadn't given me that emergency kit before we went to Ireland. I never could have . . ."

Sarah's voice caught in her throat as she recalled how narrowly her husband had survived being stabbed with a poisoned knife by their re-embodied enemy, Arán Bán. Her friend's tincture had neutralized the deadly substance meant to kill Kevin. This was the stuff of nightmares and still affected her if she put her attention on the event.

"*A chara*, you know I've told you that was F. M.'s doing," said Róisín, reaching across the bar to hand Sarah a tissue. "Debbie and I were merely the messengers."

"Yes, and I will be forever grateful to all of you," said Sarah as she dabbed her eyes. "And to Lucky for giving Kevin a job—actually many jobs, when you count keeping the books."

"A task the man was more than pleased to delegate, I can tell you," Róisín interjected with a laugh.

Sarah grinned and continued. "Yes, keeping the financial books, selling real books next door, helping Lucky with maintenance, and spending time with the college students. Kevin is a man whose every dream has come true."

"Don't forget this other rather important dream," commented Debbie looking down at her friend's blooming body.

"That is impossible," answered Sarah. Her hand automatically stroked her belly and her eyes glistened in the perpetual glow she emanated. "The babies are definitely making their presence known. And . . . well, can I tell you both something that is a bit strange?"

"Of course," the women said together.

"You know we're all about strange," laughed Debbie. Then her expression sobered at the faraway look in Sarah's eyes. "This isn't serious, is it? Are the babies okay?" She instinctively reached out to take Sarah's hand.

"Oh, no problem with the little ones. In fact, I can feel them growing daily—and not only physically. I'm not sure if what I'm sensing is their energy or mine or a combination of the three of us, but I'm starting to have visions."

"You've been doing that since I've known you," smiled Debbie.

"Yes, but these are different. They're not specifically about Kevin or me, although I can feel that we are or will be involved later."

Róisín nodded. "You've had more of an otherworldly look about you since *Bealtaine*. What's going with you, *a chara*? You can tell us anything."

"Then I will. Debbie, have you heard from Glenna?"

"That's an odd segue, but, yes. She called me the day before she left for Ireland, but I haven't heard anything since then. I thought I might get a postcard, though I imagine she's completely enthralled with sightseeing. I certainly would be. Did you know she met F. M.?"

"Really? Where? When?"

"At the Guggenheim, the day you encouraged her to go to a gallery to collect her thoughts about accepting the offer she received through that letter from Ireland. Inspired advice, I'd say."

"I'm so glad," said Sarah. "Maybe I helped her after all."

"Of course you did," added Róisín. "And you'll help her even more when the time comes."

"It's odd. My voice of inner wisdom said that our next commission from Saint Germain was beginning, but then nothing else has happened with Glenna."

"Consider that your commission is working on invisible planes," Róisín stated simply. As Debbie had described only moments earlier, she went very still. Her voice took on a tone of quiet authority.

"You'll be prompted when it's time for you to act in the visible world. Glenna must heal some deep wounds before she can find her way to the Friends of Ancient Wisdom. She and her twin flame have hurt a-plenty in both their hearts. Those will mend when they figure out their priorities and decide who they want to be in this life."

When she paused, Sarah said wistfully, "I remember being very fond of Glenna. I'd like to be good friends this time around."

"You will," said Debbie quietly. "We all will."

"You've remembered who she was when we were together in Ireland, haven't you?" said Sarah with a wink. "You see things before I do and then wait for me to catch up."

"Which you do very quickly," said Debbie, squeezing her friend's hand.

"And maybe my spending time with you, Róisín, will help me improve my skills."

"Of course," said the woman, "as long as you remember F. M.'s guideline: 'As each one requires.' We always give *An Síoraí*, the Eternal One, time to work out the details of our service."

The three women laughed together and Debbie changed the subject.

"Sarah, you had a story to tell us. Something about strange visions?"

"I do. And in light of our conversation, I'm thinking perhaps our commission is coming to life after all."

Róisín answered Sarah's implied question with a subtle nod. "Go on, lass. I believe you have the right of it."

Sarah stood up for a minute to stretch her back and roll her shoulders. Debbie gave her a concerned look when she steadied herself with a hand on her friend's shoulder.

"I'm fine. Just needed a bit of a stretch, that's all." Sarah resumed her seat and her story.

"I've purposefully not put my attention on Glenna since our conversation at *Bealtaine*. The last thing I wanted to do was intrude on her path. So what's strange is that I'm having visions of her current experiences in Ireland—right now—almost as if her life were unfolding before my inner sight. And not only this life, but the important past life that Debbie and Glenna and I shared.

"Now I know why I felt such an immediate connection with her. She was Gormlaith, the lovely woman who was head bard at *Tearmann*. She and Alana were very close and were a wonderful support to each other after Ah-Lahn was murdered. Gormlaith went through her own heart-breaks. I can actually feel her heart as we're speaking about her."

"I remember her well," said Debbie. "It was unusual for a female to be chief bard, but she was very accomplished. And Riordan, the love of her life, was Ah-Lahn's fellow druid and best friend."

"Exactly," agreed Sarah. "I believe that while Glenna is in Ireland, she's going to meet whoever Riordan is now in this life, and I don't have a good feeling about that reunion. Not that the love they shared won't spark again. I believe it will. But I'm worried about their future and I don't know why—other than what Róisín just told us about their having some deep wounds to heal."

Debbie was about to offer some additional information about the identity of Glenna's twin flame when Róisín suddenly hurried from behind the bar. "Debbie, hold onto Sarah and—both of you—shield yourselves. I think a big clue to the future just walked through the door."

Ten

A commotion at the front door caused the two women to turn abruptly on their bar stools, nearly spinning them off their seats. Debbie grabbed Sarah as their mouths fell open and they uttered a gasp in unison.

A. B. Ryan and his fiancée, Ursula, pushed their way through the group of shoppers who had come inside, out of the icy wind that blew in behind them.

Every muscle in Sarah's body tensed. A shiver ran up her spine. Although A. B. was acting like the politician she and Debbie had worked for, from his appearance she knew him instantly as Arán Bán, the person who had tried to murder her husband last December in Ireland.

Irish temper flaring, if she'd had a weapon, she would have been tempted to hurl it at him. Instead, she clung to Debbie and did her best to visualize a sphere of violet and blue light around them both. "Saint Germain, help us," she said emphatically under her breath.

A. B. and Ursula were expensively dressed. He wore a charcoal top coat that emphasized the sheen of his thick grey hair. Her coal-black tresses were pulled back in a severe knot, and she was swathed in ebony fur (which, disturbingly, reminded Sarah of her panther spirit guide's coat). They could have stepped off the screen of a *film noir* movie—a study in black and silver.

"This is the coffee shop," A. B. declared loudly as they entered, gesturing with a grand sweep of his arm. His companion looked thoroughly bored, which he seemed not to notice as he strode further inside, orating like the master manipulator of New York politics he'd been for decades.

"Does a decent business," he said as if he knew all about Fibonacci's, "but not enough to keep the place open. Once we demo the block, we'll put in a Starbuck's for the condo tenants. Not a big one. A sop to the neighborhood, that's all. The restaurant will take up most of the corner. Definitely no need for that ratty bookshop. Let's go over there anyway. I heard there's a ballroom upstairs. Totally impractical, but I want to see it before I wreck it," he laughed lewdly and shook his head. "There is something repugnant about this whole place."

"I want a coffee," demanded Ursula.

"Okay, tell them what you want, but hurry up. I want to see the owner before my meeting and . . ."

A. B. pulled up short. His cobalt eyes went wide, then narrowed to a serpentine slit. Sarah shuddered against Debbie, but she pulled herself up straight. Her hands went to her belly as the man ogled her obvious pregnancy and snorted at her sarcastically.

"Well, little lady, looks like somebody got to you in a big way. Rudy didn't tell me you worked here. 'Course, it's hard to get anything useful out of that kid. Debbie, you, too? What a crew! Do you do windows?"

"I don't . . ." Róisín's steady hand on Debbie's shoulder stopped her from firing back at A. B.'s rudeness.

Anything she might have said was interrupted by Kevin's brisk approach. He had felt a tidal wave of malintent enter with A. B. Ryan.

Instantly responding as the spiritual warrior he was, Kevin sealed his aura in white light and walked purposefully to Sarah, immediately placing himself between her and their mortal enemy.

Although he was all too aware of who had intruded upon his sanctuary, he was astonished to look into a pair of eyes that focused on him with a hatred less than human. He gathered his energy into his heart and calmly leveled his own gaze at the man who, time and again, had tried to abort his sacred mission.

"Ah, here's the great protector," scoffed A. B.

Kevin noticed that his voice wavered slightly, but the man pulled himself up with a shake of his head, as if to banish the image before him. Kevin was supposed to be dead. A. B. cleared his throat and regained his arrogant tone.

"I see you've recovered from that little nick I gave you in Ireland. I might have known you two would be in the middle of my plans." He looked around angrily. "Where's that guy, Lucky? We need to talk."

As A. B. attempted to move further into the room, several members of the Friends of Ancient Wisdom rose from their tables and, standing like a phalanx of seraphim, began silently invoking a shield of light between their friends and the aggressor.

Visibly surprised at being confronted with such a display of unity, A. B. took a step back. A look of concern flashed across his brow.

Róisín took note of this small retreat and addressed him—speaking slowly and deliberately, her green eyes flashing, her voice like a sword.

"The owner of Fibonacci's is not here. If you wish to speak with him, you will make an appointment. We do not welcome loud disruptions in our place of business." She stood shoulder-to-shoulder with Kevin—imperturbable, like a flaming white candle.

A. B. was momentarily still, then his eyes narrowed. He dismissed Róisín with a hiss and turned the full force of his attention on Kevin. He pointed a malicious finger at the man he despised above all others.

"You tell that weasel, Lucky, that my best offer is about to drop another ten grand. If he doesn't sell by the end of next week, I'm having the bank foreclose on his loan."

When none of his listeners reacted, he grew further incensed and raised his voice. A whip of energy spewed from him.

"Oh, yes, little people, I can do that. Just like I can have this miserable property condemned. Then you'll have nothing." He spat out the word. "Nothing, do you hear? And none of you can do a thing to stop me!"

His wicked laughter echoed throughout the coffee shop. Sarah swore she felt the rafters shake.

"Come on, Ursula, let's get out of this rat trap. The management is making me sick." He grabbed her by the elbow, nearly spilling the very hot latte she was sipping.

"Let go, you fool! You almost ruined my new coat." Ursula snarled at him and slapped away his grip. Her long, darkly polished fingernails scraped the back of his hand like a claw and he winced.

She spun around without paying for her beverage, angled her head over her shoulder with a knowing smirk at Sarah and Debbie, and sashayed out the door. A. B. stomped after her, fuming like a storm cloud full of thunder and fury.

Debbie hopped off her bar stool and hurried to the front window in time to watch him climb into the back seat of a chauffeured limousine. She couldn't see Ursula, who had preceded him into the vehicle. But she could tell from the dark energy swirling around the two of them that they were yelling at each other as the car roared away from the curb.

She stood for a moment, leaning against the door to steady herself. Her whole body was shaking from the barrage of negativity she had witnessed. She noticed that Rudy and his fellow college students were gone—presumably into the bookstore.

Then her inner sight opened to reveal a conflagration of spiritual presences she had not noticed in her determination to hold onto Sarah.

The entire coffee shop was bathed in scintillating waves of light. She lifted her gaze and saw, rather than the shop's antique tin ceiling, a heavenly vault where rings upon rings of angels were arrayed. Each one held a sword aloft. Their eyes were flashing with spiritual fire.

When Debbie looked around the room, she could see that she, Sarah, Kevin, and Róisín were all surrounded in a sphere of translucent blue flame—the spiritual energy of protection and power. The focused thoughts and prayers of the Friends of Ancient Wisdom had created this manifestation of light.

These wonderful compatriots remained standing at attention. They were solemnly gazing up at the rings of angels that only now began to dissipate. The ceiling came back into view and the Friends returned to their seats—though each one was facing Róisín and Kevin.

Debbie let out a deep sigh and breathed a prayer of thanks to *An Síoraí*, the Eternal One, for the gift of this vision. Finally able to walk on steadier legs, she rejoined her friends at the bar in time to help Kevin get Sarah seated in a chair.

He stood behind her, his hands on her shoulders. She had gone very pale. Ursula's parting glare had been a knife in her heart.

"My God, I have never felt such evil in this life," said Debbie, shaking her head. "No doubt about A. B. Ryan being Arán Bán. I'm amazed I never recognized him when I worked for him."

"F. M. said he cloaked himself so none of us would see him for who and what he really is," explained Sarah.

"He must not feel the need to be so controlled now," commented Debbie. "Or else all that anger is making him lose control."

Sarah suddenly shuddered and turned pale. "No, I don't think anger alone is the cause. When he confronted us in Ireland, I wondered if he had merged with his druid self the same as Kevin and I merged with Alana and Ah-Lahn. Now I'm sure that's exactly what happened. A. B. Ryan *is* Arán Bán. I know it in my bones."

Kevin, Debbie, and Róisín all looked at her in amazement.

"I believe you have the right of it, *a chara*," said Róisín.

"Which means we'll have to be even more vigilant than we thought," said Kevin. He kept his hands on Sarah's shoulders, as much for his own sake as hers. Then he added, "Thank God Lucky wasn't here today."

"Where is Lucky?" asked Debbie.

"Last night he and I agreed that he wouldn't come in this morning," said Róisín. "We had a very bad feeling about today. Now I know why."

"We've got to do something to protect Fibonacci's from that man," said Sarah. Her voice was weak, but emphatic. She felt emotion welling up in her body. She would not let it be fear.

Debbie felt her dear friend's determination. "Let's move to the back where we can talk." Moving behind the bar, she made a large pot of hot tea for the four of them to share and joined them at the large table which the philosophy students had vacated.

For a few minutes, everyone sat in silence, their minds searching for answers as each one contemplated Sarah's revelation about the startling event they had just witnessed.

Exactly what was Arán Bán up to?

Could he really have Fibonacci's condemned?

At last, Kevin spoke. "Róisín, do you know when the bookstore and the coffee shop were built? Is the entire block the same age?"

"I don't remember for certain, but Lucky will know. Why?"

"I think we need to dig into the building's past right away. If we can prove its age, we might be able to get it designated as a protected landmark. That will allow it to be renovated, but not destroyed. The historical society might even decide that the whole block is protected against rezoning or whatever it is that Arán Bán intends."

"Lucky tried that a couple of years ago, but nothing came of it," said Róisín. "I wonder if A. B. Ryan had a hand in denying our application, even then."

"That's possible. Regardless, let's try again," said Kevin, doing his best to be encouraging. "Maybe F. M. knows something or someone who can help us. In the meantime, where's Rudy? Did he go to the bookstore?"

"I expect he ducked out as soon as A. B. and Ursula barged in here," said Sarah. "I wonder what he meant by Rudy not saying much about Fibonacci's. How would they be acquainted?"

Her color had returned, but she sighed and rubbed her stomach. Rudy's knowing A. B. Ryan could be serious, even dangerous.

"I'll ask him next time I see him," said Kevin solemnly, sharing her thoughts. Was this scenario a replay of Arán Bán's manipulation of Ah-Lahn's son, Tadhgan? He hoped not. He'd thought they were making progress with Rudy. Clearly there was more going on here than met the eye, especially if the lad was involved with the man who was their sworn enemy.

Kevin gazed around the room and felt his heart expand in deep appreciation for the Friends of Ancient Wisdom who were his trusted compatriots in this face-off between light and dark. No one doubted that battle lines had been drawn.

He stood up and bowed to them, palms together at his heart. "Thank you, Friends," he said sincerely. They returned his bow and beamed their own appreciation to this man who was displaying a power of which he himself might not be fully aware.

Kevin put his arm around Sarah and helped her to her feet.

"Come on, Hon," he said, "we've got to get you home. Debbie, thank God you were here today. Róisín, please tell Lucky I'd like to speak with him first thing in the morning."

"I will. I can feel his eagerness to see you, too," she agreed. "Now, get yourselves home. We'll all pray about this. I know there's a plan."

Eleven

Ireland! I'm in Ireland! This isn't a dream!" Glenna exclaimed to herself. She was finishing unpacking and trying to decide how to spend her first afternoon on the Emerald Isle.

She had thoroughly enjoyed a light lunch served by Fiona, the cheerful owner of the inn called *Teach na beannachta,* and then retired to her upstairs bedroom.

The chirps and trills of birdsong wafted in on a soft breeze blowing through the lovely lace curtains that graced her open dormer window. She could see the harbor only a few blocks away. Clearly, today was much too inviting to waste in napping.

She checked her appearance in the antique mirror whose painted frame matched the sage green dressing table across from her bed. She decided she was none the worse for wear after her travels and ventured out to explore the quaint seaside village that was to be her home for three weeks.

Dingle Town was a riot of maytime flowers, a child's paintbox of color in bloom. At the windows of residences and shops, flower boxes overflowed with marigolds, pink petunias, blue forget-me-nots, and multicolored pansies. Front gardens were bursting with purple and red flowers she couldn't name. Ivy, furze, and rhododendron bushes and, surprisingly, palm trees flourished in abundance here in County Kerry's temperate climate.

Even the buildings that snuggled side by side along the narrow, winding streets were painted in vivid Easter-egg colors—the better to distinguish business from business and residence from residence.

"If I ever own a house, I'm going to paint it royal blue with white trim and a bright yellow door!" Glenna declared to the sea birds who gaily called and wheeled overhead.

She thought her heart could come no nearer to bursting with the exhilaration of being in Ireland, until she heard and then saw the little girl—a stunning little redhead with bottle-green eyes. She looked to be about six years old.

She was standing by the famous statue of Fungi the Dolphin, whose bronze image holds pride of place on the harbor strand. Her teacher and classmates were chatting to each other, ignoring her completely while she sang at the top of her lungs.

Glenna was enthralled at the purity of the child's voice and her unabashed joy in the rapturous song that flowed from her with the ease of breath. She seemed not to notice the crowd that had gathered around her and was genuinely surprised when they clapped at the conclusion of her song.

Apparently, she had been waiting for someone and beamed as soon as she noticed a lovely young woman hurrying toward her. Judging by the woman's equally green eyes and slightly darker red hair, Glenna was certain this was the mother. She swept her daughter into her arms, twirled her around, and then set her on her feet.

Glenna was delighted to watch them skipping along the pavement, hand-in-hand, and entering Murphy's Ice Cream Shop a few doors up the block. As a cone seemed the perfect addition to her afternoon, she followed them into the busy store and ordered a scoop of Dreamy Creamy Caramel.

Not wanting to intrude, yet feeling she must at least thank the little girl for her song, Glenna stepped up to where mother and child were sitting.

"Your daughter has a beautiful voice," she said to the mother. The little girl edged closer to her parent and focused intently on eating her ice cream. The mother patted her child's knee and smiled. "She does, yes. 'Tis a gift from the angels."

"I believe that is true," said Glenna, her eyes suddenly misting. "Don't let anybody ever take away your joy in singing, sweetheart," she said to the little girl. "You've made my day."

"You're an American," said the mother. "Do you sing?"

"I do back home," said Glenna. "This is my first day of vacation."

"Enjoy your holiday," said the young woman. The little girl looked up from her ice cream and graced Glenna with a smile that felt like a ray of recognition, a window into the past.

"Thank you, I will," was all she could say as speech abandoned her. She nodded to the two radiant redheads and quickly left Murphy's in favor of a bench by the water.

There she sat for the better part of an hour, watching the comings and goings of boats both large and small, while pondering that surprising glimpse into another time when she and children sang together in the pure ecstasy of music for its own sake.

"Ah, Glenna, you're back in time for tea." Fiona greeted her warmly when she returned to the inn. "Come sit, *a chara*, and meet some of our guests. The German couple are still out sightseeing. You'll see them tonight or in the morning. We're a regular United Nations this week.

"This is Ruth. She's a teacher from the U.S., like you. John is a student from Sweden. He's new here today as well. And Imogen is from Donegal. You'd think she wouldn't need to stray from such a lovely place, but here she is. To paint, is it, Imogen?" The woman nodded and beamed a smile.

"Hello everybody," said Glenna, taking a seat at the large wooden dining table that was spread with an embroidered cloth, rose-patterned china, and an abundance of tea, coffee, and baked goods.

She surprised herself by accepting a cup of tea and a warm scone. "I shouldn't," she protested weakly. "I've probably gained five pounds already with all the sweets I've consumed. But they look so good."

She shrugged and slathered butter from the local dairy on the fresh pastry, topping it off with homemade strawberry jam.

"Yum! Fiona, these are the best I've tasted so far."

"There's plenty more, whenever you're the slightest bit peckish," said her hostess, then laughed at Glenna's puzzled expression. "That means hungry, *a chara*. And here's a letter for you. A lass dropped it by while you were out."

Fiona reached into her apron pocket and handed Glenna a small envelope, hand-addressed on lavender paper with a linen finish. Inside was a note card with a delicate *fleur-de-lys* watermark embedded in the quality stock. Her heart leapt as she read:

> *Fáilte*, Glenna.
>   We are pleased to welcome you to the Dingle peninsula. F. M. has told us a bit about your upcoming theatrical adventures. *Comhghairdeas!* (Congratulations!)
>   We look forward to getting to know you while you are here. Please join us tonight for a mighty *seisiún* at Kennedy's pub on the waterfront, Strand St. The three of us will be playing.
>   *Beir bua* (Best of luck),
>   Cormac, Saoirse, & Ciara

"Apparently I need to start learning some Gaelic. Or I guess you call it 'Irish,' don't you?" Glenna said lightly, looking up from reading. "I know *fáilte* means 'welcome' and they translated 'congratulations' for me. What is a *seisiún*?" She said the word as 'see-shun.'

Imogen from Donegal gave her a patient smile. "It's pronounced 'session' or 'seshoon'. 'Tis our Irish word for an impromptu gathering of local musicians. Our pubs are famous for the quality of trad—that is, traditional music. I've heard these folks play and they're very good. I'll be glad to go with you tonight, if you like."

"How do you say 'thank you' in Irish?" asked Glenna.

"*Go raibh maith agat*," said Imogen, "and you're most welcome. Don't worry about the pronunciation, you'll catch on."

Glenna beamed at the woman's instant generosity and felt her shoulders relax. She hadn't realized how much anxiety about finding her way she'd been carrying. Now, on her first day in Dingle, she'd been entertained by a singing angel and she had met a fellow traveler who knew the language. She could feel F. M.'s people gathering her in.

And gather her, they did. The entire town seemed to enfold Glenna in a soundtrack of welcome. Even as a singer-actress in New York, she had never been surrounded with so many truly gifted musicians. There was a quality about these Irish players she couldn't quite identify—a depth and a sweetness that poured through their music, especially from the ones who were F. M.'s friends.

Every night for the next week she could be found in one or more of Dingle Town's many pubs. As promised, Imogen accompanied her to Kennedy's for her first night on the town. After that, Glenna was more than comfortable going alone or with others from the inn who wanted to join her.

Sometimes the tunes and the conversation kept her in a single pub, listening intently, talking to the locals and tourists who shared a table or adjoining seat at the bar. She was tuning her ear to the lilt of Irish still spoken here in the Gaeltacht. And she was trying to identify that special quality of being that had eluded her, even on Broadway.

On other nights she sampled the atmosphere in a variety of establishments. Each had its own personality—a reflection of the proprietors, who often lived in upstairs apartments. Glenna was struck by the pride of ownership she observed and felt from these folks. They were deeply engaged with their businesses and their customers. The dedication was palpable. She was noticing the same connection in many of the other business owners in town.

Very quickly she began to recognize familiar faces of people she met in the shops that she explored as eagerly by day as the pubs she visited in the evenings. Dingle was a haven for artists who worked in every possible medium. Her friend, Imogen, had been here several times before and knew most of the painters and artisans whose galleries they visited together.

Most mornings, after one of Fiona's hearty breakfasts, Glenna went for a long walk. As she strolled along narrow streets or sat watching boats coming and going in the harbor, she savored the experience.

Handmade jewelry, pottery, stained and blown glass enticed her eye from shop windows. Delicious aromas from bakeries and restaurants tickled her nose. She luxuriated in the textures of handmade woolens.

She felt like a thirsty sponge, soaking up every sensation of this enchanting place where fate or fortune had landed her.

She had to admit the weavers were her favorite. After her first night walking home from Kennedy's pub in her thin blouse, khakis, and light jacket, Glenna had quickly realized she would need more substantial clothing for an Irish summer.

Friends had told her to pack some sweaters, but she simply could not bring herself to bulk up her suitcase with heavy clothing when the temperature in New York City was pushing ninety degrees Fahrenheit.

The following morning she stopped first at the studio of a weaver whose gorgeous sweaters and scarves were displayed to show off the woman's unique designs. Glenna disciplined herself and bought only one cardigan and one pullover. She knew she would be back.

Then she went next door and bought two hats and a scarf made by another local artist. As someone who made her living acting and singing, she knew enough to keep her head and throat warm in the damp breezes that blew off the North Atlantic.

A week later she received an invitation from her new musician friends, Cormac, Saoirse, and Ciara. "You've got to hear this accordion player," they urged. "We've been privileged to join a few *seisiúns* with him, which is grand. But we often end up just listening. He can play any tune and sings with a voice that'll break your heart."

Glenna needed no further encouragement. When she arrived at the pub where the man was playing, the room was already packed. Fortunately, her friends had saved her a tiny space up front where she squeezed in between them. She was amazed to see the man had not one, but five accordions.

"They're tuned to different keys," explained Cormac, whose instrument was the *Uilleann* pipes. "I've played a bit of accordion myself, but I've never experienced anybody like him. That's the thing. You don't just hear him, you feel him in every note."

Cormac was correct in his description, though not by half. The man played and sang his first tune soft and slow, like a lullaby. Glenna thought it was lovely, but nothing she hadn't heard other nights. Then he kicked into a series of jigs and reels that demolished any smugness she might have had about her knowledge of traditional Irish music.

His energy electrified the room. Here was a heat not generated by outward display. It boiled up from the man's soul. His entire body danced the music. He didn't just play his accordion, he channeled the wild Celtic spirit that no invader had ever conquered.

When he lifted his clear tenor voice in a traditional *sean nós* song— that haunting Gaelic *a cappella* style—Glenna felt her own soul catch fire. He wasn't only singing, he was being sung.

Had she ever felt that in her own performances? Only a couple of times, but then she couldn't reproduce the effect. She didn't know where it came from or how it happened. Yet this accordion player captured—or was captured by—this incredible energy, even when he played a gentle love song.

Glenna knew there were performers like this on Broadway, but she'd never really noticed them. Something about Ireland was opening her to see and feel in a way she never had before.

She realized now that this same total engagement with their art was what she had witnessed in her musician friends and in the little red-haired girl, and that drew her to some of the artists in town, though not to others. These were the ones who lived their art—their passion. The Gaelic word, *paisean*, even sounded the same.

Here was a universal truth—a uniquely human potential for soaring to the heights as an instrument of some divine eros that poured out through the artist's expression of pure soul essence.

The result was nothing less than unconditional love which flowed from the abandonment of self-consciousness, affect, or sense of limitation that would keep the artist earth-bound.

Now Glenna knew what she must bring to her role as Portia. She had to open up her own soul to the character Shakespeare had created so that the spirit of Portia could move through her like a flame that would ignite every time she took the stage.

By the end of the evening, she could hardly speak. She bid her friends a hasty *slán* (good bye), and rushed back to her room at the inn where she could process the vibrations that reverberated through her—body, mind, and soul.

Almost since the day she had arrived in Ireland, she'd been writing a few lines of verse and song. Now a full-fledged poem poured out as her soul's profound response to being swept up into the man's electrifying aura.

The Celt & His Music
Five instruments
Five voices
Five bellows like lungs
Five extensions of a fire
in the man and his music—
born of battles, voyages, storms,
and loves to break
the heart wide open

Played on the very threshold
of life and death,
the cliff-edge of existence
where time is naught and sound
is the fullness of the soul

Who can hardly bear to live,
except it dare not die
for love of the tune
that begs it breathe again
for one more day of music,
called out like a warrior's
cry for freedom,
as if this were his final,
passionate moment on earth.

The hour was late, and still Glenna couldn't sleep. She felt reborn, illumined, set aglow with her own art, with the magic of theatre that had drawn her to the stage as a child.

Here was the power the ancients had danced upon their altars in rituals of transformation. That's where theatre had begun—as sacred ritual designed to convey the peaks and perils of human existence and to "alter" both actors and audience in the process.

Glenna was ready now. She knew it. Bathed in the flush of inspiration, doubt in her ability to play Portia dropped away.

Now she understood what had been missing from her high school drama class recitation of Portia's much-repeated speech: *The quality of mercy is not strained.*

She had been given poor marks for a flat, mechanical performance. Not this time, she vowed. If she could infuse her Portia with the *paisean* she had contacted here in Dingle, the powerful energy and presence of Shakespeare's beloved character would light up the stage.

A week remained before she would take the Bus Éireann to Dublin to begin rehearsals. She still had plenty of time to finish memorizing her lines. And to take the hike up Mount Brandon that F. M.'s friends had promised her would be a life-changing experience.

Twelve

Ventry Beach was a much less serene place than Rory remembered from his boyhood visits. Nowadays there was a large caravan park near the entrance where crowds of campers and day visitors lined the beach. Many more cottages, like the one he was lodged in, dotted the drive from Slea Head to Dingle Town.

Nevertheless, he found it was possible to wander into less populated areas farther up the beach where he could walk or rest in hopes of finding peace of mind and answers to the mysteries of his dreams and visions.

Today's bright, mid-morning sun sparkled on gentle waves making lacy patterns in a thousand shades of pearl and white, which, amusingly, made him think of ladies in long skirts, paddling in the shallows, risking their hems in the ripples that dared to catch them unawares.

Distant green hills lay placidly amidst banks of clouds that parted, exposing blue sky, then falling back to earth to cool and shadow Ireland's longest stretch of sand. Watching the ever-changing interplay of sky and sea and land soothed Rory as nothing had accomplished in many months.

As he had done most mornings for the past two weeks, he made himself a couple of sandwiches and a thermos of strong black tea, and stuffed them with some wrapped cheese, sausages, and an apple into his day pack. Thus armed against hunger and thirst and well-clad in an Irishman's instinct for layers, he had walked the two blocks from his cottage to a niche in the dunes where tall grasses made a natural shelter from the stiff breezes that often blew off the Atlantic.

Rory was glad the air was calm today, though he was not opposed to walking in the wind. Many a day he had relished leaning into the strong gusts that whipped and swirled across the length of Ventry Beach—almost as if he were pushing against the hand of destiny.

He had not meant to be resistant, but there it was. Some unseen force wanted his attention and, despite his intriguing encounters with F. M. Bellamarre and his congenial assistant, Phelan, for the first few days of Rory's sabbatical he had been unwilling to consent to whatever message that force was trying to convey to him.

Instead he had set his teeth against the wind and stalked as if hunting for prey until his legs gave out. Then he would sit wherever he stopped to eat his lunch and watch the waves—sometimes for hours—until he felt the soft rhythm of Ventry's surf ease its way into his pores.

On bright blue mornings, like today's, he would strip down to his shorts as soon as he got to the shore and stride right into the shock of cold surf, letting the water rise up around him in a chilly embrace. In those moments, the sea was a comfort, a nurturing, motherly presence that offered him relief from the questions about his future that he could not seem to resolve.

Swimming in the ocean, he had to focus on being alive and aware of currents that might pull him out too far or simply pluck him under the restless waves. It was good to be so one-pointed. He always came back to shore with a clearer head. The more he swam, the longer the sensation lasted. As of today, nearly at the end of his second week, he was feeling much less anxious.

He had brought his bicycle with him on the back of Phelan's SUV. Last week he had ridden the entire thirty-mile Slea Head Loop. Another exercise in focusing. One had to be a strong biker, which he was, and pay attention as you rode. A wandering mind could get you knocked into the sharp branches of fuchsia hedgerows, battered against ancient stone walls, or tossed off a cliff by one of the ubiquitous tour buses that squeezed around Dingle's narrow, twisting roads.

The challenging bike ride had done him good, yet it was not enough. Father Crispin had told him to give his mind a rest, and so he was doing. But he still felt uneasy. He was sleeping better at night, but his mind was not really calm—almost as if memories that held important messages were lurking, just out of reach.

Rory and his brother, Craig, had particularly loved riding horses by the sea—both at home in Donegal, where they had enjoyed brisk canters on the dark sands of Tullagh Beach—and here at Ventry.

Four days ago he had found a stable within walking distance of his cottage. He was pleased to discover their herd was made up of Irish Cobs—the native breed considered by many to be the best horse in the world because of their docile temperament, sure-footedness, and straight-forward honesty.

Exactly what I need, Rory had said to himself as he strolled out to the paddock to meet the horses.

Within minutes he'd had no doubt as to which horse he wanted to ride. Her name was Bevan, meaning "Fair Lady"—a gorgeous bay with a mahogany coat, long black mane and tail, and the feathered feet characteristic of the Irish draft horse.

"She's a smart lass, is our Bevan," said Hugo, the guide who helped Rory pick out the appropriate English tack for his size and weight.

"The other horses respect her, as she mothers them a bit and keeps them in line. She's patient with beginning riders, but she does like to pull out the stops once in a while. Since you're an experienced rider— and a Celt to boot—she'll like you. We'll give you some time to get your seat back before you go galloping on the beach, but when you do, she'll give you plenty of speed."

Ah, yes. Here was the therapy Rory needed. He had noticed it that first day in the presence of the sweet-tempered horses. He could feel the shift in his entire being the minute he began to groom Bevan. She was a beauty. Keen awareness. A kind, but no-nonsense lady. He could tell that from the look she gave him.

"You've got issues, boy-o," she'd seemed to say. "No worries, there. We'll work them out together."

And so they did. Slowly at first—Rory easing out the kinks after not riding since he'd been living at the monastery. Horse and rider becoming accustomed to each other's energy.

Bevan relaxed as she felt Rory take the lead a good rider knew to do. He awakened to the grounding presence of thirteen hundred pounds of patient intelligence under him, waiting for his signal that together they would know how to take on the five miles of glistening sand and surf that stretched before them.

On the third day, as he was cinching Bevan's English saddle, she turned her head and fixed him with what he would always remember as "the look." In fact, he could have sworn she winked, as if to say, "Today, boy-o. Today we fly!"

The sky had been a clear, robin's-egg blue overhead, circled by fluffy clouds in the distance where early afternoon sun was only beginning to play hide and seek. The tide was out, leaving a wide swath of sandy beach with easy waves swishing gracefully toward land from a glorious, teal-blue sea. Rory was in heaven.

Only two other riders, both women, had joined him and Hugo that day, and they all knew what they were doing. They rode slowly down the trail to the beach, carefully avoiding the stretches where swimmers and fishermen enjoyed the lazy waves. Once they passed the first big curve in the beach, they began to canter.

Rory had felt the energy building in his body, mind, and soul. He knew Bevan sensed it, too. Her muscles were bunching, force gathering like a rocket readying for lift-off. Then Hugo shouted, the horses surged forward, and they were off in a flash, galloping as if their lives depended on reaching a sacred destination!

Hooves pounding on the sand. Hearts matching them beat for beat. Salty air teasing the nostrils of riders and mounts. Ocean water splashing up to the horses' withers as they ventured further out into the surf where land and sea became one—men and women flying across the strand in complete harmony with their steeds.

When they finally reined in at the very end of Ventry and let their horses play in the slightly rising tide, Rory was ecstatic. Beyond exhilarated. Filled with the buoyancy of love for life he had not felt in many months. Here was the vibrancy that prayer and chant had given him as a lad and in his early novitiate, but that had ceased to invigorate him.

This feeling of being incredibly alive was what he had been missing. The sense was in his body again. But where to find it and how to retain it? As much as he loved horse riding, he knew that was not his vocation.

And what if this elán was not the will of *An Síoraí*? What if his debt had not been paid? He could not begin to guess. He could only pray that what he was seeking was also seeking him—and that they would find each other within the next week before he must return to the monastery and report his decision to Father Crispin.

Today's rising tide reached Rory's outstretched legs, rousing him from his recollection of yesterday's adventure. He longed to ride again, and might do so before he had to leave. Yet something told him that yesterday was special. The felt sense still reverberated through his body.

Remember this feeling and build on it, an inner voice told him.

The wind kicked up, prompting him to gather the remains of the lunch he had barely touched and walk back to his cottage. When he arrived, he made himself a fresh cup of tea and took out his journal.

"Not a lot of self-discovery recorded so far on these blank pages," he remarked aloud to himself. Which was fine with him. He was grateful that the leaves of F. M.'s gift had been free of the lines that could be so demanding when you had nothing to inscribe on them.

On an empty sheet you could scribble a few fragments of thought or paste bits of leaf or flower petals to remind yourself of a pleasant wander through a neighbor's garden. You were not goaded by straight lines to write something deep and well-formed.

Ireland didn't move in straight lines. Rory had known that truth from the cradle. He didn't intend to go linear at this stage of his life. However, he did have something to say to the blank page, so he began to write.

I feel her every day now, like a waking dream. She's walking beside me, sitting with me on the dunes at Ventry, sharing my thoughts, my musings of the past, my fleeting wonderings about the future.

Did I know her as a druid? I know I did. But who was she and what did she do, looking so lovely in her gold torc and her blue dress? Druids wore white, or so I've read. The bard's color was blue.

My lady was accomplished. I know that by her bearing. She is no one's fool. Does she think me a fool? I pray not. She loves me, that I know. I hear her singing to me now and then. A song we wrote together and one we share as the melody of our unity.

Here is the song I hear her sing:

> Come dance with me!
> Spin 'round and 'round
> where time turns into timelessness
> and forever spirals on Life's great wheel.
>
> Male and female are we now,
> flame and water, water and flame.
> You are the spark; I am the tinder.
> I'll be the sun, you be the moon,
> for we are souls that sail to sea
> across the ocean of *An Síoraí*.
>
> What a lively dance is this:
> spinning into luminous realms,
> weaving garlands 'round our shoulders
> opening our hearts to playful spirits
> who come to puncture pompous displays,
> and carry us off on clouds of laughter,
> singing songs only fairies know.
>
> Come dance with me in Life's sweet play!
> Your smile's been tucked away too long.

A firm knock at the door brought Rory back to the present. He looked at the clock on the wall. Five o'clock. Nearly supper time. That would be Phelan, showing up with another batch of groceries. He also had a message.

"Are you up for an adventure?" he asked enthusiastically as Rory opened the door and let him in. He began putting away the bounty he had carried in a large crate.

"Sure, why not? What's the plan?"

"F. M. is inviting you on a hike up Mount Brandon. Tomorrow promises clear weather, though we know how long that can last here in Dingle." They laughed together. Predicting Irish weather was an art known only to those who could smell the shifts in barometric pressure or feel it in their bones.

"Be ready by eight o'clock and I'll pick you up here. F. M. says he'll meet us at the carpark at the foot of the mountain. Don't worry about food. I'm packing lunches, so you won't starve."

"That'll be grand. Thanks. Does F. M. ever ride with you?"

Phelan shook his head. "He always declines, saying his transportation is arranged. I've often wondered if he flies. He's that much of a magus, for sure. Trust me, if F. M. has chosen to take you under his wing, you're safe—as long as you're honest with him and yourself."

"I'll remember that," said Rory quietly.

"I know I don't have to tell you to wear your strongest hiking boots. The land's steep and rough on the mountain. But full of blessing, if you know where to look. *Slán*, my friend."

"*Slán abhaile*, Phelan."

The next morning at 8:00 a.m. sharp Rory strode out the cottage door and climbed into the passenger seat of Phelan's SUV.

"Thanks for being on time," said his friend.

"Of course. Father Crispin always said, 'All we have in this life is time.' I try not to waste mine or anyone else's."

"Not everybody understands that. F. M. is a similar model of temporal and spiritual thriftiness. As soon as he's finished the matter at hand, he's off to the next."

"I noticed that about him at Lough Gur. Moves like the wind, the man does. Or more like the mist."

The two young men shared a laugh.

"Before we get to the trail, there's something else I'm supposed to tell you about F. M. and his philosophy," said Phelan.

"Grand," said Rory. "I think I'm ready for more today."

Phelan glanced at the man whose company he would have enjoyed, even if Rory hadn't been assigned to his care.

"F. M. wants you to be aware that those who make the most progress under his tutelage are the ones with the most generously loving hearts. Those not given to the mediocrity of sticky human sympathy, but rather those possessed of the intention to let each one discover their True Self and be that—without impediment. For that is freedom and liberation of the soul."

Rory let out a deep sigh. He could feel his heart receive the idea that he was not given to the kind of sympathy that pulls people down rather than lifting up their souls.

"*Go raibh míle maith agat,* Phelan. These insights are an unexpected help right now. Your friendship is an unexpected help."

"*Tá fáilte romhat,* Rory. You know you're very welcome. 'As each one requires,' you'll hear F. M. say. For some reason you are especially important to him. When I asked him about his interest in you, all he would say is, 'Time is short. He must be ready.' Ready for what, I don't know. Perhaps we'll find out when we're with him today."

Both men were silent for a few minutes as their vehicle gained elevation on the approach to Mount Brandon. Behind them the Three Sisters Peaks rose up out of a blue-grey Atlantic that, from this distance, appeared more serene than its actual nature.

"Are you going on the hike today?" Rory asked as the road narrowed and they neared the carpark. "Seems like you ought to have some relief from staying with the car."

"I am, yes. The parking's plentiful and safe at the foot of Mount Brandon, so I can leave the car. I'm eager to climb to the summit or as close as we can make it. I haven't done that since I was a lad and came up here with my Da.

"F. M. told me he has a bit of a mission in mind for the day, so I've come prepared. I can tell you, the man sets a brisk pace."

That he did. True to form, F. M. was waiting for them when Phelan parked his SUV beside several other vehicles already lined up in the ample carpark. Mount Brandon was a popular climb for serious hikers, most of whom were already on the trail.

After a warm, though brief, mutual greeting, the three men shouldered their day packs and crossed to the trailhead. F. M. turned swiftly onto The Saint's Trail, known in Irish as *Cosán na Naomh*, and set off—clearly a man with a purpose.

At first the two younger men engaged in friendly banter to which their companion did not respond. F. M. was unusually quiet, as if pondering some deep matter. Though his body walked just ahead of them, he seemed far away in spirit.

The man can be as remote as a skellig, commented Rory to himself. Then he decided that silence was a better way to appreciate the feel of a holy mountain under his feet. Phelan seemed to agree.

The air was crisp and cool this morning, the sky amazingly blue above. Rory felt his senses sharpen as his body found the rhythm of ascent. Mount Brandon was indeed a steep climb. You had to keep your wits about you to avoid stepping into a ravine washed out by the frequent rains that made the Irish landscape an ever-changing work of Nature's art.

But keeping one's wits was what the path was all about, wasn't it?

Thirteen

"Hurry up, *a chairde*," urged Saoirse's boyfriend, Cormac. "It's nearly ten. If we don't start up the trail soon the weather may change before we get down."

"Coming. Ciara's putting on her boots and I want to be sure Glenna has what she needs."

"I'm good, Saoirse, honest," said Glenna. "I've got a hiking stick, a pack filled with enough food for a week, my phone, my journal, and Girl Scout survival training in case we're attacked by bears."

"There's no need to be sarcastic, *a chara*. All the world may be a tidy flat stage to you actors, but the mountain is tricky in some places. Stay with us and keep a white marker in sight in case we get separated for any reason. Lots of hikers strike out on their own, but the markers are there to keep you away from the deepest wash-outs.

"The large crosses you see mark the fourteen stations. They're regularly spaced and make good resting places. You can stop to catch your breath as you need, but don't fall too far behind us. I expect Ciara and I will walk with you most of the day. Cormac is determined to make it to the top. He's the mountain goat. I'm more of a lamb, myself."

Her boyfriend snorted. "Some lamb. You should hear how she bleats at me, Glenna. More like an old ewe."

Saoirse gave him a look that would have melted the glaciers that formed the mountain. Cormac grinned, grabbed her around the waist, and kissed her mightily on the lips. "There! Now be safe, *mo mhuirnín*. I'll meet you back here, if not at the top."

Glenna and her friends soon found their own rhythm. Ciara and Saoirse walked with her until they reached the second station of the cross where they stopped to look back at the view of the dramatic Three Sisters peaks that appeared to rise straight out of the Atlantic.

"You're doing grand," said Saoirse. She turned her head toward the summit, catching sight of Cormac striding up the mountain with a spring in his step. Even from here, she could tell he was in his element.

"Go on, you two. I can tell you want to. I'm fine walking at my own pace," said Glenna. "There are so many people on the trail, if anything serious happened to me somebody would notice and find you. The view is so incredible, I don't really want to go much further."

"If you're sure," said Ciara. "F. M. would not be pleased with us if we lost you up here. He is rather depending on having a healthy Portia for his play."

"Honestly, I'm fine. This is a perfect place for me to stop. To tell you the truth, I've never been much of a hiker. I'm already getting hungry and I can feel my journal calling me."

With more assurances that their friend wanted to stay put, the two women headed up the path, chatting happily in Gaelic. Their voices faded quickly, leaving Glenna to herself. She found a gently sloping draw where she was sheltered from the breeze and still able to extend her gaze out to the blue Atlantic that lay serenely in the distance.

Ciara's mention of F. M. and her soon-to-begin rehearsals as Portia made Glenna think of the lines she had been memorizing—and of the dream that came to her frequently of the man she knew she would love beyond all others—if she ever found him.

Or would he find her? In *The Merchant of Venice*, Portia's suitors are not allowed to woo her. Instead, they must choose between three chests or caskets. Whoever selects the one that contains her picture wins her hand. Other suitors have tried and failed. She prays that Bassanio will succeed, but she cannot coach him. She says to him in her mind, *If you do love me, you will find me out.*

"Will you find me out, my darling? I pray you will." Glenna spoke aloud to the beloved whose identity only her soul knew.

Bringing her mind back to the breathtaking landscape before her, she pulled out her journal and began to jot down some impressions of how her body, mind, and soul were coming together on this holy mountain. She opened her heart to the spirit of Saint Brandon, known as the Navigator because of his great voyage to unknown lands in the sixth century AD, and let the words flow out in a poem that felt like praise.

> The whole world feels at peace here
> Where soft eyes detect Michael's misty skellig
> Rising as an apparition in the distance,
> Saved for those who sense before they see it.
>
> Could Eden be more tender
> Than dainty heathered tufts of greenery
> And tiny, four-petaled, sun-lit flowers
> Scattered as Nature's votaries
> Offered to reverent pilgrims.
>
> Here is my soul's cathedral
> Alone with Brandon all around me
> Intoning his prayers
> That bring my heart to tears.
>
> I imagine his spirit gone out walking
> To and fro with every traveler,
> Even though he long ago
> Became the very earth
> Where his soul rests still in blessing,
> Now one with all he blesses.
>
> Seen and unseen are dancing
> In Wisdom's native knowing—
> Like the bird who asks, "What's flying?"
> When lifted up by the Good Saint's exhalation.

Glenna had no idea how long she stayed in her verdant shelter, only that several hours had passed since her friends left her. She was still comfortable, except for the growing need to relieve herself.

Better not wait, she thought.

She looked around and decided she could hunker down in the wash-out to her left and do her business before anybody saw her. And if they did, oh well.

Cormac had been right about the weather. The sun was lower in the sky now and dark clouds were gathering to the south. The Atlantic had lost its blue luster and was beginning to look quite grey in the fading light. She'd worn plenty of layers, so she wouldn't get cold. She had an umbrella in her pack. She always carried her raincoat so she wouldn't get too wet if it started to rain. But she did begin to worry.

Why had she been so eager to have her friends go on without her? Why did she think nothing would happen to her out here in the middle of nowhere? What would she do if they somehow missed her on their way back down the mountain?

Realizing that she should move up closer to the path, she stood up too quickly. Her foot slipped on a patch of mossy grass. A sharp pain shot up her leg from her ankle and she sat down hard.

"Ow, ow, ow! No, no, no, no, no! This can't happen," she cried out loud, rubbing her ankle. She clenched and unclenched her fists and tried to move her foot.

"Good, it's not broken. Get a grip, Glenna." She dug out the arnica gel she always carried and rubbed it on her foot and leg. She did actually have some Girl Scout survival training, and this was the first step in preventing bruising or soreness.

Now what? She had to get to the path. She pulled her belongings together, shouldered her day pack, and hoisted herself up to standing with her walking stick.

Slowly and gingerly, she hobbled back to where she thought the path was. But as she looked around for white markers, the looming clouds suddenly became a thick mist that obscured all landmarks from sight. She was completely and terrifyingly lost.

"Fair play to you and F. M. for making sure we got an early start," said Rory. He and Phelan were making their way down the mountain. For strong young men, the round trip up and back was three or four hours, so they were only several yards above the third station of the cross when the mist engulfed them like a thick, damp blanket.

"We'd best stop and see if this will lift," said Phelan. "We usually get a good breeze about now. That should blow off the thickest mist. Let's hope so anyway. I remember one time . . . "

"Sh-h-h. Do you hear that?" interrupted Rory.

"What?"

"I thought I heard a woman singing."

"You're joking."

"No, I can hear her. It's a song I know. An old one from long ago. I can't imagine anyone singing it out here in the damp."

"Are you sure the altitude hasn't fogged your brain?" Phelan knocked playfully on Rory's head.

"No, I definitely hear something. Can you see at all?"

"Not much. If we're careful we can keep going, but mind your feet."

Rory was amazed that Phelan couldn't hear the woman's voice, but at least his friend believed that *he* was hearing something. Gradually they made their way down the mountain, and the mist did clear some by the time they reached the second station of the cross.

"I know you'll think I'm daft, but now I hear the sound behind us. And it's not a woman singing, she's calling for help."

"I hear it now," said Phelan.

"She's over here," said Rory. Moving over the ground as if he were following a homing beacon, he found her. She was huddled with her raincoat hood pulled up over her head. Her voice was extremely tired, but she had not given up calling out.

"*A chara*, are you all right?" said Rory, bending down and putting his hand on her shoulder. "We heard you calling. Are you hurt? Here, let's have a look at you."

He tipped up her chin in his hand and brushed her hair away from her face. Her hood fell back and her eyes went wide as she stared at him.

He pulled back his hand from her forehead and stood up sharply. He spun away, then back again, rubbing the back of his neck.

"You! It's you. How can that be? Are you real?"

"You found me. You found me. I can't believe you found me," said Glenna weakly, a dazed look on her face. Then she grimaced. "Ow!! And, yes, judging by this pain, I am very real."

"I thought I heard you singing," said Rory, staring down at her.

"More like howling. Can you get me off this mountain? I don't know where my friends are. Do you have a car? I need to go home. I'm sorry I'm babbling."

"You've had a shock, that's all," said Phelan. Then he looked over at his companion who was fixated on the woman's face. He appeared to have two shocked people on his hands.

"Rory, pull yourself together, man. Let's get her safe. Look, the wind is up. I can see down past the gate. Can you stand, *a chara*?"

"Not really. I managed to lean on my stick, but I think it's bent."

Rory scrubbed his hands over his face, shook his head, and kicked himself into action. "Here, Phelan, take my pack. I'll carry her on my back and you can catch us if I stumble."

His friend and Glenna both frowned at him, but then Phelan agreed. "You're right, lad. I'll take the lead and we'll go single file."

Glenna was glad she had relieved herself while she had daylight to do so. If she was going to ride piggy-back on a stranger—who clearly was no stranger at all—she certainly didn't want any accidents.

Somewhere in the process of her being lifted onto Rory's back they exchanged first names and then fell silent in the awkwardness of recognition that neither of them could quite believe.

Part way down the mountain, Phelan offered to carry Glenna, but Rory declined, saying with surprising firmness, "No, she's mine to bear." He hoisted her further up on his back and said reassuringly, "Don't you worry, lass. I won't let you down. Not this time."

She seemed to understand his deeper meaning and clung to him with all her might.

After a harrowing thirty minutes, two tired young men and Rory's very bedraggled piggy-back rider reached the paved path to the carpark. They were heading for Phelan's SUV when Saoirse and Ciara ran up to them, their exclamations tumbling out on top of each other.

"Oh, my God, Glenna, where've you been?"

"We were sure you'd have walked back to the car when the temperature started to drop. Then that mist enveloped the mountain and we couldn't see a thing."

"Are you hurt? You must be. Oh, *a chara*, I'm so sorry we left you."

"Can you bring her over here to our car?" said Saoirse to Rory, whose eyes were glazed and cheeks red from the exertion of carrying the woman he had dreamed about down the mountain.

As Saoirse opened the car door she looked past the young man who was easing Glenna onto the back seat and exclaimed again, this time in surprise at seeing a dear friend, one of many in Dingle who were acquainted with F. M. Bellamarre.

"Phelan, is that you? What are you doing here? Did you come up with F. M.?"

"We did, yes. This is Rory." Phelan nodded to his companion who was kneeling beside Glenna, holding her hand while she drank a cup of tea that Ciara had fetched from her thermos.

"We were on our way back down the mountain when we heard Glenna calling for help. She twisted her ankle. We don't think it's too bad, but she does need to get back to her lodging as soon as possible."

"I hate to ask," said Saoirse, "but can you take her? We have to wait for Cormac. I'm sure he went all the way to the top and probably had to stop until the mist cleared. We got a really late start today, so I don't expect him for another hour. Oh, but don't you have to wait for F. M.?"

"He sent us on our way hours ago. Said he was going on over the Brandon Ridge. You know how he is. He'll find his way back to wherever he's staying with no trouble."

"We'll see you then. *Go raibh maith agat*, Phelan. *Slán*."

"*Slán abhaile*, Saoirse. Ciara. Get yourselves and Cormac safely home and don't worry. We'll take care of your friend. Rory, stop mooning over Glenna and help her into the back of my car. She can stretch out there. We've another quarter hour to reach her inn, but she'll be fine."

Within minutes Glenna was bundled into Phelan's SUV where she went instantly to sleep and dreamed of being rescued by the love of her life from a fate she had long feared might come upon them. Now she was safe. He had found her out, at last.

"You lie back now, *a chara*, and don't trouble yourself." Fiona was fussing like a mother hen. She had fed Glenna some of the creamy vegetable soup that her guest decided was the best food in Ireland. She was now tucking Glenna into bed after making sure she took a hot bath with some kind of amazing herbs that soothed away the day's stress and most of its pain.

"Your young men said they'll check on you tomorrow. They were sorely worried about you, especially the handsome blond one. My, if I had to twist my ankle to be brought home by the likes of him, I'm thinking the ache might be worth it," Fiona said with a wink.

Glenna felt her face redden. She grinned in bashful agreement.

"You rest well now," said the woman who already seemed like family. "If you need me during the night, you can ring this little bell—like a grand lady in her boudoir. I don't want you getting up before you're steady on your feet."

"*Go raibh míle maith agat*," said Glenna wanly. "I'm sorry to be so much trouble."

"Oh, see, you're better already if you're thanking me in Irish." Fiona beamed and tiptoed out, only partially closing the door.

Glenna closed her eyes and snuggled under the cozy comforter her landlady had added to her blankets, though nearly an hour passed before she could fall asleep. Her heart and mind were still filled with amazement. He was here! Her beloved had found her! She was safe at last!

Fourteen

On their way back to the Ventry cottages, the two men agreed that Rory now had need of a car so he could visit Glenna as often as possible. He might go to her on his bicycle, but he couldn't very well ask her to ride on the handlebars for a shared outing.

"I'm sorry I can't loan you mine," said Phelan with genuine regret. "And the closest car hire is in Tralee. I'll ask around, but don't get your hopes up."

Rory was truly in despair as to how he was going to visit Glenna. On a good day, Ventry to Dingle Town was a thirty-minute bike ride, and he would arrive looking like a thoroughly disheveled refugee. Not an appearance he wished to present to the woman of his dreams.

He went to sleep praying for a miracle and the next morning found one in the form of a note in his kitchen.

> Rory, I understand you have need of an automobile. A friend of mine is on holiday elsewhere and is pleased to give you the loan of his vehicle for the next several days.
>
> Best wishes, F. M. Bellamarre

A set of car keys rested next to the note. Rory rushed outside to find a roomy, silver-blue SUV parked by the cottage. He could hardly believe his good fortune.

"*Go raibh míle maith agat,* F. M.!" he shouted and could have sworn he heard, "*Tá fáilte romhat,* you're welcome," in return.

Despite his eagerness to visit Glenna, Rory disciplined himself to eat some breakfast. At what he considered the respectable hour of ten o'clock, he hopped into the SUV's driver's seat, started an engine that purred, and pulled out onto the road that surely was leading him to his destiny.

When Rory entered Fiona's sunny private parlor—so they would not be disturbed by the other guests, the landlady told him—he found Glenna already seated on one of two love seats upholstered in bright floral patterns. Matching curtains fluttered in the soft breeze that wafted in through open windows.

The setting should have made him comfortable. Rory was aware only of the wild dance of butterflies going on in his belly.

Glenna gestured for him to sit in the love seat across from her and began to pour tea from the abundantly furnished tea service that was arranged on a low table in front of her. Rory wondered at her apparent calm. She looked at him with a steady gaze. Then he saw the vein pulsing in her neck and knew she was as jittery as he.

"Milk or lemon?"

"Milk, thanks." She added a splash and handed him his cup.

"Scone?" She held out a plate of Fiona's delicate rounds.

"No thanks, I had a large breakfast," Rory lied. His mouth was so dry, he couldn't have swallowed a morsel. They each sipped their tea. He noticed she also took milk in hers. Should he speak or would she?

"Thank you . . ." They blurted out at the same time, then laughed at the ridiculousness of nerves.

"Shall we start over?" said Glenna. She set her tea cup on the serving table and gripped her hands together on her lap. Rory kept a firm hold on his own cup.

"I'm Glenna Morrissey. American, actress, here on vacation for another week before I start rehearsals in Dublin. I'm playing Portia in Shakespeare's *The Merchant of Venice* at a replica of the original Abbey Theatre."

American women are certainly direct, thought Rory. He took a careful swallow of tea so he didn't choke, set down his cup, and began his own introduction.

"I'm Rory Ó Donnell. Irish, dairyman, history teacher, here on sabbatical for another week before I return to the monastery where I've lived for four years."

"You live at a monastery?"

"I do, yes."

"Are you a priest or something? You don't look like a priest."

Glenna's heart sank. "Please, *An Síoraí*, don't let him be a priest," she pleaded silently. How could they possibly be together if he was a priest? His next statement gave her some hope.

"I'm more of an 'or something' at the moment. I've been studying to become a priest, but now I'm not sure I'll continue. I haven't taken formal vows yet. I'm here to decide if I'm going to." He wrinkled his brow.

"And you don't really want to talk about it, do you?"

"Not at the moment."

The room fell awkwardly silent. Rory finished his tea and tried again. "You must be a serious actress if you're doing Shakespeare."

"Not so serious. I've been performing in musical theatre on Broadway. My show closed a few weeks ago and I was offered a starring role in a new show that isn't ready yet. Then I got this weird letter and I met F. M. Bellamarre and . . ."

"You know F. M.?" What were the chances? thought Rory.

"Yes, do you?"

"He's the main reason I'm here."

"He's the main reason *I'm* here. Are you beginning to feel like you've been set up on a blind date?"

"I do, except we're not so blind, are we? I've dreamed of you."

"And I, you." They looked at each other as if willing the answer to a mystery to float out through the other's eyes.

Glenna finally broke the silence. "How shall we handle this?"

"If your ankle wasn't injured, I would suggest we drive to Ventry Beach and take a good, long walk. Perhaps another time."

Rory tried to hide the disappointment in his voice and decided he was out of small talk. He got up from his seat and turned to leave. Glenna reached over and touched his hand.

"No, let's go now. My ankle is fine. Fiona told me to keep it elevated, but honestly, I think it would feel better if I walked on it. She put some herbs in my bath last night that almost completely dissolved the pain."

"Must have been from the packet Phelan gave her when we dropped you off. F. M. handed it to him yesterday before we parted ways on the mountain. 'You'll need this later,' is all he said."

"Interesting. When I first met F. M. in New York, he said he was an alchemist. He's certainly good with herbs, isn't he?"

"He is that, and much more," Rory said thoughtfully.

Glenna stood up and walked to the parlor door that led into the hallway. "Will you wait while I go upstairs for my hat and jacket? I'll only be a minute. I'd like that walk on the beach."

They spent the remainder of the morning together, walking and talking on Ventry Beach until they both realized they were starving. Glenna's ankle proved to be rather tender after all, so they adjourned to Rory's cottage where he fed her an impromptu lunch of store-bought soup and cheese sandwiches.

They talked about their families and what they liked best about their work. Glenna took particular note of his enthusiasm for cattle and morning prayers, but not necessarily the history classes he taught. She thought that odd, since he clearly knew a lot about Ireland's past.

Afternoon faded to evening. Rory invited her to dinner at his favorite seafood restaurant for a hearty meal they agreed they both needed. As they nibbled a shared dessert, the topic they had skirted all day came to the fore.

"What did I look like, when you saw me in your dreams?" asked Glenna. She could feel her heart glowing in the company of this man she already knew as the dearest companion of her soul.

"You were beautiful. You are beautiful," Rory corrected himself and reached for her hand. "We say, *tá tú go hálainn* in Irish."

"*Tá tú go hálainn.* I like that. Go on."

"Your eyes were the same crystalline blue then, and they sparkled when you saw me. Your hair was longer, about the same dark blonde.

You wore it in a braid down your back. You were often dressed in a sort of royal blue—like the sweater you had on yesterday. And you usually wore a circlet of intertwined gold around your neck."

"A torc. I know. You wore one, too, in my dreams." Glenna's eyes took on a faraway look as she remembered the vivid recollection of their mutual affection. "I thought you looked like a god."

Rory nearly choked on his sorbet. Glenna's hand flew to her mouth. "Oh, my, what have I said?"

Rory cleared his throat and grinned. "I think you should say more. I'm rather liking your dreams."

"Well, it's true. I though you looked like a god with the sun behind you and your hair blowing in the breeze. We were at a big wedding." She blushed at his raised eyebrows.

"No, not ours. Some dear friends were getting married and you were officiating. You were wearing a long white robe, with a torc, and a medallion signifying your position as . . . as, a druid. You were a druid. I never realized that before. Was I a druid, too?"

"I don't think so. I looked up the colors and it was the bards who wore blue. I think you were a singer and storyteller—a *seanchaí*."

"I believe you're right. I was singing at the wedding. I remember you smiled at me when I finished. Like you're smiling at me now."

Her eyes met his and she felt herself sink into his arms, even though he sat across the table from her, lightly touching her hand. Despite wanting to stay in this bliss forever, she stifled a yawn—as if she was finally relaxing from an internal stress she had not realized she was carrying.

"We'd better get you back to the inn," said Rory. He quickly paid for dinner and helped her into her jacket. "Ask your landlady if she has any more of F. M.'s magic herbs so you can soak your ankle tonight. I'd like to take you on a walk along the cliffs tomorrow. There's something special I want to show you."

"That sounds lovely. Shall I ask Fiona to pack us a lunch?"

"You don't like my cooking?"

"Your lunch was perfect, and I think Fiona's will be better."

They both were quiet as Rory drove the short distance from town to

Teach na beannachta. He pulled the car up to the front and turned off the engine. He wanted to sit with Glenna for hours. Anywhere. Forever.

However, not having words to express the rush of emotions he suddenly felt rippling through his body, he got out of the car and walked around to the passenger side to let her out.

She startled when he opened the door. She had been deep in thought, remembering, wondering. Not daring to hope, and fearing the future for reasons she could not fathom.

Rory took her hand and pulled her gently out of the car. They stood face-to-face, looking at each other with a combination of affection and bewilderment.

"How do you say good-night, my faithful friend, to someone you've known for centuries and have only just met?" asked Glenna, feeling strangely awkward because Rory was still holding her hand.

"*Oíche mhaith, a chara dhílis,*" he said. "That seems a good place to start, doesn't it?" He lifted her hand to his lips and then released it.

"It does," agreed Glenna. "Thank you for dinner."

"You're very welcome. I'll pick you up tomorrow after you've had your breakfast. Sleep well, *a chara.*"

"I will. You, too."

The view from above Clogher Beach was spectacular. Here was the Wild Atlantic on full display. Rough waves hurled themselves against jagged cliffs with an intensity whose raw, primal power stunned Glenna.

Rory led her up a long incline to the very edge of the cliffs, though not too close, he warned. The relentless ocean eroded the land from underneath so that an unsuspecting hiker might find herself falling, fatally, to the rocks below.

The wind blew savagely here. It was so strong that Rory had to hold onto Glenna to keep her upright. They stood in their first embrace, buffeted by the gale-force wind and, for a few moments, noticed only how their hearts kept time with each other as if they had known that rhythm from long ago.

"Come with me," said Rory at last. "There's something else over this way." He took her hand and led her back several dozen feet away from the cliffs to a broad, grassy field. "We'll rest here for a while. Let yourself sink into the land and tell me what you feel."

Glenna was rather surprised at what seemed her companion's suggestion of a reclining embrace, but she followed his lead. He had released her hand and was stretched out on the grass, hands behind his head, a look of utter contentment on his face.

She lay down in the grass. It was incredibly soft. The land seemed to cradle her in the subtle warmth of small plants that gathered the sun's heat and held it next to the earth. She looked up at white fluffy clouds sailing gently across a deep blue sky. Then she felt it.

The ground was quivering. The pounding surf was reverberating into the land, even though they were safely away from the cliff edge. The earth was absolutely alive here, carrying on a dynamic conversation that had gone on for millennia.

"I can almost hear them, can't you?" said Glenna softly, still looking up at the sky.

"Who?" Rory had been watching her, enjoying her reactions when he saw from her half-closed eyes that she was deep into the experience.

"The rocks, the sea, the wind. I can hear them conversing, comparing their power and debating who is older."

"That's lovely, *a chara.*" Rory lay back down in the grass and was silent for a full minute. Then he cleared his throat and said rather quietly, more to the sky than to Glenna, "I know we've just met—again—but have you thought about sex?"

Glenna's eyes popped open and she turned her head to fix him with a look of utter surprise. "Have I thought about sex?!"

She raised up on her elbow and turned her body toward him, doing her best to speak calmly. "Well, yes, I have. I am a healthy, twenty-six-year-old American woman. We do consider such things."

"With me, I mean. Have you've considered sex with me?" Rory matched her posture and looked directly at her.

Glenna now sat up cross-legged, her hands on her thighs. She stared back at him, very seriously. "Are you accusing me of impure thoughts? I wouldn't dream of deflowering a monk, if that's what you mean."

Rory was sitting now, too. "You make me sound so medieval."

"Isn't that what living a monastic life is like?"

"I suppose you could say so. I guess that's part of the attraction. Living apart from the world. To join the monastery you have to be free of family ties and other obligations, which in many ways is a relief. It can also be stifling, as I have begun to discover. However, until I come to a decision about making a profession or not, I'm still under my vow to live *conversatio morum*—in the manner of life appropriate to a monk."

"I understand that."

"I didn't want to disappoint you, that's all. I thought I should be clear about my, uh, un-availability."

"I'm not in the habit of jumping into bed with someone I've known for two days—even if he is the man of my dreams."

"Fair play to that. And just so you know, I am not totally without experience. I've only been at the monastery for four years."

Glenna felt herself blushing ferociously. "Can we table this discussion, please? I cannot believe I'm having a conversation about sex with a monk."

"I shouldn't have brought it up." Rory flopped back down on the grass and stared at the sky.

Glenna crawled over to him and made him look at her. "Yes, you should have and I'm glad you did—sort of. We're adults. We know there is something remarkable between us, and intimacy is bound to become an issue. Especially when you bring me to this place brimming with raw, primal energy."

"My mistake. I wasn't thinking." Rory grinned at her. "Honest."

He stood and pulled her to her feet. "Point taken. At least we know where we stand on this particular adult issue. We'd best get going now. The weather's changing and we don't want to be out in an open field like this if a storm hits."

For the remainder of that day and the next, neither of them said anything further about the delicate subject of sex. They were more than content to be together as new-found friends who were far from ready to be intimate.

Glenna's ankle had swollen some over night, so they decided to drive around the peninsula, taking in the sights that she had not visited yet and that Rory had not seen since he was a boy.

Their hours spent together slipped by as they marveled at how they seemed to have always been a couple. They would both remember these days as a magical time. An interval of innocence and growing affection that, at the time, they were certain would last them all the days of their lives.

Fifteen

The date was June 3, their next-to-last day together. After tomorrow they would ride the same Bus Éireann to the Limerick station. From there, Glenna would go on to Dublin, where members of the Aeon Repertory Company she was joining would pick her up. Rory would take a different bus to a local *garda* station where one of his brother monks would collect him for the short drive back to his monastery.

They didn't talk about leaving. Instead, they went for another walk along Ventry Beach. The day was fine, the breeze soft off the sea, the waves gentle, the sand warm beneath their bare feet.

Despite the lovely day, Glenna was feeling nervous about the lines she was expected to know perfectly when rehearsals began on Monday. Rory said he would be glad to run them with her, so they found a spot sheltered by the dunes and got to work.

After they had run several scenes, Rory was genuinely encouraging. "You've nothing to worry about, Glenna. I'd be proud to say I know you if I came to your play."

"Would you come to Dublin? Not for the first week, of course. I'll want to be sure I'm not a disaster. But after that, would you come see me? I hadn't thought that was possible."

"It could be. If I can, I'll come, yes. Will you visit me when you're finished with your play?"

"I will, if you want me. Where will you be?"

"I don't know, but I'll send you word. What is it Portia says, *If you do love me, you will find me out.* I'll make sure you can find me."

"That's so lovely. You are a lovely man, Rory. I'm glad I know you."

Glenna was sorely tempted to lean over and kiss him, but she held herself in check. She took a deep breath and turned back to the script.

"I am having trouble with this one speech. I know the status of women in the late sixteenth century was very different from today, but I can't imagine Portia being so instantly subservient to Bassanio—even though she says she's *unschooled, unpracticed.*

"Basically, she's led a sheltered life, but since her father's death, she has been *lord of this fair mansion, master of my servants, Queen o'er myself.* Then she gives it all up in a single speech:

> Happiest of all, is that her gentle spirit
> Commits itself to yours to be directed
> As from her lord, her governor, her king.
> Myself, and what is mine, to you and yours
> Is now converted. . . .
> This house, these servants, and this same myself
> Are yours, my lord's. I give them with this ring.

"It seems like she's making herself a commodity, and I can't reconcile that with the intelligence and independence she exhibits only a few pages later when she takes on Shylock in the big trial scene."

Rory took the script from her hand.

"If I were Bassanio, although I might not have originally wooed her except for her money, I wouldn't want her to be a commodity. I think he would want her to remain in charge of her estates. He wouldn't have the background to manage her wealth. I believe Portia is wise and merciful enough to be gracious to her husband, to empower him equally as she, herself, remains empowered.

"She proves she's a shrewd thinker in the trial with Shylock. If Bassanio truly loves her, he wouldn't want her to be diminished by their marriage, just as she wouldn't want him to be emasculated by her wealth. Their individual power only increases with their union. They are different in many aspects, which makes them perfect partners. They create a whole as each completes the other."

"As long as they are loyal to one another," added Glenna.

"Well said, my dears." They looked up to see F. M. Bellamarre standing before them, his violet eyes bright, a halo of light sparkling around his head from the sun behind him. They had not heard him approach.

Rory and Glenna instantly rose to their feet. This was the first time they had been together in the Master's presence and they were in awe that he should visit them. They both had many questions they hoped to ask him about the meaning of his bringing them together.

"How lovely to see you," exclaimed Glenna.

Rory offered a seat on the blanket they had spread. "Will you join us, Sir?"

F. M. declined with the slightest of bows. "No, thank you. If I may suggest, let us retire to your cottage. We have some matters to discuss that are better considered in a less vigorous setting."

Even as he spoke, the wind picked up. The sky, which had been clear, darkened suddenly. They had barely arrived at Rory's cottage when a steady rain began to fall.

Once they were settled on the homey leather sofas in the cottage living room with a warm fire burning brightly on the hearth, F. M. smiled at the two young people who were seated across from him, holding hands. His violet eyes twinkled as he addressed them.

"Before I comment on Shakespeare's lovers, may I say that you both did well on Mount Brandon. I am pleased to note your appreciation of the little 'blind date' I arranged for you."

Glenna and Rory looked down at their joined hands and grinned sheepishly. So the Master had, indeed, arranged their dramatic reunion.

"Now, to your thoughts about Portia. She is no more a commodity than is Bassanio. Agreed, he is without funds of his own. Nevertheless, he comes to her with all of himself. She is merely stating the ideal bargain in a marriage contract—one hundred percent to one hundred percent.

"When we marry, we share our graces and our debts. We come to each other with our blessings and our burdens, and we share them equally. We pledge our troth as surety for our mate in sickness and in health, in karma both positive and negative.

"And in the case of twin souls, such as Portia and Bassanio—such as you, Glenna and Rory—the joining of one another's strengths as support for your inevitable human weaknesses is a union of cosmic importance."

Rory stroked Glenna's hand. They looked briefly into each other's eyes and smiled.

F. M. sat for a moment, gauging the two souls before him. "I believe some explanation is in order before we proceed," he said in the friendliest of tones. "Are you aware of the significance of the twin soul or twin flame relationship?"

"I know it means we were together in past lives, like soul mates. People with whom we have a strong affinity. Like Rory and I do. We have dreamed of each other."

Rory felt the warmth of the Master's presence and remembered how he trusted the man. "Is this what you wished to discuss with us?"

F. M. rose from his seat and stood by the hearth. The fire appeared to flame up behind him. Glenna could swear that he grew in stature. His voice became more melodic than usual. His figure gave off a radiance that lifted them to a state of refined awareness. There was no doubting they were in the presence of a powerful adept, a great master.

Long ago, before you knew to count time, your two souls were created in a starry nursery as a single ovoid of light. Much like the formation of a human embryo, that sphere began to vibrate and spin until the great T'ai Chi of masculine and feminine was formed. Still unified, but differentiated.

After a while the two halves divided, forming two separate identities, identical in all but the polarity of plus and minus.

It was then that the Great Law sent them forth in Divine Love to realize the perfection of male and female, and then to return having gained their individual mastery to create the greater wholeness of twin flames united in the strength and wisdom of perfected love.

Unfortunately, many soul pairs did not succeed. Most who are alive today have been struggling on the path of reunion for many centuries, because of their karma and because there are forces at work in this universe who viciously and with great determination oppose the union of twin flames.

These dark forces know better than the children of light the power of bringing together two souls who began as one. And so they do everything in their power to prevent couples, such as yourselves, from meeting and facing the trials that precede the fulfillment of your dreams and your cosmic destiny.

The Master paused briefly. He could see that Rory and Glenna were riveted by the images his explanation was creating in their minds.

"Will you hear more, dear ones?" he asked in great kindness—to which they merely nodded their heads in assent.

Masters of Wisdom, who are known as the Great White Brotherhood because of the white light that surrounds them, have a mission for the two of you. However, you must first work out who you are as individuals and determine if you can truly pledge your undying loyalty to one another.

As your teacher, I cannot force. I can support, instruct, illumine, and suggest—but the decision to follow the path of your divine plan is yours alone. Only by the wise exercise of your love and the determination of your free will can you succeed on the path of soul freedom to which you are commended.

There are others like you. Pairs of twin souls whose union is key to the victory of Divine Love on this planet and beyond. If you choose to become a part of our community, you will help one another. Although you can expect to be mightily opposed in the coming months as you pursue your individual work, you will not be alone.

I will be with you in your endeavor. You may not see me or recognize me in the guises I employ in my service. However, please know that as long as you are loyal to one another, you are under my protection. Will you join in this vital endeavor?

Rory squeezed Glenna's hand and they answered in a single voice,

"We will."

"Thank you, my dears. May your path lead you always in the intimate awareness that you live in the palm of a divine hand. My love goes with you both."

The vibrant energy in the living room began to fade. F. M. bowed to the wide-eyed couple and departed as noiselessly as he had arrived.

It was still raining, so they settled in next to the fire with mugs of hot tea and the scones Glenna had brought with her from Fiona's.

After their amazing interview with F. M., Glenna felt herself basking in a new openness with Rory, who was sitting next to her on the sofa. Her eyes sparkled with affection as she turned to him.

"You've told me about the cows, your daily routine, and chanting with the other monks, but you haven't said much about teaching history. Is that something you're questioning?"

"It is, which is odd. I started out my career as a history teacher. That's what I did before I felt called to the monastery. I'm good at it. The students tell me I make the subject come alive for them. Some even call me the *seanchaí* monk. The strange thing is how alive the events of Irish history have become for me of late.

"I've always had a sense of stepping into events of the past when I was teaching, but recently I've had trouble stepping back out of them. There are a couple of eras that I gloss over now."

"Such as?"

"Such as the Viking invasions of the early ninth century—particularly the ones when they started venturing up the Shannon River. At first they only raided along the coasts. Later they figured out that their boats were shallow enough and the river deep enough so they could sail right up into our heartland.

"I stopped going into detail when one of the students asked me about the plundering of Clonmacnoise, the great religious and commercial center that was located in the middle of the country, on the eastern bank of the river.

"I started answering his questions and all of a sudden I began to shake so violently I had to excuse myself. I was hyperventilating, gasping for breath, and in the throes of a weird kind of soul pain that was truly terrifying."

"I can't imagine."

"Neither could I, and I never wanted to experience that again. However, I did—but not in the classroom. A few weeks ago I had a dream about the same event and it was very personal. Lots of bloodshed and loss of life, including my own, and people I loved very, very much."

Glenna hesitated. She intuitively knew the answer to her question, but she wanted to hear his response. "Was I there?"

Rory did not respond immediately. When he did speak, it was softly, as if admitting the truth brought back the pain of those terrible events.

"You were. We were to be married. Many monks and nuns were in those days. You were a female scribe, which some nuns were."

"Really?" said Glenna. "I thought only monks were scribes."

"Most were, but some very able nuns did extraordinary work in the Irish scriptoria. I was in the armed militia—a soldier who was supposed to protect the community, but I failed."

He took both her hands in his. His eyes were moist, his voice urgent. "I don't want to lose you again. Not like that. Not ever."

"I feel the same, but how will we manage? We're leaving in two days. You have a big decision to make, and I'm about to play the role of a lifetime. I desperately want to be with you, but right now I don't see how our being a couple can mesh with events we've already set in motion. Still, there must be a way or F. M. wouldn't have gone to the trouble of reuniting us on a misty mountainside. Do you see a path for us?"

Rory's eyes went suddenly dark and he furrowed his brow. A cloud passed over his countenance.

"What is it? Have you changed your mind?"

"No, but you may change yours when I tell you what I feel I must. I have a story that I've never confessed to anyone, not even to my abbot, Father Crispin. Will you hear it, even if it makes you not want me?"

Glenna shuddered. What could possibly deter her from wanting this man she had finally discovered as the twin of her soul?

She willed herself to be calm. "Of course, dearest friend of my heart. I will hear whatever you have to say."

Sixteen

"Do you mind if I sit over here while I tell you?" asked Rory. He moved to an easy chair adjacent to the leather sofa where they had been sitting together. "I'm afraid I need a bit of distance to do this."

"Of course," said Glenna, trying to quell the ripple of apprehension that gripped her solar plexus. "Are you sure you want to do this? I don't think I'm qualified to hear your confession. Why haven't you told your abbot?"

"I was afraid he wouldn't let me join the monastery, and I had to get in. Becoming a monk was the only way I knew to expiate the sin that was mine to bear."

"You really are a very strict Catholic, aren't you?" Glenna couldn't help saying out loud.

"Does that concern you?" Rory could tell that it did.

"More than it should, I guess," Glenna admitted.

At the moment, she was feeling considerably out of her spiritual depth. Then she saw the pleading in his eyes and relented.

Here was the man who had, only days ago, summoned his outer strength to carry her, injured, off a very steep mountain. Now she must summon her inner emotional strength to help him across what felt like a plunging abyss.

"I'm sorry, Rory. Of course, tell me whatever you must. Apparently, we have some storms to weather together. We may as well start with a big one."

Rory took an enormous breath and began to unfold to Glenna the events that had led him to choose a life of seclusion and prayer. And that he feared would keep him bound there for the rest of his life.

He looked off into the distance, remembering all too clearly the shock and sorrow that had ripped through his body when he first learned the secret he had kept from all but the one who caused it.

As I told you the other day, I have lived at the monastery for four years. Before that I taught history for two years after college.

It was while I was in college that I met Deirdre. She was, as American lads would say, a 'knock-out.' Raven black hair, alabaster skin, startling navy-blue eyes that I thought spoke of great depth of character.

To my profound disappointment, we didn't connect at first. She was getting her degree in chemical research. She was incredibly smart and I could tell she didn't consider me her type.

During the one conversation we had, she seemed to find my spirituality old fashioned. Oh, yeah, she told me, she'd been raised Catholic, but she didn't really go for all that ritual stuff or a pope telling her what to do with her body.

That should have been my warning, but I soon forgot the flicker of danger that pricked my mind at the time.

I lusted after her for a while, but eventually decided that my infatuation was school-boy foolishness. However, two years later we met again at a party and struck up a conversation about post-modern philosophy, which we were both mad about at the time.

Soon after, we began dating, casually at first. Eventually, we became intimate, though we never lived together. Things got more serious—at least for me. In fact, I was getting ready to propose after I returned from a holiday visit with my aunt in Galway.

However, when I got home and spoke with Deirdre on the telephone, she was surprisingly remote and begged off getting together for a few weeks until she could finish what she described as a demanding research project.

I was disappointed, but understanding. I tended to be very accommodating of her wishes in most matters. We didn't see each other for nearly a month.

Our next date was to attend an art exhibit and have a meal after. I thought she looked pale and drawn, but I figured she'd been working too hard on her research project.

She was reserved at the exhibit and at dinner. By that time, her behavior was making me uncomfortable, and I was running out of conversation. Anyway, for some reason, I decided to talk about history—a subject we had shared a passing interest in.

I had been reading about Ancient Rome and had come upon a disturbing and very detailed account of infanticide as it was practiced by all classes of society. If a child was deformed or simply unwanted, it was left out on a mountainside to die in the elements. The subject was still on my mind, so I brought it up, assuming she would share my discomfort over what I had read.

'How could anyone do that?' I said passionately. 'To end an innocent life because it's inconvenient? I cannot fathom anyone aborting a baby—ending a soul's opportunity to be whatever God intended.'

Deirdre's body went rigid and she looked down at her half-eaten dinner. 'I did,' she said very quietly.

'You did what?' I asked, not quite understanding.

'I had an abortion,' she said flatly.

I was shocked but, because I loved her, I was prepared to forgive what I was sure had been a difficult choice, most likely when she was very young.

'That must have been a terrible decision,' I said. I reached over to touch her hand, but she pulled away.

'Not really,' she said with a tinge of defiance. 'I didn't mean to tell you. But now that you've brought it up, I guess I have to.'

She didn't even hesitate, as someone might before confessing a regrettable action. She said with the same tone as if she were ordering dessert, 'I was pregnant and I got rid of it while you were gone.'

When she saw the utter disbelief on my face, her eyes went dark, hard, angry—like she was daring me to challenge her. I couldn't believe what I was hearing.

I felt myself falling into a deep, deep well. I could hear myself talking to her like I was very far away. 'You killed our child? A life we created between us? You had no right.'

'I am a modern woman,' she said emphatically, raising her voice so that other patrons looked over at us. 'I have every right to make a choice for my own body.'

I grabbed the sides of the table to stop from shaking. I lowered my voice and leaned across at her.

'You absolutely had the right—when you decided to have sex with me. But you've made a choice for a body that wasn't yours. You chose to end a life that wasn't yours. That baby was as much a creation of my body as it was of yours.'

I started putting two and two together and realized the signs had been there for some time.

'How far along were you, Deirdre?'

'About twelve weeks, I guess.'

'Was there a heartbeat?'

She looked down and poked at her food with her fork.

'Look at me, Deirdre. Was there a heartbeat?'

She raised her head and rolled her eyes as if this whole conversation was a total bore. 'I suppose so.'

I didn't want to ask the worst question of all, but I had to know.

'Was it a boy or a girl?'

'There were signs of female genitalia.'

'Listen to yourself,' I almost cried out. 'How can you be so clinical?'

'I *am* clinical, Rory,' she said, throwing up her hands. 'I'm a chemist. I look at things realistically. And, realistically, my career would have gone nowhere if I was saddled with an infant. Besides, it wasn't a baby yet.'

'How can you say that? I would have supported you, found a way to raise our baby girl, even if you didn't want her. You talk about choice. You took away my choice to be a father when you killed the life we created. That God created between us.'

'Don't throw that religion stuff at me, Rory. If you're so stuck on God, why don't you marry him?'

With that, she threw down her napkin, grabbed her purse, and stormed out of the restaurant. I sat there for ages, completely stunned, not knowing what to do. And then I made my own choice.

I promised *An Síoraí*, the Eternal One, that I would pay the price for the life lost, for the soul-potential aborted. I would dedicate myself to the celibate life of a monk. I had once considered the priesthood when I was very young. Now I would take the path of spiritual obedience. It was all I could do.

"I am so sorry," said Glenna softly. She had been holding her hands to her chest throughout his agonizing story.

Her heart ached for him. His eyes remained dry. His body was fiercely rigid in his determination to tell her every detail. She could feel the devastation that blanketed him like a shroud. Still, she could not understand why he had taken the guilt upon himself.

"Rory, the abortion wasn't your fault. If Deirdre chose not to tell you she was pregnant, what could you have done?"

He stood up and rolled his shoulders and began pacing around the room. "But it *was* my fault. I wasn't as careful as I should have been. I was too eager for a sexual relationship. And I was too arrogant to pay attention to a strong intuition that our being together was not a good idea "

"We all make mistakes, Rory. I made one."

His eyes went wide. He looked at her aghast.

"No, I never had an abortion. I couldn't have done that for any reason. But I'm sorry to say that I did drive one very desperate friend to her appointment. I'm sure she thought abortion was her only option, but I know there were people who would have supported her and who would have adopted her baby. I could have helped her find them, but I didn't. I felt guilty for a long, long time—as if I had abetted the murder of an innocent."

"Then can't you understand how I feel? If it hadn't been for me, that child wouldn't have been conceived. Her blood is on my hands. Until I believe that *An Síoraí* has forgiven me, I can't leave the monastery."

"But if that's true, then why did F. M. help us find each other if we can't actually be together? Why would he tell us we have a shared mission if we're only going to remain apart?"

"Maybe this is part of my punishment. Perhaps being a monk—and now a reluctant monk—hasn't been enough to balance the sin. Perhaps I have to bear the pain of meeting you in the flesh and then giving you up."

"I don't believe that for a minute," declared Glenna. She was trying to reason with Rory, but he wasn't making any sense. Why was he being so stubborn? Wasn't her love for him enough? She could feel panic beginning to rise in her and she was powerless to quell it.

Rory moved back to the sofa and sat beside her. He took both her hands in his and looked pleadingly into her questioning eyes.

"Please understand me, my dear friend. I love you, Glenna, but I can't be with you until my debt is paid."

"I do want to understand you, truly. But how will you know if you've been forgiven? Why can't you just confess to your abbot and be absolved?"

"We're not living in the Middle Ages," said Rory firmly, "and this is not a single sin. This is lifetimes. I know it. When Deirdre left me sitting in that restaurant, I felt like I was drowning in the chaos of war, in the mayhem of genocide practiced against innocent life that I was supposed to protect, but didn't."

"Maybe you couldn't," offered Glenna, grasping for some point of common ground. "Did you ever consider that forces were beyond your control?"

"There is always something we can do," insisted Rory. "There has to be." He was on his feet again. He walked to the fireplace and stood exactly where F. M. had been with them, only an hour earlier.

"Right now, being a monk is the only recourse I have. Believe me, this is a hellish place that I would not willingly drag you into. This is my karma to balance."

Glenna reached a breaking point as lifetimes of feeling victimized by Rory's abandoning her bubbled up to the surface of her consciousness, blinding her to everything but an ancient sense of injustice.

"And you've decided that you know how to balance that karma without asking your abbot or F. M. or anybody. Don't you see that I'm already in this situation with you? What happens to you happens to me. I feel that in my heart. I'm here for you, Rory. I love you as the other half of myself. After everything the Master told us, can't you accept that?"

"He also said that we each have to work out who we are as individuals. Glenna, there is nothing I would more gladly accept than your love. I know you want to help me, but I don't think you can."

"Then you'll break my heart, and I'm not sure I can forgive you for shutting me out. You think you know best, so you've made the decision for both of us. You're doing to me exactly what Dierdre did to you. Aborting our love before it has a chance to be born."

"Glenna, that's not it at all. I . . . "

"You know it is. And until you see through your own pride, I can't talk to you. I think you'd better take me back to the inn. I need to be alone now, and I expect you do, too."

Seventeen

Two days later, Glenna was curled up in her seat at the rear of the Bus Éireann coach away from curious glances of other passengers who might be tempted to inquire if the young American traveling from Limerick to Dublin was sad or unwell.

In fact, she was so sad she was practically ill. When Rory had dropped her off at the inn the night before last, they had agreed that they each needed a day to themselves. To pack and take care of last-minute preparations for their trips.

Of course, that was a lie. Either one of them could have packed in an hour this morning, had they been determined to squeeze out of yesterday every last minute together.

But they couldn't bear seeing each other, only to be reminded of the impasse they had reached—the obstacle of a vow Rory believed he could not break and that Glenna believed *An Síoraí*, the Eternal One, would not ask him to keep.

In fact, Rory had driven over to *Teach na beannachta* yesterday morning. Glenna had heard his voice in the hallway when Fiona answered the door. She'd already given the landlady instructions in case he braved the harsh winds of their emotional storm and made an appearance.

"Ah, Rory, good morning to you, lad." Fiona summoned her most cheerful greeting, though the young man standing before her had all the cheer of grey clouds on a winter's day. "I'm afraid Glenna's having a bit of a lie-in this morning, so she can't see you right now. Nerves, I expect, about her big adventure in Dublin."

"That's fine, Fiona," said Rory quietly. "I only came by to leave her this letter. Will you see that she gets it? I can't stay. I'm off tomorrow myself and I have a lot to do before then."

"Of course I'll give her the letter, lad. Will you take a few scones with you? They're fresh this morning. Wait one minute and I'll get you some—as a parting gift." She hurried off to the kitchen, leaving him standing, most uncomfortably, in the entryway.

Glenna had heard every word. It was all she could do not to rush down the stairs and throw herself into Rory's arms. But she didn't. She couldn't. And right at the minute when she thought she might change her mind, Fiona returned with a bag of scones for the man who was leaving her as he had done so many times before.

"*Go raibh maith agat,* Fiona. I'll not forget your kindness."

"*Slán abhaile,* Rory. Get yourself safely home. We'll be glad to see you, whenever you return."

Glenna had read Rory's letter a dozen times yesterday. By now every word was seared into her memory. Yet here, alone on the bus, once more she took it from her journal where she had tucked it between the sheets of her own desperate musings.

Somehow seeing the words written in his careful hand brought him closer, even as part of her wished they had never found each other in the mist on Mount Brandon.

Glenna, *mo chroí,*

I know I have hurt you. The very thing I would not have done. Not for the world. Not again.

Yesterday you asked if I couldn't simply confess to Father Crispin and be forgiven. Now that I have told you my story, it seems easier to tell it again to my abbot. So I will, very soon.

I beg you to be patient with me, dear friend. I pray that one day I may be worthy to call you my darling.

As soon as I know my mind and that of *An Síoraí,* the Eternal One, I will let you know. Until then, I hope you will think of me kindly and hold me in your heart as I hold you in mine.

—Rory

P. S. I'll not burden you with conversation tomorrow. If you want to arrive early at the station and take a seat in the back of the bus, I'll come later and sit up front.

May you achieve every success in Dublin. I know you'll be brilliant.

Even though Glenna had buried her nose in her play script this morning, she'd felt Rory enter the bus. She didn't look up. She didn't need to see him to sense the agony in his heart. Hers felt the same. They were matched in emotion, that was sure.

She'd kept her head down until she was certain he had glanced in her direction only once before taking his seat up front near the driver.

The back of his head was clearly visible to her, but she purposefully did not gaze at the blond hair that was mussed from the cap he had hastily pulled off. She made herself stop thinking about smoothing that hair or holding a comforting hand to his brow. Those were vain imaginings, and she willed herself to stop.

When the Bus Éireann pulled into Limerick station, she busied herself with a magazine. Unfortunately, she made the mistake of raising her eyes at the exact moment when Rory looked back in her direction before descending the steps.

The regret on his face made her breath catch. She looked away, but could not stop herself from watching him through the window—which broke her heart all over again.

His face brightened immediately when he saw his brother monk who had come to pick him up. The two men embraced and walked away from the bus as if Rory's world had never been turned upside down by meeting the woman of his dreams.

Of course, Glenna could not know the force of will he had had to summon yesterday to stop himself from rushing up the stairs to her room at Fiona's inn. He could not say what he would have done once he got there. All he knew was that he wanted this woman with him always, but for now that was not possible.

Glenna also could not have known that Rory had felt her attention on him as they rode the bus from Dingle to Limerick, even as she tried not to think of him sitting a dozen rows in front of her. The pain he sensed radiating from her nearly broke him, but he steeled himself, finally breathing a sigh of relief when he saw his friend at the bus station.

Glenna knew none of this. What she did know was that she was determined not to weep all the way from Limerick to Dublin. Instead, she pulled out her script and focused her full attention on rehearsing the speeches that were beginning to feel like a part of her own being.

Only when she repeated Portia's pledge to Bassanio—*Myself, and what is mine, to you and yours/Is now converted*—did her heart agonize in the grief that threatened to overwhelm her.

But Bassanio must woo Portia, Glenna firmly reminded herself as she read through the famous trial scene. He may have been the love of Portia's life, but he was a lot of trouble. (Just like Rory.) And he had betrayed her by giving away her ring to the young attorney—Portia disguised, but to Bassanio's perception, a stranger.

Well, if Rory O'Donnell couldn't accept that they belonged together, as F. M. Bellamarre had made clear, then Glenna Morrissey didn't need him. She wasn't going to beg anybody to love her. She'd opened her heart to him and he'd broken it. She could just as easily close the door on that heart and cauterize the wound, lest it distract her from the work ahead.

She had a career to think of. Wasn't that why she'd come to Ireland in the first place? Playing Portia had to be reason enough for her to remain in the Emerald Isle, even if her own Bassanio was unwilling to play his part.

And maybe, just maybe, this whole meeting was meant to show her that her soul's other half was on a different path for this life and that she was meant for the stage.

With less than an hour to go before her bus reached Dublin, she thought of sending a strong prayer to F. M. about her predicament with Rory. Then she noticed the signs for Kildare, seat of Brigid, her mother's favorite saint and the goddess who brought the rainbow light to Éire.

When a rainbow suddenly appeared through a break in the clouds, she took it as a sign and prayed fervently, "Brigid of the mantle, encompass us," while the bus sailed on toward her future as a serious actress.

Eighteen

Glenna realized she must have dozed during that last hour. When she awoke, she thought for a minute she was back in New York.

The smell of diesel engine fumes, the noise of car horns and loud human conversation, the atmosphere that was crowded with the rush of people in a hurry to get to or away from somewhere or something all reminded her of the city in the States that never slept.

She wondered if Dublin did.

She also found herself wondering what Rory was doing at this moment, but managed to slam her will down on that thought. No point in tormenting herself.

In no time, she was exiting the bus and being cheerfully greeted by another of F. M. Bellamarre's many friends—a pert young woman who identified herself as Celine, the director's assistant and stage manager.

Her black hair was cut short, like a pixie, which matched her diminutive stature. Her movements were quick, precise. Her bright blue eyes darted just as quickly, appearing not to miss a single detail of whatever life presented her.

Celine's multi-hued tunic worn over black leotard and tights gave her the unmistakable air of theatricality. Glenna looked down at her own black jersey top and leggings, and the floral scarf tossed cavalierly around her neck, and laughed to herself. Aren't we theatre people all so very recognizable to each other?

She returned Celine's warm greeting and climbed into the passenger seat of her companion's well-used hatchback.

"Please, tell me everything," she said eagerly as Celine negotiated Dublin's heavy midday traffic. "F. M. was rather spare with details. All I know for certain is that I like and trust the man, and I am to play Portia."

"Our producer definitely has a presence about him, doesn't he?" said the pixie woman with a quick glance in her passenger's direction. "I always want to bow to him."

"I know," agreed Glenna. "I sometimes catch myself about to bob him a curtsy. He's regal, noble, and yet humble—like a master adept of ages past."

"Oh, I think he's a master adept of ages present," said Celine with a wink. "Whenever he's with us, I try to pay very close attention to what he does and says. He understands Shakespeare like nobody I've ever encountered. Merlin—that's our director—gets the most time with him. When he returns from one of their meetings, he's all a-glow with enthusiasm and fresh insights."

"Our director is named Merlin? Like the magician?" Who are these people? Glenna wondered.

"He is, yes. Merlin Wolffe—though that's a nickname F. M. gave him. I should let him tell you the story, but he's very busy right now. I'll share what I've heard."

"Please."

The story goes that some years ago F. M. was producing a play at another Dublin playhouse. The theatre was old and the equipment not in good shape. The afternoon before opening night, an entire bank of stage lights went out. The lighting crew scrambled up on the catwalk, but could find nothing obviously wrong.

Martin (that was his name then) decided to have a look. He was up there for about twenty minutes, fiddling with wires until the lights came back on. They blinked a couple more times during the afternoon, but every time he went back up, they came on and finally stayed on.

When F. M. was told how the simple fact of Martin's presence appeared to snap the lights back into action he said, 'Why, you are a veritable Merlin!' and the name stuck.

"That's a great story. I look forward to meeting Merlin," replied

Glenna. "What about the theatre? It's a replica of the original Abbey?"

"It is, yes. An elderly couple with a lot of money—people F. M. had known for decades—decided that Dublin needed to rekindle more of its theatrical legacy. The new Abbey is a wonderful space and they have the Phoenix for more intimate productions. But neither theatre feels particularly historical. So the Rooneys . . ."

"The Rooneys?! Caroline and Seamus Rooney?"

"You know them?"

"Only indirectly. I'm related to them—second or third cousins or something like that. I'm just amazed at the synchronicity, that's all. Please, continue."

"Well, the dear old folks passed away a couple of years ago, but they did live long enough to see their theatre building completed and one play produced before they took off for higher realms. It was a labor of love for them and still is for those of us who are connected with the Aeon. It's cozy and we like it that way."

Celine stopped her aged compact in front of a plain grey building that might have been a hotel at one time. "Here's where you'll be living during our run. Nothing fancy, but certainly adequate. The apartments are minuscule, but you'll have your own bath and kitchenette—a plus for us poor actors.

"There are places to eat a little or a lot around the corner and close to the theatre. I'll give you a tour later. Let's get you settled and then we'll stop by the Aeon so you can have a look around before we bombard you with people and expectations tomorrow morning. Rehearsal starts at nine o'clock sharp."

Celine's enthusiastic efficiency appealed to Glenna's own sense of professionalism. She smiled as her guide steered her upstairs to the studio apartment that was possibly the smallest she had ever seen. The only space with a door was the bathroom that held only a toilet, tiny sink, and equally tight shower stall. Still, the apartment was sunny.

"You're right. This is, uh, tiny—and it's absolutely perfect," said Glenna with her most appreciative smile. She was determined to be as upbeat as this woman upon whom she already knew she could depend.

She set her suitcase on the single bed to unpack later and, like a pair of whirlwinds, she and Celine were off to the theatre. If Rory did not want her, at least she was welcome here.

"Oh, how totally charming!" exclaimed Glenna as they pulled up to a brownstone building. The structure looked exactly like old photos she had seen of the original Abbey Theatre as it had appeared after being completely remodeled and furnished with electricity in 1904.

As Celine led her through the building, she could see that every detail had been perfectly replicated—from the stained glass windows by the front entrance, to the harlequin-pattern tiled flooring and tapestry upholstered side chairs in the vestibule.

Authentic dark wood balustrades led up carpeted stairs to the balcony and down to the auditorium. The only nod to modern comfort was the replacement of hard wooden benches in the back of the main level and the balcony with upholstered flip-up seats that matched those closest to the stage.

" 'Tis a bit like time traveling, isn't it?" remarked Celine as she directed her guest into the auditorium and onto the stage.

Glenna gazed out on the empty house that would soon be filled with the audiences she rather desperately hoped she would please. For an instant she felt the air shimmer with memory. Had she acted in the old Abbey in the past?

"Yes," she agreed. "There's no moldy smell of an old building—as if they'd only recently finished the remodel. I keep expecting W. B. Yeats or Lady Gregory to appear at the back of the house and give me notes on my performance. How ever did they manage such accuracy?"

"Archival photos and drawings still exist, and a wonderful digital model has been produced. But, truth be told, the Rooneys simply consulted the akashic records."

"I know I should remember what that term means," said Glenna, "but, I'm sorry, I don't."

"No problem," answer Celine. "It means the energetic patterns of everything that ever happened in a place or in the consciousness of in-dividuals. Those impressions are absorbed and recorded in the ethereal substance called *akasha* which fills all space. That's one reason when you visit certain places, you get a feeling of positive or negative energy. Until someone clears that energy through prayer and the invocation of spiri-tual light, the pattern remains.

"These records can be seen by adepts or people like the Rooneys who have developed their inner sight over many incarnations, including this one. They were long-time students of esoteric teachings. They stud-ied alchemy with F. M. for many years and eventually attained remark-able skills that let them access akashic records like you and I would open a book. Does this surprise you?"

"Very little about the associates of F. M. Bellamarre surprises me these days," said Glenna with a sudden intuition. "Were they members of his Friends of Ancient Wisdom?"

"Indeed, yes. We all are. I assume you are as well, or F. M. wouldn't have sent you to us. Theatre is magic, Glenna. I know you know that. But I'll wager you've never felt the likes of what you're about to experience here at the Aeon."

Nineteen

There was definitely magic at the Aeon. Any trepidation Glenna might have felt about her first day of rehearsals vanished in the warm camaraderie of these Friends of Ancient Wisdom, who just happened to be theatre people.

Celine grinned at her as soon as Merlin Wolffe, the director who was obviously also her brother, stepped onto the stage where the entire company was seated on folding chairs. The director and the stage manager were the image of each other.

Although his hair was considerably longer than hers—reaching to his shoulders—his eyes were the same piercing blue, his features as finely drawn, his movements as quick.

Whereas Celine looked like a diminutive pixie, Merlin had the appearance of an elfin prince—dressed in black jeans and t-shirt, a bright purple scarf tossed casually around his neck. He was slim with refined, expressive hands and a melodic voice that carried effortlessly, filling the empty theatre with a dynamic enthusiasm that Glenna found infectious. She was totally in awe.

"Welcome Aeon players and crew, one and all," proclaimed Merlin to a round of appreciative applause. " 'Tis grand to see you brave souls returned for another production. Our most ambitious acting challenge yet—*The Merchant of Venice* by our beloved Bard."

More applause. An oddly familiar way to reference Shakespeare, thought Glenna—especially in Ireland, not England.

"Fortunately, the incomparable Connor O'Riley has agreed to play Shylock." Generous applause and some foot stomping.

"Our own Derek O'Brien will be Antonio. Fair play to you, my man, for submitting yourself to Shylock's *merry bond*."

Connor reached over to his fellow actor and, grinning wickedly, pretended to choke him as Merlin continued.

"Since Shane McManus has not lost his looks, he will play the famously handsome Bassanio." Oohs and aahs greeted this announcement. Glenna laughed when she saw Shane turn bright red.

"And I'd like you to give a special Aeon welcome to Ms. Glenna Morrissey, who—at F. M.'s request—has come to us from Broadway to play our Portia."

"Brave lass," declared a deep voice as others applauded. Glenna turned to identify its source as a robust young man with reddish blond hair and leaf-green eyes that were full of mischief. He was sitting next to Celine with his arm around her shoulders.

"She is that, Grady," agreed Merlin. "And I know you'll all make her feel welcome. Glenna, you'll get to know the names of this motley crew as rehearsals progress, though there will be a test at the end of the week." Merlin gave her a wink and continued.

"Finally, I want to introduce my sister, Celine, who will be acting as my assistant and stage manager throughout the production. Most of you have worked with her before. Fair warning to those who haven't. She doesn't miss a thing, so you'd best be on your toes."

"Truer words were never spoken," agreed Grady, rolling his eyes. "If all the world were an actual stage, our Celine could manage the whole of it."

"Glenna, you will observe that Grady has been type cast as Bassanio's loquacious friend, Gratiano," said Merlin with a grin. "Good luck managing him, Celine." More laughter rippled through the company with a few slaps on the back for Grady.

"Now, to business," said Merlin as soon as the laughter subsided. He rubbed his hands together—a man relishing the task before him.

"F. M. sends his warmest greetings to you all. He had hoped to be here today, but pressing matters have called him elsewhere. However, he has promised to pop in now and again, as his other responsibilities allow."

That statement drew another wave of chuckles from the company.

Apparently the man's mysterious comings and goings were as well known here as they were to her, observed Glenna.

"F. M. wants you to know that he looks forward to seeing the play, as it is one of his favorites. He also asked me to convey to you his desire that you pay particular attention to the theme of the letter of the law versus the spirit of the law.

"I also feel confident pointing out F. M.'s own profoundly merciful character. I can understand why he loves *Merchant*. No pressure on you, Glenna," (everyone chuckled) "but our mutual success with the trial scene is pivotal to the message of the play. I know you'll all do famously."

Merlin clapped his hands again. "That's enough with preliminaries. Let's take a fifteen-minute break and be back for a first read-through."

Glenna started to rise from her chair, then noticed that everyone else remained seated.

The elfin director suddenly put one foot on the adjacent chair he had not sat in and assumed the character of a sea captain—his left eye closed as if patched, hands on his hips, his voice growling like an old pirate, "Then it's off to yer oars, me hearties. We open in two weeks!"

Glenna was in theatre heaven. Hours and days of rehearsal flew by as if guided by a divine hand. Merlin and the other cast members were impressed with her preparation for her role as Portia. They welcomed her as one of their own and began to speak freely about their experiences with F. M., whom they openly acknowledged as their personal master of ancient wisdom.

In this rarefied atmosphere, Glenna began to discover insights and a level of intuition she had not known she could attain—in her personal life as well as in her performance.

As her new friends discussed the possibility of seeing beyond this plane into other realms of existence, she felt her consciousness expanding, the understanding of her dreams deepening. She did not mention that she might have been a bard in a former embodiment, but she felt sure that if she did, they would not have thought her daft to say so.

She was also fascinated by the penetrating discussions they had about the meaning and significance of Shakespeare's controversial play.

At the beginning of rehearsals, Merlin had explained that he was approaching *Merchant* as a timely commentary—not only on racial prejudice, but also on the deadly nature of hatred as expressed by Shylock and many of the other characters.

"If you hold onto hatred, it will rot and kill you," he said, quoting an actor he admired. "Though Antonio is the target of Shylock's enmity, the fact that he loses his ships could be seen as his own karma—the return of bias he has expressed toward the Jews for many years.

"At the end of the play, we will be showing both Antonio and Shylock as victims of their own animus. To me, that's a message the Bard wants us to convey."

"In the last scene Portia tells Antonio that three of his ships *are richly come to harbor.* Doesn't that mean he's redeemed?" asked Derek.

"We can certainly explore that in your interpretation. I've often thought the Bard had a soft spot in his heart for Antonio," said Merlin. "His kinsman, Bassanio, loves him dearly. They would do anything for each other."

"And just so everyone knows," said Derek, "Merlin, Shane, and I have agreed that we're playing them as brothers. Some productions have portrayed them as lovers, but my reading of the play and a conversation I had with F. M. tells me their devotion is filial, not even remotely sexual."

Merlin nodded and continued, "Antonio is definitely being given a chance at redemption, whereas Shylock is reduced to nothing. Not even his own religion is left to him. One thing you might consider, is that Antonio's soul has been scarred by the death he has escaped and the animosity that he, himself, has practiced against his fellow man."

"I wonder if any of the characters learn from their shared experience. Shakespeare doesn't tell us. Perhaps the audience will be enlightened," suggested Laoise (Lee-shuh), the actress playing Nerissa, Portia's lady-in-waiting.

"I think we'll leave the instruction up to the Bard," said Merlin with a chuckle. "Our job is to tell the truth of the story and be as entertaining as we can manage. I have faith you'll manage brilliantly."

Glenna deeply appreciated the company's collaborative approach and the artistic freedom it gave her. She had never felt her own creativity so trusted or encouraged. She threw herself into her role, doing her best to embody the same passion she had observed in the musicians and other talented artists she had met in Dingle.

Although she had vowed that she would focus solely on her career, once the play opened, she found her thoughts turning to F. M. Bellamarre and the instruction he had given her and Rory. He'd said they must be loyal to each other in order to remain under his protection.

We're not doing very well in that regard, she admitted to herself. In her mind, she had managed to make their separation all Rory's fault. But that was hardly fair. At least he was being true to his promise to *An Síorai*, the Eternal One. She might not agree that such a vow was necessary, but who was she to judge? And who was she being true to?

Was she being true to Portia and the merciful justice she stood for?

Often, in the midst of a performance, Glenna would have the distinct sensation of another force, almost a separate being or spirit, acting through her. There were times during the trial scene, when she would feel the presence of such power balanced with wisdom and mercy that she was nearly moved to tears.

An actor must learn to channel the playwright's intention through her emotions, not be overwhelmed by them, Glenna reminded herself in those moments. She was learning a great deal about staying out of the way of the spirit of Portia so that whatever she wanted to convey to audience and company alike would come through.

This was more than magic. This was transformation, and a few other "trans" words, such as transmutation and transcendence. Glenna felt as if she were being remade into a different person.

In that light, she worked harder at not thinking about Rory. It was too easy to fall into dark old hurt and frustration. Especially since he had sent her not a single word.

Yet there were times when she wished she could talk with him about her experiences on stage. He wasn't an actor, but he was an excellent storyteller. As a kind of fellow bard, she felt he would appreciate hearing her stories.

Since she couldn't speak with Rory, she decided to imagine she could speak with F. M. Bellamarre. From what Celine was teaching her in the private conversations they had about the Friends of Ancient Wisdom, Glenna knew that the link between master and sincere student could never be broken.

She did not expect to see their master. He had said she would not. But, somehow, she had an intuition that she could communicate with him through her journal.

One morning, early in the play's run, she made an important discovery. The night before she had been puzzling over how to handle a situation with the young actress who was playing Nerissa. Several times recently she had noticed Laoise trying to upstage her in a couple of their many scenes together.

"What shall I do?" she had written in her journal before retiring.

The next morning she awoke with the answer on the tip of her mind, as if the Master had responded personally to her inquiry. Except that the response had a distinctly feminine vibration.

She knew that F. M. held a particular fondness for the soul qualities that Portia displays. Could there be an actual being who had inspired the Bard? Grabbing her journal and pen, Glenna began to write:

Your Nerissa is not malicious. She is unsure of herself, though she would have you believe otherwise. She is intimidated by Portia's presence, which moves through you, yet is not you. Take a lesson from Portia and show Laoise the justice of mercy. Ask for her opinion, and you will have a friend for life in this actress. And an unseen friend, as well.

With such vivid instruction, Glenna took immediate steps to do as suggested by whoever was prompting her. She would invite Laoise to lunch that very day. And, as divine intervention would have it, she ran into the lass as they were both leaving the apartment building.

"Laoise, hi," Glenna said cheerfully. "I'm on my way to grab some lunch. I don't want to sit alone today. Will you come with me?"

The actress's face brightened. She had a winning smile that matched her name's meaning—"radiant girl."

"I'd like that very much," she agreed, clearly pleased to be invited.

Anyone watching the two actresses walk around the corner to the company's favorite pub might have pegged them as sisters. Although Laoise was a brunette, they were of nearly equal height, and a similar quality of élan emanated from them as they chatted.

Glenna was relieved. Any concern she had about this being a difficult conversation melted away as she and Laoise shared stories about their background and previous acting experience.

"I don't know if you are aware that this is my first Shakespearean role," Glenna confessed. "Portia is a far cry from singing and dancing on Broadway."

"You'd never know it," said Laoise with genuine sincerity. "I've been with Aeon Repertory since we opened and I'd say you're better than some of the classically trained actresses who have played here."

"That's good to hear," said Glenna as she felt a nudge from her intuition. "I do have a question for you about our characters."

"Ask away." Laoise brightened again.

"Portia relies heavily on Nerissa for support and friendship. My sense is that they may have grown up together, like sisters. Nerissa understands Portia's predicament better than anyone. I'm wondering if we could show more of their relationship, in little glances or touches in difficult moments. That kind of thing. Any ideas?"

Talk about opening the floodgates! Glenna thought to herself later.

Soon the two were laughing and experimenting with line readings and gestures, exactly as Portia and Nerissa might have done. After that night's show, several other actors, and Merlin himself, commented on their performance.

"You've brought out a new freshness between the two characters that I really appreciate," he said. "Well done, both of you."

"Thank you, Portia!" Glenna said aloud when she returned to her apartment. Somehow she was not surprised to sense a certain, "You're welcome!" waft its way into her heart.

With this success as encouragement, she began a ritual. Every night before going to sleep she would write a few lines in her journal. Sometimes, she wrote only a note of gratitude for an especially appreciative audience.

Other nights she posed a question—for example, what to do about the actor playing one of Portia's suitors who began taking his role a bit too personally. In this case, she found a way to thank him for his attention while pointing out that one of the ladies on the costume crew found him very attractive.

And at other times, she wrote a simple prayer for Rory. She could not seem to shake the sorrow over him that was coupled with an odd sense of injustice that felt as if it stretched back for millennia.

However, she could ask *An Síoraí*, the Eternal One, to help Rory find his way. Despite F. M.'s assurance that they were twin flames, she could never quite bring herself to add "back to me" to her request.

The further she got into the play's run and away from her time with Rory, the less certain she became that she wanted him back. At least that's what she told herself.

Twenty

As time progressed, Glenna also found herself penning little prayers or requests on behalf of other members of the cast and crew. She had never thought of herself as a "helper," but these days she relished the suggestions for small, anonymous acts of kindness that appeared in response to her journal inquiries.

Was this the kind of service F. M. had meant for her and Rory to perform? she wondered. She might never know, but she was delighted to make a difference where life had planted her—and without anyone noticing what she was doing.

Of course, the highly perceptive Celine did notice.

"I see you, Glenna," she whispered warmly one night as she made her rounds before curtain time. "Your secret's safe with me. I just wanted to say that I think you're a lovely fairy godmother. I'm grateful to F. M. for sending you to us."

Tears welled up in both women's eyes as they smiled at each other's reflection in Glenna's dressing table mirror. Celine gave her a quick peck on the cheek and resumed her duties as stage manager.

"Ten minutes," she called out to the women's dressing room before she delivered the same message to the men across the hall.

"No pressure, but we have a full house tonight and some important press in the audience. The critic for the *Sunday Independent* doesn't often review us. The fact that he's here is exceptional. Break a leg, everybody!"

Glenna was pleased to hear that the common wish for a great show was popular on both sides of the Atlantic. She intended to do just that. The other cast members did as well. Spurred by the possibility of an excellent review, the company rose to the occasion and gave one of their best performances.

If the weights (called legs) at the end of the theatre curtain had been made of wood, as in former times, when the curtain was raised and brought down quickly during the rousing applause, those wooden "legs" surely would have broken.

Glenna's efforts paid off particularly well. Her earlier reviews for her Portia had been good. This one was spectacular.

Surprise & Delight in *The Merchant of Venice*

No actress in her right mind begins her Shakespearean career as Portia in the Bard's enigmatic play, *The Merchant of Venice*. Yet that appears to be exactly what the charming American, Ms. Glenna Morrissey, has taken on as her premier role in our fair country—which has not always looked with kindness upon plays, however great, from our neighbors across the English Channel.

Much to our surprise and delight, we find in Ms. Morrissey a Portia in full command of the role—first in her innocence as a self-described *unlessoned girl* who immaturely mocks her suitors for their peculiarities of personality and foreignness. And then later in her depth and intelligence, insightfully portrayed in the famous trial scene.

Many consider Portia's famous speech, *The quality of mercy is not strained,* to be the pivotal moment on which hangs the ultimate power of her character. While truly one of the most exquisite of all Shakespearean arias, these lines have been so mangled by so many actresses (professional and amateur alike) as to make one cringe in anticipation of another pedantic or too emotional recitation.

Thankfully, Ms. Morrissey spares us that torment. She delivers Portia's wisdom with a deft touch and a clear understanding of her character's purposes that reveal to us why Bassanio has chosen well in his pursuit of this woman.

The brilliance of this Portia ignites the trial scene in her prosecution of the law as she leads Shylock, by the law, to prove in open court his intention of taking Antonio's life, thereby seal-ing his fate in receiving *more justice than thou desir'st.*

Here, at the high point of dramatic tension, Ms. Morrissey summons a voice that flashes through the audience like a flame in her *Tarry, Jew. The law hath yet another hold on you.*

Indeed, this actress's performance creates the perfect foil to an extremely adept Shylock who, in his past portrayals of the Jew, has overpowered other less capable Portias. In Ms. Morrissey we see him countered fire for fire—and are grateful to have witnessed such a match-up.

I believe I may have attended a true *Merchant* for the first time in my long life as a theatre critic—and doubt I may ever again observe the work so perfectly interpreted. One wonders if the spirit of the Bard himself may have had a hand in creating so stellar a production.

Glenna e-mailed a copy of this review and two others to her agent, Mel. He immediately shared the great news with Roland Newhouse, who sent his congratulations, but no comment about his proposed show that was "guaranteed" to make Glenna a star.

"How odd," she exclaimed aloud to her apartment, as if an unseen presence were listening. "I feel not a ripple of pleasure or encouragement from these remarks. Merely being in this play with these incredible people is reward enough. I would not trade this experience for all the Tony awards in New York City!"

The upshot of Glenna's success turned out to be odd, indeed. Newhouse sent his regrets that he could not spare the time to attend the play. However, the following week, who should appear at the theatre but A. B. Ryan, accompanied by a woman he introduced as Ursula.

Glenna supposed her to be his mistress or trophy wife. The woman exuded that air of expensive self-absorption she had seen on other young-ish females who slink in and out of black limousines in the company of rich and powerful older men like A. B. Ryan.

In her four-inch stiletto heels, Ursula was nearly as tall as her companion. She was clad in a long, tight, black sheath dress that was slit to mid-thigh. She was thin as a wraith, smug as a woman who controls a rich man's wallet, and about as charming as a black widow spider, which she closely resembled.

A. B. insisted on coming backstage before curtain time to wish the company well. He particularly wanted Glenna to know that he had flown in from New York specifically to see her—due diligence for his future investment, he said.

He thrust out his hand to her so obviously that she could not avoid shaking it. A shiver of energy ran up her arm and she tried to pull her hand away. But he held on and focused his cobalt eyes on hers in a way that made her very uncomfortable.

She could feel that penetrating focus on her throughout the play, along with the daggers she was certain Ursula was projecting at her. She got through the performance, but considered it her worst to date. By the time the curtain fell on Act Five, she was exhausted.

"Glenna, are you okay? I thought you were going to faint before the trial scene." Celine had hurried into the women's dressing room and pulled up a chair next to where Glenna was removing her make-up.

"Not really. That A. B. Ryan and the harridan he brought with him packed a wallop of energy."

"I am so sorry. We shouldn't have let him backstage, but the man was a bulldozer. He pushed past us like he owned the theatre. I promise it won't happen again."

"I doubt he'll be back. In a way I hope he gives Roland Newhouse a bad report on my performance. Even if their show turns out to be a 'Go,' I don't want to be in it. That man gave me the creeps. At one point I felt—no, I don't even want to say what I felt. The vibration he put out was really dark."

"We'll get you home and you can forget all about them. See you out front in ten, okay?"

Glenna nodded as her efficient friend hurried off to take care of the thousand details she juggled every night. She turned off the dressing table lights that made her look ghostly pale without make-up. She folded her arms on the table and lay down her head with a sigh. She did not try to stop the tears that spilled down her cheeks.

Despite being surrounded by wonderful people like Celine who shared her love of theatre—and who were teaching her a lot about alchemy and mystery school teachings—she suddenly felt desperately abandoned and alone.

She had been in Dublin for four weeks and had not heard a word from Rory. They had not promised to write, but he'd said he would let her know if he moved out of the monastery. No news must mean he was still there.

She couldn't get a sense of him, as if their connection had evaporated into the ethers. Was he even thinking about her? She had considered sending him a note, then decided not to. Would he contact her with any problems? she wondered. Probably not.

She thought of Bassanio's betrayal of Portia's trust by giving away her ring—and worried that Rory was becoming likewise disloyal.

Anxious thoughts filled her mind.

Had he decided that pursuing their relationship as twin flames and members of F. M.'s Friends of Ancient Wisdom was more than he could handle?

Did he not love her after all?—vivid dreams not withstanding.

What if something had happened to him? He could have had an accident. None of his people at the monastery would know to contact her. Not that she cared. Except—damnit!—she did care.

Imagined disasters continued to flood her mind until, disgusted with herself, she sat up and pushed them away. She heard Celine calling from the hallway and quickly dried her eyes.

Worry was a waste of time. She still had four weeks before the play closed and she had plenty of money left to buy a plane ticket back to New York.

Mel had told her she was in considerable demand—now that she was an "acclaimed international Shakespearean actress." She'd snorted at his hyperbole. But if he was right, she could return to the States on a professional high note and carve out the next phase of her career.

She would simply pretend she'd never met Rory O'Donnell and that her heart wasn't breaking in the emptiness of his silence.

Glenna grabbed her bag and followed Celine out into the cool night air. She felt her spirits lift immediately.

She would *not* to fall prey to A. B. Ryan's unsettling energy which she could sense was still swirling around, trying to gain a foothold in her consciousness. With everything she had going for her, she would *not* let him or that woman, Ursula, bring her down.

Twenty-One

For most of the remaining weeks of the play's run, Glenna succeeded in putting Rory out of her mind. Playing tourist on her Mondays off helped considerably. She was determined to soak up as much of Ireland's urban center as she could. She might never be here again.

She strolled along the lush pathways of St. Stephen's Green and went shopping on Grafton Street's brick-paved pedestrian mall. She visited Dublin Castle and meditated under the soaring, creme-colored Gothic arches of the Chapel Royal.

She spent hours exploring St. Patrick's grand cathedral and thought herself mightily blessed when a visiting girls' choir filled the space with the soaring melodies of medieval chants sung in their crystalline voices. She'd felt enfolded in the presence of angel choirs.

She had meant to visit the Guinness Brewery, but was so moved by the transcendent experience, she had returned to St. Stephen's Green and simply walked and walked, contemplating the music of her soul that she was finding in Shakespeare's Portia.

The most impressive sight, which stayed with her for days, began early one misty morning when she stood in line at Trinity College to view the breathtaking genius of the Book of Kells.

Glenna appreciated the excellent modern displays that explained how the vellum pages were laboriously prepared from calf skins—a process that was difficult and possibly toxic—before the first letter could be inscribed on the surface.

Large images of many of the more famous pages displayed the incredible detail and marked sense of humor the scribes left for those who would view their craftsmanship a thousand years later. All very impressive and a gift to humanity.

However, it wasn't until Glenna came face-to-face with the actual Book of Kells, opened to a new page each day and safe under protective glass, that she stepped back in time.

Suddenly, she could feel her fingers holding a goose-quill pen for lettering or one of many different-sized paint brushes—some with only a few bristles for coloring the thinnest lines.

She unconsciously rolled her shoulders to ease the stiffness in her back and neck, and the tension in her right arm, as she labored over an oak table in a scriptorium, doing the holy work of preserving the Gospels for future generations.

Had she worked on these very pages? Probably not. But she had been a scribe. She knew that now as surely as she knew her own name.

Centuries after her embodiment as a bard, she was still telling stories. Now in print. A practice the druids had eschewed, but which Irish monks had perfected in glorious pictures and illuminated words the world had never seen and would not again for many years.

When Glenna finally made her way out of the exhibit, through the magnificent Long Room Library with its massive, wooden barrel ceiling, through the gift shop, and out into Dublin's noisy streets, she knew she had been given another glimpse into her past.

The devotion that sustained her and her fellow scribes had seeped once more into her blood, into her bones. Yes, she could summon that resolve again—now that she knew what it felt like.

As Glenna had felt upon departing the Guggenheim museum, she returned to her apartment a changed person. And was glad of it.

"One more show, *a chara*." Derek, the Aeon Repertory actor who played Antonio, stood behind her chair at her dressing table. Most of the other actors had already gone home, but Derek had the lovely habit of offering congratulations or encouragement to anyone who might need it after a show.

He rested his hands fondly on her shoulders and smiled at her in the mirror they both faced. "It's been a pleasure, my dear. I hope you'll join us again. Why not stay in Dublin? We'd be glad to include you in the repertory company."

"That is very sweet of you, Derek," said Glenna. "I'd love to stay, but my agent in New York has several auditions lined up for me in a couple of weeks. I really need to get back to the States. I've been gone since the middle of May. I guess I'm actually a little homesick."

"We'll surely miss you. I wish you all the best in your career. You've got what it takes, *a chara*. Don't give up."

"I won't. And maybe I will come back sometime. You never know."

Glenna was collecting her belongings when she heard her name being called, rather urgently.

"Glenna! Will you come up to the vestibule! There's somebody here who says he knows you!" Celine was shouting so she could be heard all over the theatre. After the debacle with A. B. Ryan, she wasn't letting any strangers into the private areas reserved for cast and crew.

"On my way!" Glenna shouted back as she left the dressing room. "Who is it, Celine? I'm not expecting anybody this late."

If she hadn't been holding the hand rail she would have tripped going up the stairs and fallen into the vestibule, landing in a heap at the feet of a good-looking young man with blond hair. At the last minute, she caught herself on the top step and held her ground.

Her eyes went wide, then narrowed. She dropped her bag and clutched the banister. All the pent-up anger and frustration she had neither acknowledged nor dissolved came spewing out in a torrent.

"Rory! You, you . . . Rrrh! I was about to call you a terrible name, but you're a monk. I can't swear at a monk. What are you doing here?"

"Nice greeting for the man of your dreams," said Rory raising his eyebrows with perhaps a bit too much humor. "I came to buy a ticket for tomorrow night. I read your reviews. *Comhghairdeas*, by the way. I'd like to see you in action before your show ends."

He couldn't help grinning at her. He wanted to rush over and scoop her into his arms, but the icy daggers shooting out of her eyes made him think better of it.

She practically snarled at him. "I've given up dreaming. My only fantasies are on stage these days. Go away. It's late. I'm tired. I need to go home and sleep for a long, long time. We close tomorrow night and I'm leaving on Sunday."

"Where are you off to?"

"None of your business. You didn't tell me where you were. You don't get to know where I'm going."

Rory could feel his spine stiffen and his jaw clench. Pushing back the anger he was determined not to let take hold of his emotions, he took a breath and began the speech he'd been rehearsing in the car for the past two hours as he rushed to Dublin. He'd made a decision. Her combative response wasn't going to change his mind.

"You're right. I did promise to let you know when I'd made a decision. Well, I made one—this morning. So now I'm here to tell you. I've left the monastery. All of my worldly possessions are in my car out front. I drove straight here as soon as I could pack and say good-bye to some really good friends. I'm leaving it all behind. New chapter, new life. I want you with me, Glenna."

She swayed slightly. He stepped forward to catch her, but she held up her hand. He stepped back and stayed where he was.

"Rory, you can't just barge in here and say such things to me. I haven't heard from you in weeks. I've worked really, really hard to wipe you from my mind. From my heart. Besides, you can't see the show tomorrow—we're sold out."

"He could sit in the control booth," Celine offered meekly. "I mean, if you wanted him to."

Glenna glared at her friend who was still standing in the vestibule.

"Oh, all right, since you've come this far. God, my head is spinning. Why did you have to show up now?"

"It was the soonest I could get here. Listen, I know it's late and I can tell your friend wants to lock up. Is there someplace I can stay for a couple of nights? I can't really leave all my belongings in the car parked on the street and I'd prefer not sleeping in the passenger seat. I can pay for a room, if there is one."

"I have keys to an empty apartment in our building. You can stay there." Celine shot Glenna a sharp look. "Oh, come on, give the man a break. He's driven all the way across the country to see you. At least hear him out."

"Okay, okay." Glenna threw up her hands and started for the door. She turned and scowled back at Rory. "Celine is parked out back. We'll drive around front and you can follow us. The building is only a few blocks away.

"When we get there, I am going to bed. I can't talk to you tonight. I'll meet you in the morning at the pub around the corner. You can have breakfast—and *explain* yourself."

Twenty-Two

The minute Celine pulled her car up to their apartment building, Glenna leapt out and hurried inside. Without looking back to see if Rory had followed them, she ran upstairs to her apartment, slammed and bolted the door as if she were being pursued by banshees.

She took a hot shower and dove into bed, determined to put Rory's words out of her mind. But, of course, her thoughts were full of what he had told her at the Aeon, despite her angry greeting.

He'd left the monastery and he wanted her with him. What had caused him to make this decision? When he'd left her at her lodging in Dingle the night before they rode the same bus to Limerick, he'd avoided any sort of commitment. Even the letter he'd written made no promises. What had changed his mind?

And could she change hers? Did she even want to? He had hurt her so many times in the past, how did she know if she could trust him now?

Rory looked and sounded like a different person. More like the radiant druid she had seen in her dreams, she thought as she turned off the light and buried her head in her pillow. She fell instantly to sleep and dreamed a dream that would change both of their lives.

Gormlaith, the chief bard in the *túath* of *Tearmann*, was on her way to the harvest celebration of *Lughnasa*. She wore her best blue gown and finest gold torc for the occasion. Her long, dark blonde hair was plaited to hang elegantly down her back.

It was important that she look her best. She knew her presence could lift the spirits of her community—a vital part of her work on behalf of her people who sorely needed encouragement in these difficult days.

Thankfully, the harvest had been plentiful, and the entire *túath* was returning to a sense of optimism for the coming winter. They were glad of the diversion, for, after nearly a year, their hearts had remained burdened by the murder of their *ceann-druí*, Chief Druid Ah-Lahn.

Gormlaith's dearest friend, Riordan, would be at the celebration. She had not seen him for several weeks, as he had been on campaign with Cróga, the chief of *Tearmann* and surrounding areas of the Brigantes tribe to which they all belonged.

As Ah-Lahn's friend and rightful successor, Riordan had taken over the responsibilities of chief druid—a position he had never really wanted, but now felt obligated to assume.

Before Ah-Lahn was killed, Gormlaith and Riordan had planned to wed. However, the community had been in such turmoil after the murder that they had delayed. The longer they delayed, the more frequently Riordan began to express doubts, eventually telling Gormlaith that he felt he was not worthy to marry her.

Perhaps his path lay in support of Cróga in the increasing number of skirmishes with their neighbors. Riordan had originally been a bard and then became a druid. Now, perhaps, the life of a soldier was more appropriate. Regardless, he could not marry her until he was certain.

When they had spoken last, he had told her not to wait for him. She should wed one of the other young men who would make her a good husband. He was sorry to hurt her, but he knew he was not fit to marry anyone. She would be better off without him.

The scene changed in Glenna's dream. Gormlaith was now an old woman. She and her friend, the druidess Alana, visited each other and shared stories about the men who were their twin flames, yet were no longer living.

Alana had been happily married to Ah-Lahn for only a few months before Arán Bán killed him. Gormlaith had lost Riordan to a soldier's life. And then he himself had lost that life in a battle against the dissolute son of Arán Bán, who for a time had swayed the druids to oppose Cróga.

The battle had been won, the son eliminated, and order restored. Riordan had been posthumously hailed as a hero for turning the tide. But for those who loved him most, that honor was no consolation.

'If only he had loved me enough to stay. If only I had loved him enough to beg him not to go,' Gormlaith cried out to *An Síoraí*, the Eternal One, as she passed from the screen of life, her heart broken for herself and her twin flame.

Glenna's dream shifted once more and this time she was not fully asleep. In her half-waking state, she saw the figure of a great Master of Light. As she focused on his radiant presence, she began to recognize him as one she had known as a beloved mentor. He spoke few words to her, but they were uttered with intensity.

Your place is with Rory. Do not let his former vacillation deter you from your *dharma*—your sacred labor—that only you as twin flames can accomplish. He is a changed man. So must you be the courageous woman I know you can be.

Seize the mantle of your True Self, my daughter.

I will be with you and your beloved amidst your trials. Have faith in my presence and in those who will come to aid you in your time of greatest need.

Do not turn from assistance when it comes, though other voices would convince you that good is evil and evil good. These are tricks of ancient forces that mean you great harm.

Embrace Divine Love and its Spirit will see you through. That I can promise, for I speak on behalf of Love in the essence of *An Síoraí*, the Eternal One.

The sun had been up for hours when Glenna finally awoke the next morning. The dreams of the night before still resonated through her being. But were they really dreams? They were seared in her memory as if an unseen hand had drawn them in fire.

Though these images were clear, her mind was not. Still groggy from the deep sleep into which she had fallen in the morning's wee hours, she wandered into the shower to clear her head. The hot spray soothed her body that felt as if it had fought a mighty battle—and then she remembered the Master's instruction.

Rory! She belonged with Rory. No matter what, the Master said they belonged together.

"My God!" she cried aloud. Would he still be waiting for her or was she too late? She snatched a towel from the rack in her tiny bathroom, dried off quickly, and threw on jeans and a warm sweater.

Grabbing her bag, coat, and hat, she hurried out the door and around the corner to the pub where she hoped the man who was her soul's other half hadn't given up on her. Only when she reached the entrance did she pause to compose herself.

The Master had said she could be courageous. She hoped to heaven that was true. She whispered a prayer to Portia's just and merciful spirit, and crossed the threshold.

Twenty-Three

The Corner Pub, est. 1823, was the perfect place to wait for Glenna, thought Rory as he sipped his strong black tea and munched distractedly on the scone he had ordered. After a sleepless night, his stomach was in knots, not ready for anything heavier.

On first approach, he'd liked the looks of the establishment. Its carved, quarter sawn oak front entrance told the truth of its reputation for not having changed much since Victorian times when it first began providing food, beverage, and conversation to soothe and enliven its clientele.

The pub's etched and stained glass windows looked to be original. Many rugby posters had survived from the nineteenth century. Photo portraits of W. B. Yeats, Lady Gregory, and G. W. Russell (the original Aeon) gave a special nod to Glenna's theatre around the corner.

The dark walnut and mahogany woodwork, well-aged bar, clusters of small tables, and deep, leather-upholstered booths offered Rory the congenial atmosphere he craved this morning.

He had arrived at half past nine o'clock. A good hour as it happened. The early-morning tourist crowd had recently finished their breakfasts and hurried off to tour the city. The late Saturday morning customers, many of them from Aeon Repertory, had not begun to trickle in.

Rory had easily found a booth with a view of the front entrance where he could watch for the woman who held his future in her hands. He could only pray that her heart did as well.

The time was now ten o'clock and, still, Glenna hadn't arrived, so Rory decided to order a full breakfast. If disappointment was on the day's menu, at least he would face it well fed.

Celine had warned him that actors tended to sleep late into the morning. He wasn't surprised at the hour, but he was beginning to wonder if Glenna would meet him as she'd promised. And if she did make an appearance, would she greet him with smiles or with the same antipathy as last night?

When she walked through the pub's front door, his concern was not assuaged. She wore dark glasses and a man's fedora hat that made her look less than approachable.

That's it, he told himself. Nice try, Brother Rory. Guess it's back to the cows, if they'll have you. He was staring into his cup of tea that had gone cold, so he missed the hopeful expression on her face. When she pulled off her dark glasses, bent down, and planted a soft kiss on his cheek, he gasped.

She seated herself across from him, and offered him a pleasant, "Good morning."

"So you've come after all," was all he could manage.

"I have, if you still want me."

Rory simply focused his full attention on Glenna's crystalline blue eyes. His expression was inscrutable, which wiped the smile from her face.

Moment of truth, he thought to himself. Would they be able to overcome the pain they had caused each other, and not only in this lifetime? The only way to know was to try.

"I do want you," he said at last, "if you have decided to hear what I need to tell you."

She returned his focused gaze, which gave him pause. Here you go, Glenna, she said to herself. Will you open your heart to this man one more time? *Yes!* came the answer from her inner voice of wisdom.

"I have decided to listen," she said and smiled knowingly when they sighed at the same time. Then she added as his breakfast was delivered, "I will be especially attentive if you'll feed me. I'm starving."

"I'd like the same, please, and a fresh pot of tea," she said to the waitress, who grinned at them. She had seen many couples resolve their differences over a good, hot meal.

"I'm happy to share." Rory pushed his plate between them and asked the waitress for more silverware when she brought Glenna's tea. "Go ahead and enjoy this while it's hot. I'll have some of yours when it comes."

After they had eaten in silence for a few minutes, he put down his knife and fork and ventured, "Are you ready to hear why I had nothing to tell you until now?"

"I am." Glenna nodded and took a deep breath. "Then I'll tell you the dream I had last night—about us."

"Is that what's transformed you back into the woman who at one time said she loved me?"

"It is. Tell me your story and don't leave anything out. I want to know everything that's happened so we can put this part of our history behind us."

She poured them both fresh cups of tea and took possession of Rory's plate. "I'll eat while you talk and then you can return the favor."

He nodded and began.

I remembered a story from before I entered the monastery. A friend I hadn't seen for a while was telling me what happened to him when he realized he'd met the woman of his dreams. 'I did what every red-blooded Irish lad does in such a circumstance,' he said, 'I broke her heart and ran.'

When I left you at the bus station in Limerick, I knew that was me down to the ground. I knew then, without a doubt, that we belong together, and that scared me more than any experience I'd ever had. Not even leaving my family for the priesthood was as terrifying. Probably because I realized that you are my destiny, and being a priest is *not* what I am supposed to do.

"Have you decided what you *are* supposed to do?" Glenna inquired tentatively.

"Not entirely, but I do know what I'm not meant for."

As soon as I returned to the monastery, I went to see Father Crispin. I had sent him a message that I was coming back and that I needed to see him as soon as he was available.

I told him about finding you in the mist on Mount Brandon and about our experiences with his friend F. M. Bellamarre—which didn't seem to surprise him.

When I told him the story of Deirdre's abortion and my vow to enter the priesthood as penance, his expression was one of the deepest compassion. After I'd finished, he closed his eyes for a moment. I could tell that what I had told him weighed heavily. He was seeking his own inner guidance, so I waited.

'Such a vow is not one I can release you from, my son,' he said at last. 'I can tell you that I believe your penance has been received and forgiveness granted. However, the actual bestowal of that mercy and your acceptance is an experience that can be shared only between yourself and *An Síoraí*, the Eternal One, who I know will speak in your heart as the truth of your being.'

"That seems very wise," said Glenna simply. She could sense Rory's body relaxing. A light was coming into his face she hadn't seen before. She was glad that he continued his story.

I wasn't surprised that Father Crispin declined to absolve me of my own spiritual communion, but I was relieved at his perception. He was also very generous in his offer to let me stay on the property until I sorted myself out.

Since *An Síoraí* had not revealed my future, Father Crispin and I agreed that I should work full time at the dairy until a clear course presented itself. That's where I've been all this time—until yesterday.

"Tell me," said Glenna as Rory refreshed his tea. "You have my full attention."

Working with the cows was the therapy I needed. They can be stubborn beasties, yet there is something about their patience in the milking stalls that inspired me. I know they're animals and they don't have complex thinking brains to trouble them with anxieties about their life plans, but they do have a sort of knowing about them.

At least the dairy cows do. It may be different with beef cattle, which I couldn't work with, never mind that my Celtic ancestors all raised cattle for the table. As much as I appreciate the taste of meat and the strength it gives me, there are times when I remember the dark brown eyes of my cows, and eating meat feels just too personal.

Glenna grimaced as she slowly chewed and swallowed the large piece of sausage she had just put in her mouth. Rory chuckled at her and went on.

I never became a vegetarian, as did many of the other monks, but the dairy cows gave me a lot to think about. It's their mothering instinct, most of all. How tenderly they nurture their young ones, if given the chance, and how they grieve when their calves are taken from them.

It's one of the downsides of the commercial dairy business.

Big industrial farms separate the calves within twenty-four hours of their birth, which is traumatic for the mums and their offspring. Cows can't keep their calves if they're to continue giving milk. Conventional wisdom is that there is less anxiety and risk of disease when the calves are removed immediately, but the emotional effects on the cows and their babies is significant.

We've taken a different approach. We let the calves stay with their mothers until they would be naturally weaned, but we mostly bottle feed them instead of letting them suckle more than a little.

This way we can harvest the mother's milk, which is her purpose, after all, while continuing to support the maternal relationship. This process is more labor-intensive and can cost more, but we're convinced our cows are happier and healthier.

Glenna's felt her heart clutch when Rory spoke of the grief of separation between cows and their calves. She had never imagined them having such human feelings.

"I hope you don't mind me telling you all this," said Rory apologetically. "It does bear on the rest of my story."

"I think it's very sweet," said Glenna. "I can see how much you care for the cows. Did you consider becoming a full-time dairyman?"

"I did. But then last Thursday I had the experience that brought me here, back to you—back to the life we're meant to live together."

Glenna looked at him tenderly, encouraging him to continue.

I was feeling inspired and relieved not to be teaching history or involved in the religious duties of being a monk. I was welcome to attend all of the services, but I didn't have to participate in conducting them. I was free to express my devotion without it being a task.

My soul thrived in the difference, which led me in fairly short order to decide I did not want to pursue the priesthood. But I still didn't know what I wanted to do. Father Crispin advised me to stay the course, which I did.

At this point I was living in separate quarters from the monks. The monastery employs several local lads and lasses to help with the farm. Some of the fellows live in rooms located upstairs in one of the dairy buildings. That is where I lodged.

Last Thursday was the turning point. I'd retired for the night and had probably been asleep for about an hour when I was awakened by a bright light that filled my room. When I sat up I saw a robed figure of a man who looked very much like F. M. Bellamarre, although he was surrounded in a shimmering radiance with rays of rich violet, ruby, and gold streaming out from his heart.

I knew immediately he was a Master of Wisdom. I began to hear him speaking to me as if we were in the middle of a conversation. Here's what he said.

'Many humans have an innate fear that if they allow a bond of love to grow too deep, they will be shipwrecked if that connection is broken.

'This is how the soul feels every time she takes embodiment. This sense of abandonment is matched only by the separation of twin flames, for that cleavage is akin to being cut off from *An Síoraí*, the Eternal One—the presence of the Divine that lives in each heart.

'Truly we are only half ourselves until we bond with the Divine Presence. If we can bring that wholeness to our soul's twin, then do we know the explosion of joy that was ours in the beginning—only now multiplied by the mastery we have gained on the path of self-transformation.

'This is the task to which you are called and which, like so many, you have misunderstood. There is sacrifice involved, though not the sacrifice you imagine.'

Rory paused to ease his throat with some fresh tea and helped himself to a bite of toast from Glenna's plate.

"As you can imagine, I was bewildered. For four years I had thought I was making a divinely-ordained sacrifice by pursuing the priesthood. The Master said that was not the entire picture."

"Did he explain what sacrifice is lawful?" asked Glenna.

"He did, with a powerful vision that showed me the error I had made many times in the past. His discourse continued."

'The human soul is a bit like your calves—knowing that as soon as she is born she will be ripped away from the source that has sustained her life. So she resists the path that is hers, thinking that, if she assumes an identity other than her True Self, she will be safe.

'She takes on the projects of others, which actually causes greater separation of the soul from her source than if she had summoned the courage to face the challenges that only she can conquer. I will show you.'

With that, the Master laid his hand on my forehead and lifted me out of my physical form and into my soul body.

Suddenly, I was standing in a beautiful chamber decorated in deep purples and golds with richly upholstered theatre seats. At the front of the chamber was a large movie screen.

The Master gestured for me to be seated. A cup of sparkling elixir appeared in my hand. I drank it down and felt my consciousness instantly quickened and refined. He spoke again:

'Attend, my son, to what you experience. There is insight here, if you will receive it.'

Images began to appear on the screen and I felt myself pulled into them, as if I were in the scenes. In fact, I was a participant in the activities, for these were all events from my past lives. They changed in rapid order, and after a while I began to detect a pattern.

Whether I was clad in the robes of a monk or nun, priest or priestess—or in the armor of a soldier—I was nearly always involved in the sacrifice of my life. Whether in battle or cloister, those lives tended to be cut short.

I would find myself in the midst of some confrontation or persecution that resulted in my death—often as I tried to save someone I loved very much. Like the battle at Clonmacnoise I described to you at Ventry Beach. These scenes were very troubling to my soul. At a certain point I think the Master saw I'd had enough.

"I'm not surprised," Glenna said softly. The energy of the akashic records that Rory was reactivating in his story felt like a dark blanket weighing her down. Nevertheless, she remained silent as he pushed on. She could see this recital was requiring a Herculean effort on his part.

The screen went dark and I slumped in my chair. Another cup of elixir revived me so that I could respond to the Master, who asked: 'What did you observe, my son?'

I thought for a moment, then said, 'More than a calf being

separated from her mother, I seemed to be a lamb led to the slaughter. Was that my calling—to be a living sacrifice?'

'In some ways, yes. Over the centuries you have gained considerable merit in laying down your life for your loved ones—though not always. Can you see why?'

'I can,' I answered. 'There were instances when I sought out danger. I drew it to myself, sometimes seeking to die a martyr's death, knowing I would be celebrated as a hero.'

'And was that courage?'

'In those situations, no. It was an ego's bravado, and in a way, cowardly avoidance of my own challenges, which involved working out the relationship with my twin flame rather than going to war.'

'Will you accept those challenges now, my son, knowing that your union will be opposed by some of the most virulent forces you have ever faced?'

I didn't hesitate. 'I will,' I said, and was instantly back in my room. I looked at my clock and not more than five minutes had elapsed. I lay awake for some time, then drifted off into dreamless sleep.

The next morning was Friday—yesterday. I immediately sought out Father Crispin and told him I had made my decision and how I came to it, which, again, did not seem to surprise him.

'My son, I heartily give you my blessing and wish you Godspeed, as does our mutual friend, F. M. Bellamarre. He asked me to tell you that his associate from Dingle no longer has need of the SUV he loaned you. Here are the keys. The car is yours if you want it—which I expect you do, as you are needed in Dublin this very night.'

Rory and Glenna sat silently for several minutes, simply gazing at each other. They hardly noticed when the waitress arrived with a second breakfast. She assessed the state of the table and set the plate in front of the man.

Rory searched his beloved's face for the answer he prayed would be there. "Do you believe me, my Lady of the Glen? That's what the Master called you."

"How sweet of him," she said with a catch in her throat. She looked down for a moment to gather herself, then gave Rory the answer that made his heart sing.

"I do believe you, my love. My dream unfolded differently from yours, but the result is very much the same. I feel profoundly transformed and committed to learning how we are meant to be together in this life and what we are meant to accomplish. Shall I tell you about my experience while you eat my breakfast? I seem to have finished yours."

"Please do. I've worked up quite an appetite."

Twenty-Four

For the next several minutes Glenna shared the details of her dream and her sense that, perhaps, Gormlaith had understood their life's purpose better than Riordan.

When she finished her story, Rory had a question for her.

"Did the Master tell you his name? I forgot to ask."

"It's amazing how much is transmitted in a single glyph. He didn't actually say, yet I felt him convey to me that when I see him in his light body I should call him by his ascended-master name, 'Saint Germain.'

"He winked at me when he explained that 'F. M. Bellamarre' is his stage name. He uses it in public until the people he contacts are prepared to accept his true identity.

"He doesn't always reveal his ascended presence. That gift is reserved for those who have made an inner commitment to join in what he calls the 'mighty work of the ages'—the reunion of souls with *An Síoraí*, the Eternal One who lives in each heart, and with their twin flames. I believe that is our sacred labor."

"So do I," said Rory. "And I have just remembered what the Master explained to me before I agreed to face the challenges that are mine to conquer.

"He showed me that for centuries I've been swinging between different types of outer sacrifice when what was needed was the balance found in what he called spiritual alchemy—the transfiguration of the lead of human consciousness into the gold of the Divine. He said our goal is not outer heroics, but inner transformation.

"He also gave me reassurance that my time at the monastery was not in vain."

'You were not wrong to become a monk, my son. Given your past lives, your penance was appropriate, and your prayers for the unborn have saved many innocents. However, you must become attuned to cycles. When *An Síoraí* signals change, you must move with the flow of Spirit.

'Now is one of those times. Do not sacrifice your twin flame's love on the altar of your fear of the past. Be a teacher, my son. Find your place in an academy that teaches the education of the heart. Love your Lady of the Glen with your total being and you will find the satisfaction you seek in the fulfillment of your own sacred work.'

"He showed me that the inappropriate aspect of my fleeing to the monastery and, in a way, hiding out was my fear of death and destruction from past events that had flooded my soul. I couldn't bear any more losses—especially not losing you. He said I have to conquer my fears and transmute those records of death and loss. It's time for me to claim my path with you, my beloved."

Rory reached across the table and took Glenna's hands in his. He looked at her intently and breathed a deep sigh.

"Spend the day with me, *a ghrá*, my love," said Rory. "Today is the Celtic feast of *Lughnasa*. I'd say we have a grand harvest to celebrate. Walk with me on the green and tell me about your life as a brilliant Shakespearean actress."

They walked and talked until early afternoon when Glenna stifled a yawn. "I'm sorry," she said. "It's not the company."

"You're tired," Rory observed with an intimacy in his voice she had not heard before. It was if he had surrendered to their love and in doing so had found an inner peace he'd not had in many a lifetime.

"I admit that am. I usually rest in the afternoons. Portia demands everything I can give her and I want to be at my best tonight. You will be in the audience, my love, and somehow I have a feeling our Master will be, too—in one form or another."

Glenna truly was at her best that evening. She gave the performance of a lifetime and she did it for her druid, her Master, and her own connection with Divine Love.

When Portia told Bassanio she is all his, the actress felt as if she would lift right off the stage.

When she delivered the Bard's famous lines, *The quality of mercy is not strained*, she knew she was speaking them into the records of many past acts of non-forgiveness which she and Rory had committed.

And when Portia promised to explain all to her beloved Bassanio, Glenna knew that tonight and throughout their travels she and Rory would share the deepest secrets of their hearts, as they had not done for a very long time.

Rory had never been to a cast party. If he had overwhelmed Glenna by his unexpected arrival in Dublin, the exuberance of her fellow actors and crew, who gathered for a rousing farewell celebration at their favorite pub, paid him double for the trials he'd caused her.

He was welcomed as a fellow member of F. M. Bellamarre's Friends of Ancient Wisdom. He felt as if he had known these people forever and said so. They begged him to convince Glenna that she should stay and act with them on a regular basis. When he confided that he had other plans for her future, they demanded details.

"You'll find out soon enough," he said in a conspiratorial voice that only those standing nearby heard over the sounds of boisterous music and laughter. He strode over to the upright piano where Glenna had been singing with some others and took her by the hand.

"Will you come out for some air?"

He quickly led her through the crowd and into the night where a full moon shown brighter than the overhead street lamps. As he turned her to face him, he felt his heart bloom with the love that had been locked there for centuries.

The moon created a halo around him, casting a silvery glow upon his light blond hair. His simple tan jacket and pants blended together in the light as if he wore a white robe. His eyes had gone wide in a luminous deep blue. Glenna gazed at him in wonder, for here was her beloved Riordan, come again. She thought he looked like a god.

"I know this isn't the most romantic spot," he said, "but I had to wait until tonight. I didn't want to shock you before you went on stage. Otherwise, I would have asked you this afternoon on St. Stephen's Green."

He took both her hands in his and knelt before her. "My darling Glenna Morrissey, will you marry me?"

"Just like that?"

"Just like that. I've missed you *mo mhuirnín.*"

"You have?"

"For hundreds of years, my darling"

"That is far too long a time. Yes, Rory, my love, I will marry you. And the sooner the better."

"My thought exactly." He got to his feet, reached into his breast pocket and solemnly recited:

> Myself, and what is mine, to you and yours
> Is now converted. . . I give them with this ring.

He lifted her left hand and slipped onto her third finger a delicate gold band set with a deep purple amethyst that sparkled as if lit from within.

"Will you wear this ring as a symbol of my pledge to you until we can be married? I thought we might have a wedding ceremony with my family in Donegal and then go to the States for your people—if you don't mind getting married twice. Whatever you like, *mo chroí.*"

Glenna threw her arms around him. "I will marry you a hundred times, my heart, and then a hundred more."

Her eyes filled as she kissed him lightly on the mouth. He kissed her back, gently at first, and then more passionately, savoring the feeling of their first true intimacy.

And then she began to laugh.

Rory held her away from him and looked into her face. A frown wrinkled his brow.

"You think my kissing you is funny? Am I that out of practice?"

"No, of course not. I rather like your kissing me. Of course, practice does make perfect, and I think we should do a lot of practicing. I laughed because I was reflecting on how I seem to receive amazing proposals at cast parties. I do hope this one turns out better than the one from Newhouse and Ryan."

"It will, if I have any say in the matter," declared Rory. He held her face in his hands and kissed her again, taking his time in this moment he could not have imagined would be so sweet.

Glenna wished this kiss could last forever, but she shivered in the night air. She had followed him outside without a wrap.

Rory put his arm around her shoulder. "We'd best go back inside. I don't want my fiancée catching cold. Besides, I promised your friends some good news, and they'll be coming after me if I don't deliver."

Twenty-Five

"Here they come," cried Celine from the pub window where she had been watching the wedding proposal she was sure Glenna was going to receive tonight. No one had believed her, but she'd insisted.

"Wasn't I the one to see them together last night? Nothing but true love could have upset our Glenna as much as the sight of Rory appearing out of the blue. And nothing but true love could have sent him racing cross-county to claim her.

"Of course, they're meant to be together. Between them they've been quite a pair of ninnies, but I believe they'll get it right this time. Does everybody have a ribbon? Good. Now hush, you lot. Let them come through the door before you scare the wits out of them."

Celine was accustomed to being obeyed by cast and crew, but not this time. The minute Rory opened the door for Glenna, cheers rang out. Glasses were raised. The couple was pulled into the pub, embraced and kissed and congratulated as if they'd won the Six Nations Rugby. Calls for "Speech, speech!" rang out.

Rory began to speak, his voice overcome with emotion. "You people are the best. I just want to say . . ."

"We can't hear ye, man," came a voice from the back. "Glenna, give us some words in your best stage voice. We know we can hear that one in the back of the house."

Everybody laughed and cheered again. "Show us the ring," shouted a female voice. When Glenna held up her left hand, Grady shouted, "You put it on the wrong hand, lad."

Rory felt his face redden. "She's an American. That's how they wear their wedding bands in the States."

"And you're a Celt, man. Buy her another ring and put it on her right hand. That way some boy-o won't try to steal her from you—no matter where you live."

"I will, then. Would you like that, my Lady of the Glen?"

"I would, very much," said Glenna kissing him soundly to another chorus of cheers. "May I speak now?" she said with a wink at the crowd who faced her. She projected her voice to the back of the pub and commotion hushed at last.

"Aye, lass, we hear ye," said Grady, who was firmly shushed by a frowning Celine.

"I must say, you're the best audience I've ever played to." Glenna choked back the emotion that welled up in her heart. She swallowed gratefully from the glass of water someone handed her and took a deep breath.

"*Go raibh míle maith agat.* Thank you very much. I love you all so much. This is the best engagement I could have asked for."

Rory grabbed a handful of cocktail napkins and wiped the tears that now spilled freely down her face. He beamed at the crowd and prepared to help her to a seat.

"Tarry, Celt!" commanded Merlin Wolffe. He grinned widely and pushed his way through the crowd. "You're not finished yet."

"We're not?" asked Glenna, a bit weakly.

"Not quite. Here in Ireland we have a tradition called handfasting. You're not officially committed to each other until you've 'tied the knot.' Celine very firmly instructed us that we were each to bring a length of ribbon to the cast party. Now we know why. Being the director of this motley crew . . ."

"And a right old druid," called a voice from the crowd.

"As I was saying," declared Merlin in his own stage voice, "I believe 'tis my place to officiate.

"Rory, stand across from Glenna. That's right. Clasp your right hands together. And hold fast as your friends make sure you stay that way." His elfin face beamed like the sun and he beckoned, "Come forward, now, you wild heathens!"

Glenna and Rory simply melted into each other's blue eyes as, one by one, their friends came forward and wrapped their ribbon around the couple's clasped hands, tying a knot wherever they could find room.

"Not too tight, Liam," said Merlin to the burly stagehand who was last in line. "I know your name means 'strong protector' but we don't want their circulation cut off." Everyone laughed and several slapped Liam on the back as he went back to his pint. He was a man of few words and a favorite of all who knew him for the strength of his heart as well as his hands.

Merlin spoke on behalf of the company.

"Glenna and Rory, as these cords are tied, so are your lives now bound together. As these knots are secure, may your love be likewise. As those present have witnessed and participated in your bonding, may you be tied with cords of love to friends around this world and beyond. And may you know within the circle of our love the fulfillment of your highest hopes and fondest dreams, wherever life may take you."

The room was silent as the lovers simply stared at each other.

"Kiss her, Celt!" cried Grady, and Rory did just that—with great feeling.

Raising the pint that Celine placed in Merlin's hand, the director sealed the celebration. "May you be blessed forever. *Slainte*."

Slainte! cried the gathering of F. M. Bellamarre's uniquely theatrical Friends of Ancient Wisdom.

The flash of light from an amethyst ring suddenly caught Glenna's attention. There, in the back of the room, was the radiant figure of a man standing alone. He was dressed in Shakespearean costume, looking for all the world like the Bard of Avon himself.

His violet eyes met hers with a mischievous glint. He held her gaze momentarily. Then, when her knowing laugh told him she had caught his meaning, he doffed his hat with the gorgeous curved feather, graced her with a sweeping courtly bow—and vanished.

For days following, Glenna smiled to herself over the little joke F. M. had shared with her as an engagement present and in expression of his gratitude for her portrayal of his most beloved heroine, Portia.

"Will you stay with me tonight?" asked Rory in a quiet voice as they walked through the moonlight back to their apartment building.

"Oh, Rory, I'm not sure I'm ready for . . . you know."

"Nor am I," he said. "But neither do I want to be separated from you. My apartment happens to have twin beds. Would that suit you?"

"Yes, I believe it would," said Glenna, who once more broke into uncontrollable giggles.

"I'm glad I make you laugh, *mo mhuirnín*, but must you do so at my expense? I'm being serious here and, instead, I find myself met with snickers."

"Oh, I am sorry," said Glenna. She clapped her hand over her mouth, which only made her snort. Rory couldn't help but laugh.

"I'm sure you won't get the connection from American television re-runs, but this reminds me of the old 'I Love Lucy' show and romantic comedies from the nineteen-fifties and early sixties. Married couples all slept in twin beds. There was never a hint of sex, even though they managed to have babies and appeared to be quite satisfied with each other."

"I don't mean for this to be a permanent arrangement," said Rory with a grin, "but since I've only recently come from a monastic life, perhaps you wouldn't mind waiting till we're married."

"As long as that waiting is not more than a couple of weeks."

"Agreed. Now gather your things and come home with me, *a ghrá*. We've a grand life before us and I want it to start right now."

Twenty-Six

Sarah's cell phone rang, jolting her from her meditation. These days her afternoons were becoming a precious time of contemplation with the two lives growing within her.

The babies were weighing heavily now. Weeks ago, she had ceased to see her feet over her belly, and she was waddling more than she thought any woman should be required to endure.

However, she was determined to carry the twins to as close to full term as possible. The longer they were in utero, the better their chances of being fully formed and healthy when they entered the world outside the safe haven of her body.

She had been expecting this phone call, though she would rather have let it go to voice mail. She did not want to speak with the man who had abandoned her to the machinations of A. B. Ryan, but Debbie had e-mailed that she should hear what Tony Argenti had to say.

"Hello," she said coolly.

"Sarah? It's Tony."

"I know."

"Do you hate me, darling?"

"Hate is a pretty strong word. But I wouldn't be talking to you if Debbie hadn't insisted."

"I wouldn't have had the nerve to call if she hadn't insisted. Sarah, I'm sorry about Boston, truly. I should have suspected A. B. would put the moves on you, but I didn't think."

"No, you didn't, and you left me alone with that man. Tony, he intended to force himself on me. I can't believe you're still working for him. I asked Debbie and she said you were. How could you?"

"Right now I have to."

"Why?"

"He knows things about me, and let's just say I'm safer making my-self useful to him for a while longer. It's a good thing I am or I wouldn't have found out what I'm about to tell you."

"Go ahead, then." She heard him let out a deep sigh.

"What you need to know is that A. B. is mad as a whole nest of hornets and he's itching for a fight. You are aware that he's trying to buy Fibonacci's and the block that surrounds it."

"More than aware. He and Ursula were in here a few weeks ago. He was insulting and demanding, acting like he owned the place."

"He's worse now. He's furious that the Historical Society is investigating your site as a protected landmark. He can't do anything while the buildings are under review, even though he stopped the process last time.

"He's dangerous, Sarah. The man's like a volcano. I've never seen him like this. He has it in for you and your husband, and hatred is eating him up. He's like a man possessed. And it's not just Fibonacci's that's got him wound up."

"There's more?"

"There is. And if you weren't still mad at me, we could have a good laugh about this part. It involves Ursula. She's had some work done, you know. Pretty sure it was liposuction, though she was already skinny, so I don't know."

"Tony, please get to the point. Just tell me the story."

"Right. Well, two days ago Rudy called me in a panic."

"Rudy? Our Rudy who works at Fibonacci's part time? How do you know him? A. B. said something about not being able to get much information out of him. How is that possible?"

"I thought you knew. Rudy's my nephew—my sister's kid—and that's a story for another time. He does some work for me now and again. He's a good kid, a bit surly sometimes, but you know . . ."

"Tony, the point?" Sarah had never had to drag a story out of him before. She was relieved when he began in earnest.

Okay. It's last Saturday and I'm swamped with A. B.'s political campaign, so I ask Rudy to pick up some marketing pieces from the printer and take them to the office. I don't expect the boss to be there, but he is. I'm driving over there when Rudy calls, all frantic. I can hear his voice shaking.

'Uncle Tony, you've got to get to the office, fast! A. B. is here. He's drunk, raging, throwing things.'

Okay, I tell him. Stay out of sight, and wait for me. I'm only a couple of blocks away. 'No way!' he exclaims and hangs up.

When I get to the office, A. B. is in a state. Shirt tail out, hair standing on end, eyes bloodshot, and a glass of Scotch in his hand. He's usually cold and calculating when he drinks, but this time he is not in control—not until he sees me walk in, that is. Then he runs a hand through his hair, tucks in his shirt, and becomes his usual oppressive self.

'Sit down,' he orders. You know that tone he uses. 'You've got to help me. Ursula has flown off to Majorca with her jewels and furs and a lot of my cash. She could ruin me if I don't get her back here.'

I'm dumbfounded, but I ask how I can help.

'Just shut up and listen,' he growls at me and tosses back the rest of his Scotch.

Sarah heard Tony take a deep breath. What was he going to tell her that was making him so hesitant?

"Here's the scoop, darling," he said at last, "and it would be funny if it wasn't potentially bad for a lot of people, including you."

"Why us?" The hairs on the back of Sarah's neck bristled and her babies stirred. What could this story have to do with her?

"I'll get to that in a minute. Anyway, here's what happened."

So, early in July, A. B. decides to take Ursula to Dublin to see an actress he and his business partner, Newhouse, are planning to cast in the musical they're producing later this year. Debbie says you know her—Glenna something.

They meet this actress backstage and Ursula is instantly jealous. She fumes through the whole play and drags A. B. out of the theatre the minute the curtain falls and the house lights go up.

She criticizes everything about the actress's performance and tells A. B. he's a fool for wanting to cast her in what should be his big Broadway debut as a producer. She keeps beating this drum until he finally starts believing her claim that she should be the star of his show.

Never mind that she has no talent or experience, she convinces him that all she needs is a bit of training and he can hire that. She tells him she's got more stage presence than that entire Dublin cast put together and that's what counts.

You know A. B. eventually does whatever Ursula demands of him, so he pressures Newhouse to come up with a few of the songs that are mostly written. The script is far from complete, but there are a couple of scenes they figure they can start rehearsing with Ursula.

Of course, she agrees. After all, she's the star. Her performance is what matters. They can fill in those chorus people later.

Newhouse acquiesces because he does whatever A. B. demands of him. They rent a studio, hire an acting coach, a dance instructor, and a musical director—who turns out to be the composer who should be writing more songs instead of teaching Ursula to sing. But, oh well.

While they're getting organized, Ursula spends several thousand dollars at a spa on massages, steam baths, facials, mani-pedis, and that liposuction, or whatever—generally being polished and pampered as befitting the star she believes herself to be.

Her training begins the third week of July and, from the start, things do not go well. Ursula is her usual overbearing, insensitive self. It soon becomes obvious that she can't carry a tune across the street, is incapable of learning even basic dance steps, and reads her lines like a robot.

The people they've hired hang on for about a week. But then last Friday there's a huge blow-up. Everybody is yelling, Ursula is crying, blaming them all for treating her badly, failing to recognize her true talent, blah-blah-blah.

I can't tell from A. B.'s ranting who storms out first, but it's a mass exodus. He tries to stop Ursula, but she hails a cab, dashes off to their penthouse, somehow manages to empty the bank account he'd set up for her, and hops on the next flight to Spain.

So now the big Broadway show is in the tank before it even gets off the ground. Newhouse swears he'll never work with A. B. and threatens to black-ball him with other producers. We know he should be careful about threatening the man, but that's his problem. He'll learn, probably the hard way.

A. B. doesn't know where Ursula is. I'd say, good riddance. But he's besotted with the woman and so angry he wants blood. He's blaming you both and vowing revenge.

'This all started when I took Ursula to that stupid coffee shop,' he grumbled. 'Every time I turn around those people are messing up my plans. This time they're going to pay.'

Sarah was silent on the other end of the line.

"Are you still breathing, darling?"

"Barely. You're not making this up or exaggerating, are you?"

"Not this time."

"What are you going to do?"

"Not much at the moment. A. B. has hired a private detective. He knows people—if you catch my meaning. They'll find Ursula. Not sure what will happen when they do. I may plan to be long gone before that tsunami hits."

"Good idea." Sarah took a deep breath and let it out with a sigh. "Thanks for telling me all this, Tony. Next time you're on Long Island, give me a call. I'll buy you a latte at Fibonacci's."

"Thanks, darling. Take care of yourself and your hubby. And do forgive me, please. I truly meant you no harm before. *Ciao.*"

Twenty-Seven

Kevin drove home as fast as he dared. With increased summer tourist traffic in the village, the police were closely monitoring speed limits. The last thing he needed was a ticket. But Sarah had sent him a telepathic signal that she needed to talk to him at home right away and that worried him.

His nerves were on edge these days. With less than six weeks before her due date, he knew the babies could come at any time. The obstetrician had told them she was planning to schedule delivery about a month early, unless the twins beat her to it.

There was also the threat looming against Lucky and Fibonacci's. There was bad energy in the air, and this concerned him more than he dared admit.

Sarah was waiting for him in the kitchen. She was having a snack which Hero and Sprite were helping her eat. They all looked up when Kevin rushed in.

"Are you okay? No pains? You look pale. Are the babies doing somersaults again?" He put a hand on her belly. Hero nudged a big doggie head under his other hand and Sprite curled herself around his legs. Kevin shook his head with a chuckle and smiled at his family. It was good to be in this circle of love.

"I'm fine, Hon. I shouldn't have dragged you home, but I couldn't tell you except in person."

"Tell me what?"

"Here, finish this sandwich for me, will you? My belly is so tight, I take a few bites, then I'm full. Not you, Hero, darling dog," she said scratching his head, which now reached the top of the kitchen table.

"Yes, you're very helpful when it comes to food," she laughed.

"Sit down, Kevin, and I'll tell you about the phone call I got from my ex-coworker, Tony."

"The one who abandoned you in Boston? What did he want?"

"Possibly to save us. I'm not entirely sure from what, but I have a very good idea from whom." She took a bite of the sandwich she had just given her husband. "Sorry, guess I'm still hungry."

"What do you think we should do?" Kevin asked after Sarah had related the entire bizarre story of A. B. Ryan and Ursula. "You're the one who knows Tony and Glenna. My main involvement is that we know A. B.—we may as well call him Arán Bán—hates me with a passion and would probably try again to kill me, if he could.

"His obsession with buying Fibonacci's is certainly a key part of the equation, but this feels more complicated than a real estate deal motivated by one man's greed."

"I know," agreed Sarah. "Do you remember my saying that I was worried about Glenna and her twin flame? Oh, maybe you weren't there when I was telling Debbie and Róisín."

"No, I wasn't," said Kevin. "I think that was before A. B. and Ursula barged into the coffee shop."

"Right. Well, Debbie and I figured out that Glenna is the reembodiment of our bard friend, Gormlaith, and I was feeling really uneasy about her. I'm quite sure she's going to meet up with Ah-Lahn's best friend, Riordan, whoever he is now, and they could be in some kind of danger."

Kevin agreed. "That's serious because Riordan is reembodied as Craig's brother, Rory."

"How do you know that?"

"Craig told me the first night I met him last November."

"And, after all this time, you never thought to tell me."

"The subject never came up. You were still in Massachusetts and, because Rory was still in Ireland, I never thought to mention it when you came home. Besides, I don't know Glenna. She's your project. I'm surprised Debbie didn't tell you, since you're both acquainted with her. And, yes, before you ask, she knows all about Riordan being Rory in this life."

Sarah huffed out a breath. Why was she always the last to know these things?

"I suppose that makes sense," she said reluctantly. "But, still, considering that Riordan was Ah-Lahn's best friend, I would have thought you'd be eager to share that piece of information."

"I was. When I first met Craig, I wanted to tell you all about the connections. But, remember, I was given very specific instruction that I couldn't share anything about Fibonacci's with you. After that I knew I'd meet Rory when the time was right. Until then, I didn't put my attention on him."

Sarah pursed her lips and sighed.

"I am sorry for not telling you, Hon," said Kevin, looking her in the eye. "Ah-Lahn and Alana were so close to Rory and Glenna. Now that we're talking about them, I can feel that connection."

"Well, you have more self-control than I would've had concerning such important personal details."

"We know that, don't we?" said Kevin with a wink, to which Sarah wrinkled her nose.

"Besides, we've had too many other important issues to discuss." Kevin reached over and caressed his wife's swollen belly. He smiled playfully. "Forgive me?"

"Yes, you're forgiven." Sarah took his hand in hers and kissed it.

"So, tell me about Glenna," Kevin prompted her.

"As I mentioned, she's been in Ireland doing Shakespeare—which is really great for her—and Arán Bán found out. That's all I know about her. I have no idea how all of these puzzle pieces fit together."

"Neither do I," Kevin agreed. "Seems like a lot of things are in flux."

"My thought exactly. I can't see any clear path for us, can you?"

"No. Until circumstances reveal themselves, we shouldn't do anything. Except maybe ask Saint Germain for advice."

Ever since merging with their druid selves, they had been able to contact the Master directly, using the mantras and visualizations he had taught them. They did not take undue advantage of this grace and sought personal audience with him only in the most challenging situations. Otherwise, they worked to enhance their own intuitive abilities so he might impress his suggestions through their higher minds. They agreed that this situation warranted a direct request.

Kevin looked intently at Sarah. "Are you sure you're up for this? I don't want you getting overly tired. You've already had a distressing day. Tony's report doesn't feel like an emergency. Maybe we should wait until after you've rested to contact Saint Germain."

"No, until we find out what he has to say, I'll just worry that we're missing something that could be timely."

"Fine. Let's go in the living room where you can put your feet up."

"Okay, but no fireplace. We'll have to do this without dancing orbs of flame. Next time we decide to have a baby, please remind me that I would prefer not to be pregnant during the summer."

Once Kevin had Sarah seated comfortably on their sofa with plenty of pillows behind her back, he set a low table in front of them both and arranged the amethyst crystals the Master had asked them to use as focuses for any rituals they performed.

He lit two tall white pillar candles and they began.

They closed their eyes and sounded the OM, visualizing a single sphere of scintillating violet light surrounding them together. Around that luminous sphere, they visualized another sphere of royal blue light. This was to protect their meditation from any negative intrusion—either from their own unperfected consciousness or from astral forces that might try to interfere with their connection to their Master.

With the OM resonating throughout the room, they began to chant the sacred Sanskrit words and ancient mantras of devotion that would invoke Saint Germain's presence.

The length of time required depended on many factors, some seen, others unseen. They would continue their invocations until the Master made his presence known or until their intuition told them that an audience would not be taking place.

In this case, Saint Germain came to them almost immediately, as if he had been expecting their call. He stood before them in a pure white robe, radiating a vibration of unconditional love and acceptance. His violet eyes sparkled when he spoke.

"Greetings, friends," he said with a gracious bow. "Please remain seated. Our conference will not take long and I wish our young mother to be comfortable."

Sarah always felt a thrill ripple through her body when he addressed them this way. Surely, there was no higher honor than to be acknowledged as a friend of an ascended master.

"Thank you for seeing us today," said Kevin. "I believe you are acquainted with the situation Sarah has related regarding our friends Gormlaith and Riordan."

"I am, and you will not be surprised to know that I am aware of many more details regarding these twin flames that I am not at liberty to disclose at this time."

"Of course," said Sarah. "My main concern is the intuition I have had for some time of an event that involves Arán Bán and his wife, Una."

She paused, surprised at what she had just said. "How interesting. I had not thought of Una until now. Of course, Ursula is Una reembodied. I will not ask why I did not recognize her until now."

"You are correct, my daughter," said the Master as he accelerated the vibration in the room so they might better receive his instruction.

All things are revealed in their own time. You are now aware that the combined forces of Arán Bán and his consort can be deadly to anyone against whom they set their minds.

With your continued acceleration of consciousness in your union as twin flames and in integration with your higher soul faculties as Alana and Ah-Lahn, you are under my protection to an extent you were not in Ireland. Arán Bán can no longer harm you without attacking me personally, which action he is forbidden by cosmic law.

He knows this and, for the time being, is abiding by that restriction. However, he is perhaps more aware than you, my dears, of the important connection yet to be made between your twin flames and those of Gormlaith and Riordan. They are not sufficiently bonded in either their physical or spiritual consciousness to seal them against whatever this adversary would perpetrate against them.

The Master perceived Sarah's and Kevin's desire to help their friends. He answered the urgency he felt from their hearts.

At this moment, your prayers and intense visualizations of light around your friends are the need of the hour. They will do much to mitigate any danger that may arise in the near future. Other than your heartfelt invocations to the angels to watch over these twin flames, I counsel you to be alert and ready to act if and when you are called.

Trust your abilities in this matter. Have faith that, together, you are able for this test. May you pass it handily. And remember, I am but a prayer away, should you need me.

Having so said, Saint Germain's light body dissolved before their eyes. The spheres of violet and blue light they had invoked dissipated and they were once more seated in their living room with a big, wire-haired dog and a sleek black cat curled up across the room, sleeping soundly on the oversized dog bed they shared.

Twenty-Eight

Following the incredible celebration of their engagement in Dublin, Glenna and Rory took advantage of spending their first night together to discuss wedding plans.

They agreed that having a ceremony for his family in Donegal and then flying to America for a second wedding that her family could attend was the perfect way to seal their commitment to each other. They also agreed that there were many sights in Ireland that Glenna wanted to visit and that Rory wanted to share with her.

"We can make a circle tour of some grand places on the way up north," he suggested. "I thought we could stop by my old monastery so you can meet Father Crispin and we can receive his blessing."

"Could we also go through Glendalough and then visit the holy sights connected with Saint Brigid in Kildare?" asked Glenna.

Rory agreed. "There are also some wonderful churches and ruins along Lough Derg, the largest lake in the Shannon River. We should definitely visit the Cliffs of Moher in County Clare. And if we go through Galway, we can stop by my aunt's house. She had quite a career in the theatre in Ireland and England and will have lots of stories to tell you."

So they set off the next morning, full of love and anticipation of the intimate conversations that traveling by car can engender. Surely there was no better way to deepen your knowledge of the person you're going to spend your life with than driving through inspiring countryside.

Since Rory was doing all the driving along modern four-lane motorways or narrow two-lane roads, Glenna was free to gaze out the window at the gorgeous Irish countryside—and at the countless reminders of the land's tragic past.

She should have remembered there would be ruins, she told herself as she counted one destroyed castle, chapel, or monastery after another. Before she left New York, she'd studied photos online and consulted a guide book or two. She'd even watched a documentary about ancient Ireland.

But just as no photo could capture the aching, shimmering green of Éire's meadows, the pearly light that bathed patchwork fields after a rainstorm, or the raw force of powerful Atlantic waves crashing against majestic cliffs, so photos had also failed to depict the sheer number of ruins that everywhere gave evidence in stone that history had not dealt kindly with the Emerald Isle.

Many of the ruins were small. Like the concentric circles of shoulder-high stone walls she had seen on the Dingle Peninsula—the only remnants of pre-Christian dwellings that had fallen into disuse centuries before. Perhaps that site, with its defensible position and spectacular view of the sea, had been claimed by a chieftain and his family—ancestors of the eighteenth-century farmer and his family who had carted off many of those same stones to build their cottage on the adjoining field.

Imagination could run rampant in conjuring stories of what life had been like in those days before more organized forces cast their greedy sights west and came in waves of Norman and English settlers who pushed the native Irish off the land that was to them as much soul as soil.

Monastic ruins were more impressive and perhaps more sinister for the extent of intentional destruction they revealed. Glenna had visited a few of them during her rambles around Dublin on her days off. But, at the time, she had not fully marked the viciousness that had laid bare the large communities which had grown up around ecclesiastical centers of learning and wealth—Ireland's substitute for towns that did not begin to form until the Vikings brought their own brand of societal organization and commerce.

Oh, yes, the Vikings had brought some progress, many would say—despite their pillaging and burning the ninth- and tenth-century wooden structures and continuing into the eleventh and twelfth centuries when thatched roofs still made stone buildings vulnerable.

But the largely unseen product of their dirty work was the destruction of priceless treasures of learning the Irish monks had created and spread across Europe, saving that continent from its own ignorance in the Dark Ages.

The heartbreak for Glenna was in viewing the brutal devastation of the religious sites—the handiwork of rapacious Irish plunderers and the sheer violence of the seventeenth century's Oliver Cromwell, the religious fanatic who fancied himself true religion's defender against heretics and idol worshipers. This was the malevolence toward a people and a culture that she could not countenance.

These were Rory's people, and now they were more deeply hers than they had been. Although her last name was Morrissey, she was an American. Her family had been in the States for generations. She lived in New York where the primary nod to Irishness was the presence of St. Patrick's Cathedral and the parade that marked his feast day on March 17.

However, spending countless hours immersed in traditional music and conversation in the pubs and shops of Dingle had begun to lift the veil of her own cultural ignorance, particularly of the Gaelic language that was reputed to be as old as Sanskrit.

Acting with the mostly Irish actors at the Aeon Theatre had folded her into the heart of Éire in a way that no tour could ever have approximated. She was a part of this land now and it lived in her. She could imagine staying here forever. Of course, that depended entirely on the life which she and Rory would build together. And where they would build it.

Rory, her beloved. Glenna sat back in her seat in the surprisingly comfortable SUV that had come to him as a timely gift from F. M. Bellamarre and gazed at the man beside her.

His light blond hair curled down his neck, the gold tips glistening in the sunlight that streamed through the open car windows. His long fingers rested easily on the steering wheel. The muscles in his arms and broad shoulders were relaxed. Those muscles had grown stronger and more pronounced under his shirt from his weeks as a full-time dairyman. Yet he still had the hands of a poet.

He turned his robin's-egg blue eyes on her and smiled.

"What are you thinking, *mo chroí*?" he asked as he steered the car smoothly around a slow-moving lorry. He'd felt her attention resting on him and cherished the way her presence stirred him, even when he wasn't looking at her.

"I'm considering if I should tell you how much I love you. How much I have loved you from the moment I first saw you in my dream."

"*A ghrá*, you fill my heart," was all he could manage through the emotion that rose in his throat. He fisted his right hand on his chest and breathed into the warmth that swirled within him.

He was tempted to stop the car, take her in his arms, and kiss her till lunchtime. Two more weeks, he reminded himself, and focused on the road ahead. The music of her voice bathing him in the knowledge of her affection would be enough for now.

The late morning weather remained fine. The sun still peeked through fluffy clouds, although they were already turning grey on the horizon. No doubt, they would have rain in the afternoon.

The air began to cool as they drove through the forests of the Sally Gap up into the Wicklow Mountains. They stopped by a wide, shallow stream cascading down the hillside where Rory said the movie *Braveheart* had been filmed.

He chuckled as Glenna snapped photo after photo on her phone's camera, and hugged her close when she stood transfixed by the beauty around them.

"I don't want to forget a thing," she said wistfully, "in case we never come this way again."

When the road descended into the lush valley of Glendalough she exclaimed, "Oh, it's like a painting!"

Sheep grazed peacefully, dotting the emerald green grass with their bodies, now wide with wool, readying them for their second shearing in a few weeks.

The monastery's intact round tower speared up in the distance, marking the place where, in the sixth century, St. Kevin had yielded to the pleas of his followers to found a monastery and a church where they could worship together.

"There has been considerable discussion as to whether or not the saint ever saw or used this round tower," explained Rory, the avid historian, as they walked around the monastic site. "Most of what remains today was built in the eleventh or twelfth century, so it's a challenge to know for sure.

"However, I've read the work of one contemporary expert who claims that these uniquely Irish towers were built much earlier. He has scientific proof that they were designed to amplify and radiate the vibrations of the monks' devotional chants into their surroundings."

"How fascinating," exclaimed Glenna. "I'd always heard they were built for defense. But that seems very unlikely. If you scurried up the ladder into your tower, you'd be an easy target to be burned or starved out by your enemies."

"Exactly," agreed Rory, warming to his topic. "And this scientist has done decades of research and field work to show that these old monks were masters of invocation and the use of sound and earth energy. In building the towers, they knew to use stone with highly paramagnetic properties that would amplify the positive energy to raise the consciousness of their community. It also made their crops thrive. You can still see how the grass grows greener around the towers."

Glenna was consulting her guide book. "Regardless of the power of their insights, the community was destroyed by fire nine times between 775 and 1071. And still the intrepid monks continued to create marvelous works of literature and art. Not even repeated pillaging could stifle the Irish devotional spirit."

She looked over at Rory in time to see a cloud pass over his face.

"What is it, my love? Is there some bad energy here?"

"No, not at all. But walking around these ruins reminds me of what Saint Germain said about my needing to transmute records of the past, especially of events when my loved ones were lost in battles. The worst of those was at Clonmacnoise. I'm thinking we should probably loop around there after we visit my aunt. It will require some back-tracking, but I'd rather make that our last stop before we drive up north."

"I'm sure you're right," agreed Glenna. "But let's not spoil our other sightseeing with nasty old records from the past. There is so much beauty in this country. I want to soak up every bit of it."

Rory enfolded her in his arms and kissed her with grateful affection.

"You're right, *a ghrá*. If the old monks weren't discouraged by their history, neither should we be. Come with me. I want to show you the building they call St. Kevin's Kitchen."

As they drove on, they continued to marvel at the proclivity of the Irish for blending their pagan past with the Christianity that, to this day, had not completely succeeded in obliterating the Celtic sensibility that the soul is free, no matter the impositions of church or state.

On the way to Kildare, Rory was delighted to share more historical details with his fascinated passenger. Here the fifth-century nun who would become a saint had built her church on the site of a pagan shrine to her namesake, the Celtic goddess Brigid. She had established a double monastery for men and women, and had even risen to the status of bishop before females were barred from ecclesiastical leadership, beginning in the twelfth century.

Glenna bought souvenirs for her mother in the market square. She and Rory meditated in the restored Norman church that stands where Brigid the bishop focused the goddess's eternal flame. They walked the quiet gardens at her holy well and visited the pilgrim center where the Brigidine Sisters welcome travelers from all over the world.

"How my mother would love to see this!" Glenna commented wistfully. "I'm glad I'll get to see her soon so I can tell her all about it while the memories are fresh in my mind."

Twenty-Nine

From Kildare they zipped across the country to Rory's monastery so he could introduce Glenna to a very gracious Father Crispin.

She couldn't help feeling that she was under inspection as he casually asked about her experience playing Portia. However, there was no hint of disapproval. She figured if he was a friend of F. M. Bellamarre he must have more than a passing appreciation for Shakespeare's works, if not for the art of acting in general.

"Rory told me that Portia was your first of the Bard's mighty heroines," said Father Crispin in his charming Irish brogue.

"She was, yes," said Glenna. "I think if I'd had any idea of her reputation and what she would require of me, I'm not sure I would have had the courage to accept F. M.'s invitation."

"And you're glad you did," observed the abbot. "I can see that in how you speak of Portia—like she's become your good friend."

"She has," said Glenna. She gazed out the window in the Father's book-filled office, then turned back to him. "The characters I played in Broadway musicals were more types than real people. I'm afraid I tended to play them for laughs without trying to discover more depth in them. That's probably why I never won the Tony Award I so coveted throughout most of my career.

"With Portia, there was a living presence about her. With each performance, she became more real to me. I began to understand why she is known as one of the Bard's favorites. As I communed with her, I could honestly feel the quality of mercy dropping into my soul 'like rain from heaven', as she says."

"That is so beautiful, Glenna," remarked Rory.

His face glowed with genuine admiration for his fiancée's gifts. And in that moment Father Crispin observed in the young man's countenance the quality he had been waiting to see. Rory's being radiated love, not fear. The abbot silently thanked *An Síoraí* that his prayers for this beloved son had been answered.

And yet, he knew much inner work remained until the lad's soul and his beloved's would be truly free. "All in good time." He smiled to himself to hear the assurance of his good friend, F. M. Bellamarre.

After midday mass and a delicious lunch with other guests of the monastery, Father Crispin bid the couple a safe journey and gave them his benediction. They were both deeply moved by his prayer and by the power of his touch when he placed his hands upon their heads as he spoke the words that carried the vibration of his own Higher Self.

May your union bring you mighty blessings
from the heart of An Síoraí, the Eternal One;
and may spirals of joy flow in and around you
as you bask in the sublime wholeness
of harmony in your togetherness.

After leaving the monastery and Father Crispin's generous presence, Glenna and Rory rode in silence for quite some time as they passed through Limerick without stopping and made their way north to the twin towns of Killaloe and Ballina.

The towns were connected by a beautiful old stone bridge at the mouth of Lough Derg. Here they spent three nights, taking day trips along both shores of the lough to ancient and more modern sites, which, Glenna was amused to discover, meant that most buildings dated from the eighteenth and nineteenth centuries.

One of their more memorable excursions was to *Inis Cealtra* (Holy Island). A small group of pilgrims who were visiting locations connected with Christian and pre-Christian Celtic spirituality invited them to join them for the day.

"You can only get to the island by boat," said their guide, "and only then when you know the boatman. Fortunately, we do. We'd be glad for you come with us tomorrow. Be sure to dress warmly. The weather's likely to be soft in the morning."

The following morning dawned a good deal wetter than Ireland's prevalent "soft" weather, but they had been warned, so they were prepared.

As they stood under umbrellas in the rain by the lake waiting for the small, open boat to ferry one group of nine passengers across to the island and return for their second group, they struck up a conversation with a friendly woman of mature years who had family connections with the island.

"Are you devotees of St. Brigid?" she asked. Her hazel eyes twinkled as if she already knew the answer to her question.

"She's my mother's favorite saint," replied Glenna, returning the woman's warm expression.

"Then you'll want to pay particular attention to her little chapel," said the woman. "At one time there were seven churches on the island. Many are completely gone, but Brigid's remains in part. It has some lovely Gothic stonework.

"We'll take a walk down by the far edge of the island and I'll show you and the others the promising stone. It's a flat rock where two people can insert an arm on either side, grasp hands, and make a promise to each other.

"Members of my family have been coming out here for many years to seal betrothals, settle disagreements, and for healings. It's a place of great power. There have been times when I felt the presence of the monks who lived here. I'm glad to share the island with you."

"I do feel something very special about this place," said Glenna as they strolled between the mostly ruined chapels and admired the care with which a few reconstructions had been done several decades in the past.

"So do I," agreed Rory. "I think the old monks are able to maintain a presence here because it's not overrun with tourists. The island sits in the middle of the lake, alone and largely undisturbed.

"I wonder if the monasteries of past ages would have emanated this kind of peace, or if they would have been humming with activity. *Inis Cealtra* might have been a very busy place in its heyday."

He took Glenna's hand and followed the other pilgrims.

"Let's find the promising stone. 'Tis a grand day for a special vow."

The group was enthralled with their fellow traveler's story about the stone. Glenna and Rory waited their turn and then knelt on either side, as they had seen other pairs of friends and lovers do.

"Give me your right hand, *mo chroí*, and hold tight," said Rory softly. "What I have to say won't take long, but 'tis important."

"I've got you, Rory," said Glenna. She felt the strength of his grasp as a ripple of unspeakable sweetness streamed down his arm, from his heart and soul into hers.

"Glenna, when *An Síoraí*, the Eternal One, spoke to me through Saint Germain, he absolved me of my fearful vow of penance and bade me make a new vow out of love—for you, my soul's own twin. Today, my Lady of the Glen, I make this promise."

> I pour the fullness of my being
> into the waiting chalice of your acceptance
> in faith that your love flows back to me,
> while waves of your devotion caress the shore
> of all that I am—body, spirit, mind, and soul.
>
> The ocean of my love knows no limits
> in the antiphon of emptying and filling.
> I become a world in order to contain the precious
> exchange of my life for yours and yours for mine,
> until we are only waves of light,
> rushing to each other in the exhilaration
> of Love's sweet alchemy of giving and receiving
> that changes us forever into eternal unity.

Glenna's heart was near to bursting with a sense of completion she never expected to feel. She squeezed Rory's hand and felt their souls lock together as she answered his promise with her own:

> My love, you humble me, you redeem me.
> I am yours forever, as I have always been.
> We shine, beloved, in the radiant fire of mutual gratitude.
> We are two candles touching an incandescent infinity.

Those with eyes to see such things noticed that where two individuals had joined hands within the promising stone, an orb of pink light now shimmered around them. Two bright flames flickered within the orb—individual, but not separate.

A hush came over the group of pilgrims and, as if in mutual agreement, they walked silently through a misty rain to the little dock where their boatman was waiting to ferry them back to the lough's far shore.

Thirty

We'd best leave early this morning," said Rory on the day they planned to visit the Cliffs of Moher and the primeval limestone landscape of The Burren in County Clare. "We're here in high tourist season, and I'm hoping we can avoid the thickest of the crowds."

"Maybe we should skip the cliffs," offered Glenna. "I confess to being a bit weary of 'touristing.' Do you mind if we save this stop for another time?"

"Actually, I do mind," said Rory gently. "I know what you mean about wanting to move on, but if we arrive early enough we should be able to walk the lesser-traveled paths and have a decent view. I want you to experience the place. There's nothing like it."

Early August's golden sunshine peeked through only partly cloudy skies, boding well for no rain. But by the time they arrived at the carpark, the wind was up. Glenna's courage was not.

"Oh, Rory, please don't take me near the edge," she begged. "And please don't go yourself. We've come this far. Let's not lose each other on a threshold we're not meant to hazard."

"We won't, *mo mhuirnín*. I've no desire for foolishness. We'll stick to the views with barriers."

As they walked well-protected paths, the raw power of the place astonished Glenna. The wind off the Atlantic roared in her ears and smelled of the damp, wave-lashed stone that fell away two hundred meters (over 650 feet) from the cliff edge to the churning waters below. She clung to Rory the entire time they were anywhere near the margin.

The sea thundered and crashed. The wind threatened to bowl them over. She knew that people had died at the cliffs and understood why.

Even standing behind the thoughtfully placed vertical flagstones known as O'Brien's Wall, they felt the elements warning that in an instant a daredevil's life could disappear with a collapsing trail.

And yet, Glenna was glad Rory had insisted on this adventure. He rewarded her courage with an evening's pub crawl in the fairytale village of Doolin where they listened to traditional Irish music that rivaled that of her friends in Dingle.

After a restful night in a tidy B&B, they made another early start to drive along the coastal route that offered dramatic views of the Aran Islands that seem to float on the vastness of the Atlantic like Saint Colmcille's intrepid monks in their open currach boats.

They stopped for tea in Fanore and then walked along the beach where the stark limestone outcroppings of The Burren flowed down to the sea. Glenna found the man-made dry stone walls most intriguing.

"They look like lace when the sun shines through them," she observed, then said teasingly. "And I thought The Burren looked like a giant mud-pie from the air."

Rory laughed at her description. "I'll have to take your word for it," he said. "I've never flown anywhere."

"I'll show you when we travel to the States," she promised. "We'll take a morning flight so you can understand why we Americans catch our breath when our plane drops down out of the clouds and Éire first comes into view.

"In fact, now that I've seen these stone walls and the landscape that birthed them up close, I have a poem for you. I began it as I flew into Shannon and it's just now completed itself. I couldn't help feeling that Ireland looked a bit like an orphan, cut off from the mainland by wild seas and high cliffs."

"And now you know that those barriers are one of the only reasons we've retained any semblance of national identity," said Rory solemnly.

"I do," agreed Glenna. "So, here's the poem."

> Set adrift from the motherland
> Like a lone calf,
> Out in the sea she floats,

Haunted home of the ancient ones
Who, generations ago,
Pushed against the nature gods
And claimed the land as their own,
Only to be claimed themselves
By the salty wind and the grey-blue sky,
Turned into the very stone
That would not yield to tyrants,
But that nestles into line under the spell
Of the wall-builder's imagination.

"Mmm," said Rory appreciatively. "You've captured the bleakness of The Burren, even though it is rich in plants and wildlife."

"I'll take *your* word for that," said Glenna. "I'm ready to move on."

"We could walk from here to our next stop," joked Rory as they made their way back to the carpark. "However, we'd miss our lunch and I want to have the afternoon and evening with my aunt."

"Do you realize we've been on the road for nearly a week and I don't think we've had anything close to a serious disagreement," remarked Glenna over a delicious chicken curry in the quaint seaside village of Ballyvaughan."

"I'd say that bodes well for our future," said Rory with a smile. "If we can spend every waking moment in each other's company while packed into an SUV with all of our belongings and sharing tiny hotel rooms, we may do well as time goes on."

"In a way, I sometimes feel as if we're picking up where we left off in a past life rather than beginning anew in this one," said Glenna dreamily."

"I pray we'll do better than that," added Rory quietly.

The hour's drive through County Clare offered a number of interesting historical sights and some striking views of Galway Bay. However, Glenna noticed that Rory seemed to be growing anxious as he navigated the increasing traffic on the outskirts of Galway City where they would spend the night at the home of his Great Aunt Finola.

He gripped the steering wheel more earnestly than on previous days and told Glenna almost nothing about the region's history. This was certainly a change from their journey since leaving Dublin.

She finally interrupted his unusual silence with a question she hoped would not reveal an unwelcome answer.

"Are you worried about introducing me to your great aunt? I hope you're not concerned about my being an American."

"Not at all. Aunt Finn will love you. I told you she was an actress. You two will get on like bread and jam."

"Then there's something else."

"There is, yes. A vibration in the air is making the hairs on my neck stand on end, as if something dark or dangerous lies ahead. I've felt that I've been transmuting the records Saint Germain told me about in the history lessons I've been giving you, so I'm not sure why I'm having this reaction."

"Nothing I've done, I hope," said Glenna.

"Oh, lass, just the opposite. I'm grateful you're such a willing student. Your love for me and your appreciation of the Irish countryside, the people, the language, the culture has helped me see my homeland with new eyes, almost as if having you with me has burned out the darkness of the past and bathed it with . . . I guess you could say, 'forgiveness.' "

"That's beautiful, Rory."

"It is, yes," he agreed. "There are times I've seen a violet light surrounding you and the places we've been. I could feel the energy lifting around us, and I've felt a sense of freedom in my soul I cannot remember ever experiencing in all my years of living in Ireland.

"I could tell it was happening naturally, so I didn't say anything. One thing I've learned about spiritual experiences is that you can spoil them by talking about them. I didn't want to lose whatever alchemy was transfiguring these familiar sights and sounds. Are you disappointed I didn't tell you?"

"Not at all," agreed Glenna. "I share your sentiment. There are experiences I've had in my life that are too deep for words. They may find expression later, but at the time they are delicate as filigree and not to be diminished by idle or even well-meant conversation."

"Thanks for understanding." Rory reached over and squeezed her hand. "You ease my mind as well as my heart, *mo mhuirnín*. We're nearly at my aunt's house. Prepare to be gathered in and well fed. Aunt Finn is a lady of generous heart and tireless energy. I used to visit her regularly when I studied history at the National University in Galway."

"Oh, that's where you were when Deirdre . . ." Glenna choked back what she was about to say. "Oh, gosh, I'm sorry. I didn't mean to bring that up. I just made the connection and it popped out."

"No, it's good that you did," said Rory. "Let me just sit with this a minute."

"Of course." Glenna waited uneasily as he turned the SUV onto what was undoubtedly a familiar route to his aunt's house, hoping she hadn't managed to ruin a perfectly lovely day.

After what felt to her like a very long minute, Rory reached over and rested his hand on her shoulder. "Don't feel bad, *mo mhuirnín*. You've done me a good turn. If you hadn't mentioned Deirdre's name, I wouldn't have realized that the whole terrible episode has been transmuted.

"I will always be sorry for the loss of a baby's life, and I pray she was given another opportunity to embody. But the personal agony is gone. The *samskara* has dissolved. Now I am absolutely certain I have been forgiven. Thank you for this gift."

Emotion bubbled up in Glenna's throat. All she could say was, "I'm pleased—for everyone's sake."

"As I was saying about my aunt," Rory began again in a light tone. "I tried to spend several days a year with her when I was a monk. Her home was nearer to the monastery than my family in Donegal, but it's been a while since I've seen her. I guess I didn't want her to notice my doubts about the priesthood.

"Most of my family thought I was mistaken in choosing that path. I didn't want to prove them right, and I knew Aunt Finn would catch the difference in my resolve as soon as I walked through her door.

"Now that I have a happier face to show her, I know she'll approve of my choice."

Thirty-One

*B*uachaill *cróga!*" Aunt Finola's ecstatic cry greeted Rory before he and Glenna reached her front door. She's got amazing strength for a woman who must be in her eighties, thought Glenna as Finola hugged her nephew then held him at arm's length, inspecting him keenly.

"Ceart go leor. Tá tú go maith."

He grinned at her Irish greeting, then said in English. "Yes, I am well, Aunt Finn. And so is my fiancée, you see here." He wrapped his arm around Glenna and folded her into this family circle. "May I present Glenna Morrissey. Glenna, my Aunt Finola."

"Och, a chara," she said taking Glenna's hands in both of hers. "Here I am carrying on in Irish. I can't help myself when I get excited, which I surely am today to see you, lad, with your beautiful lady. Come in and welcome. The tea's set to brew and Cook made scones this morning."

"You two go on in," said Rory. "I'll bring our bags and join you in a minute." With a wink, he whispered to Glenna, "Didn't I tell you?"

She nodded and smiled, following in Finola's wake. The woman must have been a force of nature in her younger days, she thought.

"Hang up your coat and go into the parlor, Glenna dear," said Finola, pointing to a cozy room to the right of her home's tiled entry way. "We'll have tea in there. 'Tis Rory's favorite room for visiting."

Glenna thought of offering to help, but she could tell that Finola was more than accustomed to serving guests in her own way. No need to intrude on a process undoubtedly refined by the woman's obvious skill and style.

Instead, she found an empty hook for her coat on the antique mahogany hall tree and made her way into an exquisitely appointed room, awash with sunshine. Lacy curtains fluttered in a soft breeze that filled the air with the scent of ivory and peach roses arranged on a side table in a large vase that appeared handmade. Glenna thought the arrangement looked like a wedding bouquet. Perhaps a hint from the grand lady?

Every surface was polished to gleaming. The furniture was antique, mostly walnut and cherry wood. Easy chairs and a love seat were upholstered in subtle tapestry patterns. The carpets were oriental silk and wool. Dozens of silver-framed photographs graced a long, intricately carved ebony table. Glenna was instantly captivated.

"Are these photos of characters you've played?" she asked as Finola entered the room and stood beside her, reminiscing as she gazed at the images of herself in numerous roles, many of them Shakespearean.

"They are," replied the lady, a wistful tone in her voice.

"That must be you as Portia. I'd recognize the trial scene anywhere."

"You know the play?"

"Intimately. I just finished a run of *Merchant* at the Aeon in Dublin. I played Portia. It was the most thrilling stage experience of my life."

"The Aeon? That's the charming reproduction of the first Abbey, isn't it? How delightful. In my time I played many roles at the theatre's modern version."

"Of course," exclaimed Sarah. "I've read some of your notices. 'Finola of the white shoulders,' one reviewer called you."

"Oh, that one. A play on my name, which unfortunately means 'white shoulders.' I've often wondered what my parents were thinking to burden a child with such a name. It was a torment in my youth, I can tell you."

Just then tea was served. Despite the elder woman's obvious agility and strength, Glenna was relieved when a girl in her early twenties carried in a tray laden with a silver tea service and enough scones for a dozen people. The girl set the tray on a coffee table on the other side of the room. Finola indicated they should be seated, with her guest on the loveseat.

"Thank you, Mary."

The girl nodded respectfully and retired, presumably to the kitchen.

"Mary is my lady-in-waiting," said Finola with a wry smile as she seated herself in a straight-backed chair that Glenna could easily imagine as a throne that no one but the great lady would dare occupy.

Like a fish to a well-disguised hook, she took the bait. "Really?"

"Indeed, yes. My family keeps waiting for me to fall and break a hip or something equally ridiculous, so I have Mary standing by to help with things like tea trays." She laughed at her own joke and Glenna joined in, immediately at ease with this grand dame of the Irish theatre.

"Please call me Aunt Finn. Everybody does. I am happy to know there is more than one reason for you to do so." She looked meaningfully at the ring on Glenna's left hand.

"So am I," said Glenna, feeling her color rise. She held out her hand for Aunt Finn to inspect the tiny amethyst that sparkled away in its gold setting. "Things have happened rather quickly. We were engaged only a week ago."

"Rory did send me a hasty note, full of the brightness I've not found in his letters for a long while. From first glance, I would say you're well matched. May you remain that way for many years. I'm grateful that my nephew has found his love at last. Where are you off to next?"

Glenna had a feeling Aunt Finn was hoping she'd say, "To church." Still, if the lady had spent many years in the theatre, she might not be overly strict in her opinion of two young people traveling together.

She wanted to assure Rory's aunt that they had always insisted on twin beds in their shared hotel rooms. However, there was no way to discreetly broach the subject, so she let it go. Rory could handle that delicate detail, should it become a matter of inquiry.

"We're on our way to Donegal to meet Rory's family. I think we've had enough of sightseeing for a while, though I'll never tire of the Irish countryside. For now, we're ready to land and figure out where life is taking us. We've one more stop—at Clonmacnoise."

A cloud passed over Finola's face.

"Do you know it? Is there something we should be wary of?" asked Glenna. "Rory particularly wants to go there." She didn't mention that he was in the process of exorcising demons from the past.

"A lot of sadness befell that sacred place. Ghosts still haunt the graveyards, no matter the busloads of tourists that swarm the ruins this time of year. Some memories take more than hundreds of feet treading holy ground to cleanse them," said Aunt Finn with a sigh.

Her face lit up as Rory entered the room.

"Now, we'll speak no more of tragedy on this happy day," she said decisively. "Here's your handsome man with a bounce in his step and a light in his eye. Give your aunty a kiss, and tell me all your plans, *buachaill cróga*," she said as she poured tea and encouraged her guests to help themselves to scones.

"What does that mean, Aunt Finn?" asked Glenna as Rory gave his aunt the most affectionate of kisses on her alabaster cheek.

"It means 'brave boy'," he answered with a laugh. He accepted his cup of tea and sat next to his fiancée on the loveseat.

" 'Tis my pet name for him since he was a babe in his mother's arms," said Aunt Finn, casting her gaze back more than thirty years to when she'd first met the little towhead who was instantly her favorite of all her nieces and nephews.

"Rory is a brave boy—now a man grown—as I'm sure you'll come to appreciate, Glenna."

"I do now, Aunt Finn. Courage is one of his finest qualities."

"See that it doesn't get him or you into trouble," she said with a grave smile. She reached out and firmly patted Rory on the knee.

What does this woman know that I don't? wondered Glenna. But then the conversation turned to more pleasant topics.

The three of them talked non-stop through tea and a fabulous dinner, prepared by Aunt Finn's magician of a cook, and on into the evening. The clock on the mantle struck ten, and they laughed at the simultaneous yawn they each tried to stifle.

"To bed with you, *a pháistí*. I know you're no longer children, but I will always cherish you as such. You are that dear to me. Cook will serve you a full breakfast in the morning so you'll be well nourished for your journey to Clonmacnoise.

"Rory, lad, you'll let me know when you're safe in Donegal. I'll phone your mother so she knows I've seen you. I'm planning to tell her she's to treat my new niece like her own daughter."

Rory and Glenna beamed, kissed Aunt Finn good night, and retired upstairs to their separate rooms, where they had been installed without inquiry as to their preferences.

Glenna sat up like a shot at the knock on her bedroom door. She had been dreaming about running away from some danger and was shaking when her door opened.

"Excuse me, miss," said a gentle voice. Mary, the lady-in-waiting, came in carrying a cup of tea. "Aunt Finn said I should wake you. Cousin Rory is already having his breakfast. He said he wants to leave as soon as you've had yours. I've brought you a cuppa. Would you like me to help you pack?"

"*Go raibh maith agat*, Mary," said Glenna, pleasantly surprised that Gaelic would be the first words out of her mouth. "Please tell Aunt Finn and . . . *Cousin* Rory?" These people were full of surprises. "Are you all related?"

"Only distantly. He didn't remember me until Aunt reminded him. I was much younger the one time we met. I certainly remembered him." She raised her eyebrows suggestively and grinned. "All the girl cousins were in love with him. A couple of the boys, too, as I recall."

"Ah, well," said Glenna. She had no idea how to comment on that statement. Instead, she quickly got out of the bed. "Please tell them I'll be right down. I packed most of my things last night, so I won't delay our journey. Thank you for the tea, *Cousin* Mary." She returned the girl's grin and hurried down the hall to the bathroom.

Back in a flash, she pulled on jeans and her favorite blue sweater and ran a quick brush through her hair. Good thing she was accustomed to fast costume changes. And wasn't it sweet that Aunt Finn had family looking out for her. She hoped her sister would do that for their parents, especially their mother, if she and Rory stayed in Ireland.

Thirty-Two

"What did you and your aunt talk about this morning?" Glenna asked as Rory steered their SUV away from Aunt Finn's cottage where she and Cousin Mary stood at the front door waving.

"Family, mostly. Everybody talks to Aunt Finn. She scolds them when they don't. If anything important is going on, she'll know."

"Like us, I suppose?"

"Definitely. You made a fine impression yesterday. She already had her list of phone calls for this morning. I think that's one reason she wanted us to be on our way. She's planning to tell everyone they're not to worry about me any longer because I've found the woman who is perfect for me."

"That's wonderful."

"You have no idea. Gaining Aunt Finn's approval is like a papal imprimatur to the O'Donnells. I'm proud of you, *a ghrá.*"

"I didn't do anything special. She's easy to talk to."

"Not everyone would say so. She doesn't suffer fools lightly. But when she recognizes authenticity in a person, she opens to it like a rose in bloom."

Glenna reached over and gently rested her hand on his cheek.

"Did she ever marry?"

"She did, many years ago, but the marriage was cut short."

"What happened? Did you know him?"

" 'Twas more than fifty-five years ago, long before I was born. He was a diplomat, as I recall the story. They met when she was doing a play in London."

"How romantic," said Glenna dreamily.

"At the time, it was a scandal," explained Rory. "He had only recently divorced his wife and Finola was much younger, a radiant ingenue who stole his heart the minute he saw her.

"My mother told me he sent her a dozen ivory and peach roses every day until she agreed to have dinner with him, which she did then every night for the next two weeks. He proposed on a Sunday and they were married a week later.

"Her play closed shortly thereafter and they stayed on in London until his next assignment. He worked for the Foreign Office, which paid him very well. She was so in love that she decided to suspend her acting career so they could be together.

"They traveled extensively for nearly a year until the Foreign Office posted him to the Middle East. I don't know what country, or what it may have been called at the time. She wanted to go with him, but he said it was too dangerous. She was not to worry, he would return in a month."

Rory paused to navigate a round-about and enter the motorway that would take them to Athlone, the town nearest to Clonmacnoise.

"He didn't return, did he?" said Glenna softly, emotion clouding her voice.

"There was an inquiry, of course, but nothing conclusive came of it. The official report was that he had been in the wrong place at the wrong time. However, people in the know suspected he'd been carrying some very sensitive papers that a foreign operative wanted badly enough to kill for.

"There was a private funeral in London, but no notices in the paper. It was as if the man simply evaporated from Aunt Finn's life."

"She must have been devastated."

"She was, but she had to return to the stage within a fortnight. He'd had debts she didn't know about and basically left her with nothing. Fortunately, she was young and much beloved by audiences and theatre companies in England and Ireland. She made a successful comeback and went on to have a spectacular and lucrative career."

"And she never remarried?"

"I once got up the courage to ask her about that. She looked at me with a wistful smile. '*Buachaill cróga*, when you find the love of your life, you'll understand how I can be content as I am.' "

Rory gently caressed Glenna's check. "I never understood her meaning until now."

As they made their way toward Clonmacnoise, the sun that had accompanied them yesterday deserted them today. The further east they drove, the darker the sky became. But with little more than a drizzle to wet the roads, neither of them really minded. If you didn't like rain, you shouldn't live in Ireland.

Glenna was always amazed at how quickly time passed when she was with Rory. They were beginning to discover the peace of being silent together, especially when driving through the Irish countryside.

The green was healing to the soul, the rhythm of the car's motion soothing to the body. They both were grateful to have found a partner who didn't require constant conversation. They crossed the River Shannon at Athlone and turned onto the road that would take them to the famous ruins of Clonmacnoise.

"Are you sensing anything?" asked Rory when they passed a sign pointing the way to the monastery visitor's center.

"No. I thought I might, but nothing so far. Are you?"

"Nothing definite, though there is a vibration in the air I can't identify. I wonder if it's because I've been seeing an image of F. M. Bellamarre and Father Crispin standing side by side."

"The two of them together? How interesting. Are they speaking or doing anything in particular?"

"Nothing specific. They're only watching. And clearly observing us."

They were silent again until Rory found a space in the carpark and turned off the SUV's engine. He blew out a breath. "Are you ready?"

"Yes, let's get a snack in the tea room and find out what time the next tour begins. The clouds are lifting. We may stay dry after all."

Despite their initial trepidation about walking the grounds where their own blood may have been spilled centuries ago, they found themselves enjoying the excellent displays in the visitor center and the wealth of information presented by the tour guide.

Most of the other visitors seemed as intent as they on understanding what had happened to this once-great center of piety, trade, learning, and craftsmanship—as the guidebooks described it.

There was definitely something eerie about walking around the old graveyard, realizing that nearly two thousand human beings had lived here at the height of the monastery's power and prestige. Unless they had been mentioned in the annals or identified by a stone cross or grave slab, those individuals were now nameless and forgotten.

Still, the site did not feel haunted, and for that they were grateful.

"Whew!" said Rory at the conclusion of the tour. "That was easier than I expected."

"Do you think that people praying here over the centuries has transmuted the akashic records you thought you might experience?" asked Glenna. "Every once in a while I thought I picked up a vibration of devotion, though nothing as strong as at Glendalough."

"After being a monk for four years, I can assure you that prayer works, but with so many cross-currents of people's consciousness walking the site, it's hard to say what's what. For many, Clonmacnoise is just another tourist attraction, so devotion is not the intention they bring with them.

"I definitely felt more energy at the round tower, but you're right. Nothing like around the tower at Glendalough. Probably because the conical stone roof is missing. Remember I told you about that scientist who believes the round towers were a type of energy conductor? I doubt that would be the case without an intact structure."

He took Glenna's hand as they made their way between clusters of visitors who had stopped along the path to inspect some faintly marked gravestones with barely visible lettering.

"Do you want to walk down by the river? I'd like to sit for a while before the weather clouds up again."

"Perfect," said Glenna. "Let's stroll over by Temple Finghin. There aren't as many people there and McCarthy's Tower still has its roof."

They soon found themselves very much alone by the ruined chapel whose unique feature was an intact round tower that was attached to the junction of nave and chancel. Around the north side of the tower was a narrow path that led down to the river.

"One thing does bother me about the history of this place," said Glenna as they walked.

"What's that?"

"Well, the Irish burned Clonmacnoise more times than the Vikings and the Normans combined. Why is that? Mostly greed, tribal rivalries, I suppose. But often there was more than plundering. I mean, who were these people? They called themselves Irish, but they seemed determined to destroy their own kinsmen."

Rory nodded. "History is full of brother against brother. Remember Cain and Abel? Humankind has been at each other's throats ever since."

"I know. Like that Munster over-king who was also a bishop and an ascetic. He was the first one to torch the monastery. He killed a lot of people in 833 AD and burned their buildings, ostensibly to purge the monks of their immoral ways, which conveniently included their considerable wealth which he had no scruples about appropriating."

"Even otherwise good people can be led astray by their beliefs," said Rory thoughtfully.

"Who of us hasn't been?" Glenna agreed. "What I can't stand is the rigid moralizing, the letter-of-the-law mentality—the lack of mercy. That's what Portia faced in Shylock. It's just so *wrong!*"

"Easy now, those people are long dead and buried. Some of them could be resting under our feet even now."

"And others like them rise up to take their places. All I'm saying is that I'd rather be faced with a straight-forward, ignorant Viking who just wants my gold and silver than with a wily adversary who wants to condemn my soul to the hell he has created in his own mind."

"Be careful what you wish for, *a ghrá.*" Rory turned around and took her in his arms. "Even though we didn't notice any strong akashic records on the tour, we know these ruins can act like portals to the past. Come sit with me awhile and let's talk about the present."

None of the people exploring the grounds of Clonmacnoise that day would have guessed that the ancient round tower that overlooked a grassy rise above the River Shannon would act as an energetic node point for the activation of a past-life record.

However, as Aunt Finn had remarked, some memories require more than the impressions of hundreds of tourist feet to transmute them. In this case, few visitors ever walked this patch of ground where in centuries past a young female scribe and the soldier to whom she was betrothed enjoyed a few moments of idle conversation whenever they had a respite from their daytime duties.

As soon as Glenna and Rory sat down on the ground and looked out across the river that had become a ribbon of shimmering silver in the rays of afternoon light that slanted between darkening clouds, the atmosphere around them began to change.

Glenna shivered and zipped up her jacket.

"Are you cold?" asked Rory.

"I feel like someone just walked on my grave," said Glenna. She shivered again. The breeze that had been blowing in from the river suddenly died completely, and a strange, greenish mist began to gather across from where they were sitting.

"Rory, hold my hand, will you? I'm starting to feel strange—like something or somebody is pulling on me, trying to get at my soul. I think you're right about this place being a portal to the past."

He grasped her hand and put his other arm around her shoulders. He felt it too. When he looked out to where the River Shannon had been in plain view, all he could see was mist.

The texture of Glenna's clothing beneath his hands was changing. Her fleece jacket had turned into the linen homespun of a ninth-century nun's habit. He looked down at their joined hands and saw his arms and legs clad in similar fabric. Their feet were simply shod in rough leather shoes for her and sturdier boots for him.

"Stand up!" the soldier cried suddenly. "We've got to get away from the river. Look there. Coming out of the mist. Do you see them?"

The nun's mouth gaped open in horror. "Dragon ships. Dozens of them. Surely not again. Not so soon. Vikings!"

"Run to the forest and hide, lass. They're only looking for treasure and people in the open they can grab for slaves. I'll fight them off if they try to take you."

"No, I'll not leave you. We've lost too many in the other raids. I will not lose you, too."

"Then stay with me and we'll run together."

The soldier tugged his beloved away from the river. The ground was uneven and there were stones everywhere. He lost his footing and they went down together, hitting their heads when they landed.

Everything went black as their souls were viciously wrenched from their bodies.

Thirty-Three

Sarah was seated at a table at the back of Fibonacci's coffee shop when her cell phone rang. Her ankles had begun to swell and she was thinking about getting up to walk around. She noticed Debbie's name on caller ID and answered on the first ring.

"Hi, what's up?" she answered cheerfully, then trembled as Debbie began to frantically pour out the news they both had been dreading.

"Sarah, you were right. Glenna's in trouble. Her agent, Mel, just called me in a total panic. His name was in her wallet as emergency contact, so the people at Clonmacnoise called him in New York."

"Slow down, Debbie. Why was Glenna at that old monastery?'

"She was there with her fiancé—Craig's brother, Rory. Glenna is getting married to Riordan, just like we thought might happen. Though not this fast. I meant to call you this morning, but we got really busy at my sister's store.

"Glenna sent me a quick text last night. She sounded so excited and said she'd have loads to tell me when they got to Donegal where his family lives. Clonmacnoise was a stop along the way."

"That's great news. So why was Mel calling you?"

"They had an accident. They stumbled, fell on some rocks, both hit their heads, and blacked out. When the authorities reached Mel, Glenna and Rory had already been helicoptered to Galway where there's a large hospital with a neurological unit.

"They're in stable condition, but they're not waking up, which has the doctors puzzled. CT scans showed mild concussions but no permanent or life-threatening damage. It's as if they were propelled out of their bodies from the blows to their heads, and now they can't get back.

"Mel said the *garda* found Rory's car with their belongings in the carpark and have secured it for now. He's flying over tonight with Glenna's father. They're both cool heads and can take care of things with the police. Her mother is too ill to travel. MS, I think."

Debbie pulled her mind back to the matter at hand. "I'm worried that whatever was troubling you is actually happening. I've tried to locate them, but my inner sight is blocked. This shouldn't be life and death, but I think it is."

"I'm sure you're right," said Sarah without hesitation. "Can you call a few of the Friends and ask them to pray? They don't know Glenna or Rory, but some of them will remember Gormlaith and Riordan. Craig for sure."

"Of course!" exclaimed Debbie. "I'll call him first. He'll want to be on that plane with Mel and Glenna's father."

"You're right," said Sarah. "I'll get Kevin and we'll figure out what to do from here."

"Okay, we'll talk soon."

Sarah groaned as she tried to maneuver her very pregnant body out of the booth. "Róisín!" she called to her friend who was working the coffee bar. "Glenna's in trouble, just as we feared. I'm sorry I can't say more, but Debbie will fill you in. Your prayers are needed in this hour."

Kevin came hurtling downstairs from the office he and Lucky shared and through the curtain that separated Fibonacci's kitchen from the coffee shop. He had felt Sarah's urgent signal and was on his way to her side before bothering to answer her call.

He found her leaning against the table where she had managed to hoist herself to standing.

"Are the babies coming?" he asked frantically. "Did your waters break? Do you have your hospital bag with you?"

"No, Hon. No babies yet, but we've got to get home. Debbie just called me about Glenna. She's in Ireland with her fiancé, Rory—the man who was Riordan, just like you said. They're stuck in a coma. We've got to help them. I don't know exactly how yet. All I know is that Saint Germain's warning is coming true."

"Okay. Here, let me help you. You're sure you're not in any pain?"

"No, I'm fine. Honest. Just get me home."

While Kevin swiftly buckled Sarah into their car, she began relaying the few details Debbie had given her.

"Do you have a sense of where they are—other than in Ireland, I mean?" asked Kevin as he sped back to their town house. He hoped the police were all at lunch. There was no time to spare.

"Everything is all misty. I can't get a clear picture of them. Neither could Debbie, and she's a much better seer than I am. I'm fairly sure they're stuck on the astral plane. Definitely not in this world. There is something or someone really sinister holding them, like they're under a spell."

"Could it be Arán Bán?" Kevin shuddered at the thought.

Sarah was quiet for a minute. "I'm afraid that's exactly who it is," she said. "While they were at that ruined monastery they must have triggered an akashic record or a state of consciousness that allowed him to grab them. Just like the raiders of monasteries kidnapped people to sell as slaves."

Suddenly her inner sight cleared. "My God, Kevin, I can feel his malevolence and their weakness. He's got them enslaved by their own karma."

Sarah and Kevin were seated in their living room, where they were accustomed to doing their deepest spiritual work. Hero and Sprite were curled up on the rug in front of them. Almost as if they're ready to play their part in this drama, thought Sarah. She and her husband were wearing their druid medallions and had changed into the white linen robes that Róisín had had made for them by one of the Friends who sewed.

"I thought I might feel silly dressing up like druids," said Kevin, "but as soon as I put on my robe I felt a spiritual mantle drop around me. I think this is a sign of how we're meant to conduct our inner and outer work, as elements of our merged selves."

"I agree," said Sarah. "Each mode has its distinctive vibration and mantle. We can accomplish our outer work as Sarah and Kevin. But for inner work that has to be done on planes other than the physical, we may find ourselves functioning more like Alana and Ah-Lahn."

"Interesting." Kevin drew out the word. "That's similar to how our Master appears as F. M. Bellamarre or Saint Germain, depending on the need of the hour. 'As each one requires,' like he says."

"I love that," said Sarah. "Perhaps we're walking in the Master's footsteps on the way toward adeptship. I certainly hope so."

Kevin squeezed her hand and nodded. "Are you ready, then?"

"I am. Let's get started."

Together they visualized the spheres of blue and violet light and chanted the invocations they used to contact Saint Germain. They said a prayer for the Master's assistance, knowing that he would lend his support.

They let their consciousness rest in full awareness of the spark of *An Síoraí*, the Eternal One, within their hearts. Their inner sight opened immediately and they soon found themselves lifting out of their physical bodies. For a brief period they traveled at great speed to another dimension where they stepped into one of the life review chambers they knew well—now in the forms of Alana and Ah-Lahn.

Unlike their previous experiences, they were not accompanied by their Master. However, the familiar goblets of sparking elixir materialized in their hands, then disappeared as soon as they had partaken of the invigorating beverage.

A faint light flickered on the screen at the front of the room, but no images appeared—only a "snow screen" that looked like an old television picture tube on the verge of expiration. They assumed they were meant to approach the grey emptiness before them, but when they moved forward, nothing happened.

"Why are we not in a scene?" asked a very pregnant Alana.

"I'm not sure, but I don't like this," said Ah-Lahn. "I know you're a brave warrior, *mo chroí*, but I don't think we should risk the babies. Not with you so close to delivery. Saint Germain, what should we do?"

Immediately a brilliant light bathed the chamber and the Master stepped into the room, standing between them and the screen.

"You are correct to be concerned, my son. Alana must not enter the action." He held up his hand before she could object.

Never fear, young mother. Your role is vitally important. You will remain here in this etheric chamber while your beloved goes into the astral scene to aid your friends of old. He will be aware of your presence and he will be able to hear your prayers, but he will not see you—so as not to distract him from his work.

You, Alana, will be fully in contact with Ah-Lahn's True Self and you will not lose sight of him. As you observe events unfold on the screen, you will invoke powerful angelic beings for the protection, vision, and transmutation necessary for this action to take place.

We are about to change history, my dears. That is, we are going to dissolve an electronic pattern that has existed for centuries in the consciousness of Glenna and Rory as a soul wound called a *samskara*.

To transmute the pattern, Rory needs to experience success in defending and saving his beloved. Glenna needs to experience being defended and saved by him. They began the process on Mount Brandon. Our mission today is to change his karmic records of doubt, fear, and death and her long-standing sense of injustice into faith in their ability to fulfill their destiny as twin flames in perfect love.

Psychologists call the action we are about to perform a psychodrama. We masters have not created this dire situation, but we will use it to effect a sort of soul-play on inner levels wherein the hero and heroine achieve a new pattern of victory in the depths of their being.

The faces of Ah-Lahn and Alana brightened with insight into their ongoing mission. Saint Germain nodded in approval at the deeper understanding his son and daughter were achieving, which allowed him to better prepare them for the current task.

This is the first of many such actions which I anticipate the two of you will perform on behalf of twin flames who do not yet possess the attainment to free themselves from the deep-seated psychological patterns that keep them trapped in lower levels of consciousness.

In this case, the level of the astral plane to which Glenna and Rory have descended is not entirely their karma—though their untransmuted substance has made them vulnerable to attack.

Placing his right hand on Alana's head and his left hand on Ah-Lahn's, Saint Germain beamed a ray of brilliant golden light into their crown chakras. He then removed his amethyst ring and held it to the center of their brows at the spot known as the third eye—a place of higher spiritual awareness and insight—and finally to their hearts, as he uttered this blessing.

By the power of An Síoraí, the Eternal One, I invoke the presence of the entire Spirit of the Great White Brotherhood. Seal these twin flames in Light and Love. Archangel Michael and legions of blue fire, protect their mission as they play their roles in a cosmic psychodrama for the rescue of souls. I AM Saint Germain and I declare that, by the grace of An Síoraí, all will be well.

Go forth now, my beloved son, Ah-Lahn. Be strong, my beloved daughter, Alana. Have faith that you are able for this test. May you pass it with flying colors.

As soon as Saint Germain's image disappeared from the etheric chamber, Ah-Lahn quickly led Alana to a comfortable chair that was richly upholstered in purple silk and situated directly before the screen.

With a look of profound love at his soul's twin, which he prayed would not be their last glimpse of each other, he turned to the task at hand. With a warrior's straight spine and eyes narrowed in calm determination, he stepped into the screen where images now came to life in vivid detail.

Thirty-Four

Alana immediately began to chant the OM and pray the prayers that Saint Germain had impressed upon her in his blessing. She felt incredibly strong and was assured that, although she carried the hope of her husband and herself in her swollen belly, all aspects of this initiation were under the protection of their Master.

Determined not to fail Ah-Lahn or Saint Germain, she placed her full attention on the screen and allowed her awareness to follow the events as they unfolded—never ceasing to invoke the light energy that Ah-Lahn was depending upon for his success.

The figures of Rory and Glenna had come into view. The two were seated in a room that was not unlike a life review chamber, except there was something slightly garish about the lighting and the shiny crimson and gold satin fabrics that decorated the walls and chairs.

"Do you know where we are?" Glenna whispered to Rory.

"No, but perhaps this druid will tell us. He looks familiar to me."

Standing before them was Arán Bán. He was clad in his most splendid druidic robes. A black crystal pendant hung around his neck on an intricately fashioned metallic chain. His thick grey hair shimmered with a silvery light that seemed to emanate from his entire form. His cobalt blue eyes were dark as midnight beneath arching brows that emphasized the solicitous smile that graced his full, sensual lips.

"Greetings, friends." His voice was silky, his tone uniquely soothing. "Welcome to the special presentation I have arranged for you this afternoon. Won't you please oblige me by enjoying a beverage of my own creation that is designed for just such an occasion."

Beakers of sweet-smelling liquid appeared before Rory and Glenna.

As they both discovered they were thirsty, they eagerly accepted the inviting drink. But as soon as they had partaken of the beverage, a strange feeling came over them and they found themselves unable to move. Rory tried to reach for Glenna's hand, but he was paralyzed and realized she was also riveted to the chair where she sat next to him.

"Comfortable?" Arán Bán asked. His lips curled and his smile became a sneer. "No? Isn't that a shame." He laughed sardonically. "Nevertheless, it appears that you will be my guests for a while."

The silvery light in his aura began to darken with streaks of black and orange as he activated a movie screen that was placed directly in front of Rory and Glenna. Neither of them could move their heads, so they had no choice but to watch the images that began to appear.

"What is happening?" Rory managed to ask, though his voice was weak and he was finding it difficult to think.

"Silence!" commanded Arán Bán. His tone was suddenly virulent. "On pain of death, do not take your attention from the screen. Watch what I show you and know that your greatest fears about your own worthlessness are absolutely true."

The couple sat immobilized while image after horrifying image appeared in quick succession on the screen. They were allowed no time to question what they were being shown. They must only witness and absorb the meaning being forced upon them by Arán Bán.

Scenes came into view of the destruction of ancient civilizations, for which he claimed they were personally to blame: Atlantis, Lemuria, Egypt, China, Mycenae, Greece, Rome. The failures of golden ages were all laid at their feet. In one particular lifetime they were members of a druidic community, destined to be together, but failing their tests for lack of determination.

Arán Bán laughed maliciously as anger, doubt, and fear rose up in their hearts and minds, binding them ever tighter to the sense of injustice that had opened Glenna to his influence and the records of bloodshed and death that had trapped Rory in self-condemnation. Time and again, they had fallen under the debilitating pressure of forces that Arán Bán and brothers of the shadow had set into motion.

When they were fully saturated with the despair he had pumped into their consciousness, he switched off the screen and began to harangue them as if he would crush the very life from their souls.

"Surrender to our eminence this day. You have no hope for a better future. You will never amount to anything. Weak, pathetic humans. You keep coming back again and again, but you never succeed. We are stronger. We have more power, greater determination than you will ever acquire. Your so-called masters do not want the likes of you.

"I spit on your pitiful belief in divine goodness. What has that ever brought you? Children of *An Síoraí*, indeed. What kind of father would allow his offspring to fall into my hands? To him you are worthless losers.

"An Irish wannabe theatre may tolerate a mediocre actress, but you will never make it on Broadway. And you, a feckless monk, an ignorant teacher, a worse defender that your supposed love could never depend upon. You could not save her from a Viking attack and you cannot save her here. Go back to the cows, if they will have you."

"Accelerate! Now!" Alana heard the command from her Higher Self and felt the power of her personal, spiritual attainment combined with Ah-Lahn's blaze into action. She immediately intensified her calls to the entire Spirit of the Great White Brotherhood—powerfully invoking the presence of Archangel Michael and his legions.

Suddenly, the sound as of a thousand voices pierced the darkness with a mighty druid leading the charge.

"Hold!" cried Ah-Lahn as he stood next to the near lifeless bodies of Rory and Glenna. His white-robed figure glowed with the radiance of a sun. A flash of royal blue flame shot from his upraised hands, shattering the walls of the astral chamber and flooding the scene with a pure, white light that vanquished the darkness.

"In the name of *An Síoraí*, the Eternal One, I say you are bound, Arán Bán! You have no power to harm these holy ones! Angels of Light, clear this forcefield now and save our Friends of Ancient Wisdom!"

Alana immediately took up the call.

"I invoke oceans of violet flame to consume, consume, consume the records of trauma, of injustice, of fear, of death! Sweep through this astral substance and free these souls! Be gone all forces of anti-Love, all hatred and murderous intent ever pitted again them, and raise them into the Light of Forgiveness!"

In response to the invocations of the druids, mighty angels swept into the arena and surrounded Arán Bán in a forcefield of blue flame, almost like a box, that rendered him momentarily powerless. Frozen in place, his face registered utter surprise that he could be so contained, even if only for a short time.

With the evil druid temporarily bound, Ah-Lahn stepped between him and his victims and called to the souls of his friends who were now clothed as the soldier and nun they had been in the ninth century. Despite their historical appearance, he addressed them by their current names, for this battle was being waged in the present as well as the past.

"Glenna and Rory, awake! Awake, I say! Be made whole by the power of *An Síoraí*, the Eternal One, and the love you bear each other as twin flames. Let nothing come between you and your Divine Source. Claim the freedom that was yours from the beginning."

Alana immediately visualized a new wave of light penetrating the scene, and she began repeating ancient mantras that had once been known to only the most advanced druids.

As she chanted, Ah-Lahn stepped to the side of Glenna and Rory. The most critical part of the rescue mission was about to unfold—for here their friends must take the action that only their own souls could accomplish.

Faintly at first, the sound of a human voice could be heard.

"You lie." The soldier groaned and murmured. Then again, a little louder, as he found himself able to move slightly. "You lie."

He lifted his head and glared at Arán Bán, who was now towering over his victims like a gigantic Viking. The blue-flame forcefield surrounding him dissolved—for the drama must be played out—and the malevolent one bared his teeth at the young man's nearly inert form.

"You lie," the soldier said again, louder still. His body began to tremble violently. He struggled to stand and then at once was on his feet, shouting into the sneering face of his oppressor, "You lie!"

"Rory!" Ah-Lahn called to his friend and tossed him a sword when he turned at the sound of his name.

In that moment, the Viking grabbed the nun's limp body and spun on his heel, heading toward the fleet of dragon ships floating on the river behind him.

"Let her go!" shouted the soldier, now in impassioned pursuit of his beloved's kidnapper.

The Viking flung his captive aside like a rag doll, turned, and raised his battle axe to demolish his adversary with a single blow. But as his arm hovered in the air, ready to strike, the young man's sword caught him in the chest, piercing his heart.

However, still very weak from his ordeal, the soldier did not move quickly enough to dodge the axe as it fell with the Viking's body, delivering a glancing blow to the young man's forehead. Fortunately, this wound was not mortal, though blood flowed from the gash.

The soldier struggled toward the body of his beloved. Was she alive? "*A ghrá!*" he called over and over. "My love, wake up. Others are coming. We must leave this terrible place."

Her eyes flickered open and she stared at him through a haze of confusion. "Where am I? What happened? Oh, you're bleeding." She reached up to touch his head, then drew back her hand when he winced.

"Never mind," he said, gathering her to her feet. "We must go! *Now!* By the power of *An Síoraí*, the Eternal One, I declare that we are free!"

In that instant, the soldier and his beloved vanished from Alana's view. The dragon ships were gone. The Viking's dead body had also disappeared. All that remained on the grassy bank of the River Shannon were the figures of Ah-Lahn standing triumphantly next to a severely diminished Arán Bán. That one's face bore a look of absolute shock that he had been denied his hideous victory.

How could Rory and Glenna have escaped? Hadn't he felt his power growing strong enough to withstand even Ah-Lahn's interference? How could he have been so hindered by mere worms who should be dead by now? He opened his mouth to curse them, but not a word could he utter. He blanched, clutched at his cape, and scuttled off into the woods.

As Alana watched the astonishing scene fade to nothing, she could have sworn the man slithered.

Thirty-Five

A h-Lahn!" Alana cried aloud as her soul's beloved twin suddenly emerged from the screen and sank to his knees at her feet. She smoothed his hair that was damp with sweat and took his face in her hands, gazing deeply into his violet eyes.

"*A ghrá,*" he said with a profound sigh. He gently placed a hand on her shoulder and kissed her tenderly.

As they embraced, their two druid presences disappeared from the etheric life review chamber—victorious and together in a new level of inner mastery that would illumine their ongoing work on behalf of other twin flames like their friends Rory and Glenna, exactly as Saint Germain had foretold.

When Kevin and Sarah came back to themselves, they were sitting side by side on their sofa, enfolded in each other's arms. It was several moments before either of them could move, and they did not immediately speak.

Instead, Kevin held Sarah at arm's length and lovingly focused his attention on this precious face he had thought he might never see again. As she returned his gaze, each one felt the profound love for their twin flame sweeping back and forth across the silver cord that linked them heart to heart, soul to soul, in the sublime flow of unity for which there are no words.

At last husband and wife settled more completely into their forms and gently began to resume life in the physical plane.

"Would you like some tea?" Kevin asked as he helped Sarah remove her druid robe which she had slipped on over her maternity clothes rather than wrestle with getting in and out of too many layers.

"Yes, my sweet husband. And don't fret about me. I'm feeling strong and full of energy. You were magnificent, my brave Ah-Lahn."

"And you, my resilient Alana. Rest here, and I'll be right back."

He was returning from the kitchen with a pot of tea on a tray with mugs and some scones when he heard his wife's voice. She was engaged in conversation with F. M. Bellamarre.

"Are you certain Glenna and Rory are still awake and not suffering any lasting ill effects?" asked Sarah.

"Indeed, your friends are well and being expertly tended by excellent hospital staff," answered F. M. "We will learn more after their loved ones are able to give us a full report. For now, be assured that your intervention on their behalf achieved its purpose.

"In that regard, please accept my apologies for not coming to you in my ascended presence. The violet light shining from your eyes attests to your having earned that communion. However, I am mindful of the exceptional amount of energy that has passed through your chakras this day. I would prefer not to overload your systems, as you soon will need all of your strength."

He smiled affectionately at the very pregnant wife and her husband who were seated before him and continued his report on their actions on the astral plane where the rescue of Rory and Glenna had taken place.

"As you may have surmised, you have won an important battle in overcoming the forces of darkness that manifest through the soul of Arán Bán. He is proving himself to be beyond redemption, but that does not mean we have won this particular war, which, regrettably, dealing with him has become.

"The legions of the Great White Brotherhood are destined to be victorious in the end, but many more events must transpire before the final curtain can be drawn on Arán Bán's activities. He has overplayed this hand, but he has not played all of his cards, as they say. His opportunity is not yet completely spent, nor is that of his consort."

"I was afraid of that," said Kevin. "Is there anything we can do now to mitigate whatever the two of them may be plotting?"

"For the time being, there is little we can accomplish by way of circumventing their conspiracies. The next move is theirs. Even ascended masters are limited by cosmic law and human free will. We must also be mindful of the capacities of our best servants. We need you alive and strong for the next engagement, which will not come for some time.

"Thus far, Ursula—Una, as we know her—has let Arán Bán assume the lead for them both. However, seeing him diminished, she may take over where he has failed. Do not underestimate her. The female, known in the East as the *shakti*, is often more dangerous than her male counterpart, more able to cloak her fangs in the appearance of sympathetic kindness—the most insidious form of treachery opposing unaware souls.

"Arán Bán is reeling from his own negative energy that has been turned back upon him. You have greatly humiliated him, for which he will not forgive you. You have also significantly weakened him, which, as you observed, came as a considerable surprise to his inflated ego.

"He is furious that you snatched Glenna and Rory from his clutches. He was well on his way to permanently damaging their souls, if not actually destroying them, which would have been a tragedy for all of us. As it is, they remain vulnerable until they can be married and brought more directly into our protection.

"They are now acquainted with F. M. Bellamarre and Saint Germain, and have received some important instruction. Gathering them into the fold of our Friends of Ancient Wisdom here in America is key."

"Oh-h-h-h!" Sarah moaned, suddenly clutching her belly.

"Another false alarm?" asked Kevin warily.

"No-o-o-o," said Sarah with a grimace. "This is a real alarm."

Later, she and Kevin would laugh at how in this moment they both totally forgot the birth class instruction for her to breathe through a contraction. Instead, she sucked a breath in through her teeth and held it until the pain passed.

"Ah, I see we are moving quickly into our next event," said F. M. as he emanated profound love and gratitude to Sarah. She did her best to respond in kind. The exchange between them was palpable and Kevin likewise felt himself enfolded in the Master's deep affection.

"May I say to you both that the initiation you have passed was purposefully timed to occur before our Sarah should become happily engaged in the duties and joys of new motherhood. By completing this action before the birth of your children, their souls were able to participate from inner levels without burdening their tiny bodies.

"In your faithful meeting of this extreme challenge, you each have accomplished a further transmutation of your own individual karma and a deeper bonding with your True Self. This achievement will strengthen your communion with my ascended presence and will ensure my ongoing protection and sponsorship."

Sarah groaned again and grabbed Kevin's hand, squeezing it so hard he winced. "This is it, Hon. You'd better get me to the hospital."

"Will you excuse us, F. M.?" said Kevin. When Sarah was able to let go of his hand, he leapt to his feet and starting patting his pants pockets, looking for the "what-to-do-when-the-babies-are-coming" checklist. He was glad to discover it had not disappeared while he was battling his ancient adversary on the astral plane.

Sensing the excitement in the room, Hero, who had slept through the entire confrontation with Arán Bán, jumped up from the cozy dog bed he and Sprite shared and bounded over to his master, who had his car keys in hand. They must be going for a ride.

"Oh, no, Hero, you're not going this time," said Kevin a bit frantically as Sprite rubbed against his legs. "Oh, my gosh, I've got to call Debbie to come take care of you two."

"I will alert her," said F. M. graciously as he rose to leave. "Go with my blessing, my daughter and my son. You will find all in readiness when you arrive at the hospital. It so happens that your obstetrician is already there, along with the team of doctors and nurses I have selected to support the entry into this world of these two very accomplished souls who are your children.

"Godspeed, friends. May *An Síoraí*, the Eternal One, go with you."

Kevin couldn't remember driving to the hospital or shouting "Babies! Twins!" to the orderlies who appeared to be awaiting the MacCauleys' arrival at the emergency entrance. That part of the evening was a blur.

As F. M. had predicted, all was in readiness. Medical staff quickly scooped Sarah into a wheel chair and whisked her off to be prepped to deliver her long-awaited children.

A courteous parking attendant inquired if he might relieve Kevin of his car keys and suggested that the father-to-be was welcome to proceed into the hospital while his car was parked in the valet lot. His vehicle would be retrieved for him whenever he and his new family were ready to go home.

As soon as Kevin identified himself to the ER receptionist, two more nurses escorted him to the room where he would scrub and prepare for his responsibilities as birth coach.

"You'll take good care of her, won't you?" he said to the male nurse who was helping him into green scrub pants and shirt. "She's had two miscarriages. You can't imagine how important these babies are to her. If anything were to happen . . ." He couldn't go on.

"Don't you worry, Mr. MacCauley. We've got everything under control. All the best people are on duty tonight. The doctor has already checked on your wife and is pleased with how labor is progressing. Here she is if you want speak with her."

"Good evening, Kevin," said Dr. Levy, greeting him with a compassionate smile. He had that "oh-my-god-I'm-about-to-be-a-father" look on his face, although she didn't remember him having violet eyes.

"I can see you're ready for action. Go on in and sit with Sarah. She wants to have a natural vaginal delivery. We're going to give her every opportunity to do just that. So far all of her vitals and the little ones' are excellent. She seems brimming with energy."

"Thank you, doctor. All I want is two healthy babies. However you get them here is fine with me."

"I believe with our team at your side we can accomplish that, Kevin," said Dr. Levy in her most reassuring tone. She had grown to love this couple and was grateful to play her part in helping them become a family.

Sarah's violet eyes glistened as she beamed at her husband who was holding two tiny bundles of life, one on each arm. She had never been happier.

Delivering two babies naturally had not been without its anxious and very painful moments. However, their arriving early had certainly facilitated the process. Going through labor helped Sarah realize, as only a mother can, that giving birth is a mighty threshold for a woman as well as for the souls being born into this world.

Fortunately, she and her little ones had hung onto each other to within three weeks of her original due date. They were strong and had already nursed a bit.

Gareth and Naimh were both doing great. So was their father. Their *father*, Sarah exulted to herself. What a miracle to say that word without fear or sorrow! They had all come through.

"What fortunate babies these are to have you for their mother," said Kevin, gazing at his wife in utter bliss. "Are you sorry your own mother wasn't here for the birth? I know she wanted to be."

"I would have been happy for her to be here," said Sarah. "But this was our night, my love. You and me and great medical people and *An Síoraí*, the Eternal One. And two souls who were determined to get here. We're a real family now. I want to cherish this moment with you and our children."

Gareth started to cry and his sister joined in.

"I guess you'd better give me the youngsters. And could you find one of the nurses to help me with them till I get used to this nursing thing? I can see I'm going to be very busy for a while."

Thirty-Six

Éire, his beloved homeland, was disappearing from Rory's view under the clouds that hid the island like a protective veil. Oh, Ireland! He felt his soul reach out once more as if he were leaving his love behind.

But he wasn't. Glenna was in the center seat beside him. She leaned across him to catch one final glimpse of cliffs and sea, now far below, as their plane pointed its nose to the sun and gained altitude. Rory was surprised that she was weeping.

"I thought you'd be glad to be going home, *mo mhuirnín.*"

"I am," she sighed and sat back to face him. "Of course, it will be great to see my family and to have them all meet you. My dad already thinks you're 'just fine'—high praise the way he says it.

"But I'm going to miss Ireland more than I can say. I feel like I'm leaving part of my soul. I could hardly bear to say good-bye to Aunt Finn."

Rory reached over and brushed a tear from her cheek. "The feeling was mutual, I can tell you. After spending these weeks with her, I could see she's come to love you like the daughter she never had."

"I feel the same affection for her. My mom has been sick for such a long time that it's been hard for her to do a lot of mothering for my sister and me. In a way, our relationship has been somewhat reversed. I don't resent that for a minute. My mom is a loving, courageous person. She hasn't let her illness get her down. Still, she's had her limitations.

"Being embraced by Aunt Finn's generosity in all things has been a balm to my soul. I love her so much." Glenna choked up again. "And you, my darling husband." She caressed his cheek. "Thank you for finding me out."

"*Tá fáilte romhat, a ghrá.* You're welcome, my love." He squeezed her hand and put his arm around her, pulling her close so she nestled against his chest. He closed his eyes to savor the deep feelings that filled his heart to overflowing. Thank God for Aunt Finn, he thought to himself, remembering. How would they have survived without her?

As soon as she'd learned about their accident, she had marshaled the family troops into action.

A cousin would drive Glenna's father, Dennis, and her agent, Mel, to Athlone to deal with the *garda* who had secured the couple's car and all of their belongings. Craig would remain at Aunt Finn's to help with physical arrangements and contacting other family members.

Cousin Mary would go to the hospital each morning with fresh scones and soup from Cook. Then Aunt Finn herself would visit for an hour in the afternoons while they recuperated from their ordeal.

Once they were released, she had insisted on them staying with her. Of course, she couldn't possibly mind if they shared a room. Not with all they'd been through. Naturally, they would be married within the week.

What neither Rory nor Glenna told Aunt Finn was that, despite her flexibility as far as their sleeping arrangements, which she had supposed meant they were already intimate in the way of today's young people, they had held to the discipline they had maintained throughout their travels.

Cousin Mary had seen to their luggage and offered them a welcome cup of tea before they settled in for the night. When they were finally alone, they had taken one look at the large and very inviting four-poster bed in Aunt Finn's best guest room and laughed.

"One more test, *a ghrá*," Rory chuckled. "Shall we abstain for a few more nights and bring honor to our marriage bed?"

"Yes, my love," agreed Glenna. "If we were to do otherwise, I feel that we might lose the blessing of the rescue we've been given. Besides, I think we both need more rest, don't you?"

"I do. So how shall we arrange this? I could sleep on the floor. Aunt Finn's carpets are very plush. Probably not as hard as a monk's pallet."

"Yes, but too hard for a man who has been battling Vikings," said Glenna tenderly. "This bed is enormous. There's plenty of room for a row of these big tapestry cushions between us. I know they're not really necessary," she winked at him, "but perhaps, a bit helpful."

Rory shifted slightly in his airplane seat, enjoying his memory of how plans had been hastily pulled together for a simple wedding, which immediately grew in size to include his parents, who had anxiously driven down from Donegal, and a few dozen relatives from around the country.

Mel and Dennis had remained in the area, taking time for some sightseeing and helping out as members of the wedding party.

Merlin Wolffe had driven over from Dublin with a car full of friends from the Aeon. They were between plays and declared that they would have shut the theatre for a weekend if necessary to see their Portia marry her Bassanio.

Weather permitting, the ceremony would take place in Aunt Finn's back garden where a veritable wedding bouquet bloomed in shades of faded pink, peach, and ivory against a bright ruby and purple fuchsia hedge that hugged the stone wall marking the border of the enclosure that shimmered like a fairy land.

As her husband basked in his recollections, Glenna sighed into his embrace. She was savoring her own memory of Aunt Finn's kindness.

"You must wear my wedding dress," the grand lady had insisted when she invited Glenna into her bedroom to show her the pale blue chiffon bridal gown her own mother had worn at her wedding in 1920.

"Irish brides traditionally wear blue, you know. Two of my older sisters wore the dress and I, being the youngest, was allowed to keep it. Over the years I've loaned it to a few nieces who were the right size, including Rory's mother. I always made them return it. Now I know why. You are its rightful owner now, my dear. May it bring you joy on your special day."

Glenna had nearly swooned as she fingered the gossamer fabric. When she slipped into the delicate garment, she and Aunt Finn stood together in front of an antique oval mirror, admiring the gown's perfect fit as mothers and daughters had done for a century.

The simple fitted bodice topped layers and layers of chiffon that gathered at the waist in a braided rosette and fell gracefully like dozens of gossamer handkerchiefs, ending just above the vintage ivory leather lace-up boots that one of the nieces had bought for her own wedding and then had given to Aunt Finn for whomever was next in line.

As the hum of airplane engines droned on like a lullaby, Glenna could still feel the thrill of her dream wedding come true. She opened her eyes slightly and glanced up at her husband. She could tell he was rapt in more memories of that fairytale day.

Rory smiled to himself and felt a warm spinning in his chest as the image of his bride came to mind. He had honestly felt his heart stop in awe as Glenna appeared to float on her father's arm when he walked her from Aunt Finn's house into the garden.

The day had been gloriously sunny, the garden redolent with sweet fragrances after an early morning rain shower. Violin and cello music had been provided by two of the female cousins.

Glenna had said something about the girls being in love with him, but he had paid no mind to that tale. He was just grateful that his brother had helped him purchase new shoes and a dark blue suit appropriate for a groom. "We can't have you looking like a poor monk," he'd teased.

The whole process reminded Rory of a wedding he had officiated at nearly two thousand years earlier—before he, the druid Riordan, had broken Gormlaith's heart by failing to marry her. At last, life was coming full circle.

Now, here they were. Husband and wife. On their way to America. She to her family home and he to a new one. A destination different for each and similarly unknown for both.

The flight across the Atlantic was pleasant enough, despite the narrow seats that cramped Rory's long legs. "Flying west in daylight is a lot easier on the body than the east-bound red-eyes," Glenna commented, trying to find a bright side to the tight quarters.

"Fair play to that," said Rory gratefully. "I'd like to not look a beggar when I meet your friends and family."

"Remember, we've known many of them before," smiled Glenna. "And we have much to thank them for."

"What do you remember about our ordeal?" ventured Rory. "I haven't wanted to talk about what happened at Clonmacnoise. I didn't want to reactivate any memories that are better forgotten."

"Nor I," agreed Glenna. "Now that we're married, I feel like we're safe to share our experience. I haven't had any nightmares, have you?"

"No, and I think I would have if our souls had been actually damaged." Rory thought a minute. "Do you recall my thanking you for bringing the Deirdre episode to mind?"

"I do. I was afraid I had upset you, but you said my mentioning her name showed you that the record had been cleared. The energy was transmuted, so you didn't feel the pain any longer."

"I think the same thing occurred at Clonmacnoise. I don't understand exactly, but I believe a huge burden has been cleared from our souls. I know we had a lot of help from my friend, Ah-Lahn."

"And my friend, Alana," added Glenna. "I remember catching a glimpse of her as our souls were lifted out of darkness and into the arms of angels. I know she was praying for us. Do you remember any details?"

Rory hesitated briefly, then closed his eyes and carefully allowed his mind to touch the dramatic events that were even now fading from his memory.

"I remember sitting with you on the river bank when dragon ships appeared. We were running away, but then we fell. The rest is a blank until I began to feel incredible waves of light all around us, waking me from a kind of stupor.

"As I struggled to my feet, I heard someone calling my name and Ah-Lahn tossed me a sword so I could rescue you from a huge Viking."

"And you did rescue me, my valiant defender. That much I do remember," said Glenna. She grasped Rory's hand and kissed it earnestly. "You killed the giant and brought me home. You were victorious, my darling. You *are* victorious."

"I am," said Rory. "I can feel the thrill of success still resonating through my body. After who knows how many embodiments, I was finally able to save you. The pain of failure is gone. My soul is free from a sense of doubt and fear I didn't even know I still carried."

Glenna added, "I never knew how angry I was at you for leaving me behind—more than once in our lives together. But you didn't abandon me to that Viking. You came after me, Rory. You redeemed our ancient history, and freed my soul to love you with my whole being, as I have always wanted to do."

"We've a new life ahead of us, *a ghrá*," said Rory.

Glenna rested her head on his shoulder and sighed. "We have, *mo chroí*, we have indeed."

Big. That was Rory's first impression of everything American. Their U.S.-made aircraft was enormous. The landscape beneath him seemed to go on forever. The mass of people moving through customs at Newark airport unnerved him.

Biggest of all was the stupendous feeling of homecoming that welled up in his chest when the couple that had rescued him and his beloved from an unimaginable fate greeted them outside of customs.

"Welcome to America!" Sarah beamed. She did not try to stop the tears that overflowed her eyes as she gave Glenna and Rory each a one-armed hug. Her other hand held tightly to a two-seater baby stroller where a pair of infants snoozed peacefully.

Kevin didn't say a word at first. He and Rory simply clasped arms in the druid's double handshake of friendship and stared at each other like the long-lost compatriots they were. Feeling suddenly awkward, they laughed, exchanged a manly embrace, and heartily thumped each other on the back.

"Thanks for the sword," said Rory meaningfully while they gathered up his one large suitcase and Glenna's several.

"You used it well," said Kevin as he helped his brother druid with their luggage. "I was proud of you. I've missed you, my brother."

In that instant, Rory knew for certain he was home. The location would not matter much. Home in the States would always be in the company of these people. Here was his soul family. They had always been connected on the inner. Now their outer relationship held untold promise for a grand future. Rory felt that truth in his bones.

"Daddy! Mama!" Glenna cried at the surprise of seeing both of her parents waiting inside the entrance to baggage claim. She hadn't expected her mother to accompany her father to pick them up. But here she was, beaming from her wheel chair.

"I had to see my girl safely arrived," said her mother answering her quizzical expression. "And her new husband. Welcome, Rory. Please, call me Noreen. I hope we'll be great friends." She opened both her arms and invited the embrace which he readily gave her.

"Thank you, Noreen. 'Tis my hope as well. Dennis, thanks for letting us stay with you."

He extended his hand to Glenna's father who enfolded his son-in-law in a bear hug, then turned aside to knuckle away the tear that trickled down his cheek.

Thirty-Seven

Rory had to admit that September on the east coast of America was a glorious time of year. Days were still warm—at times a bit too warm. Skies took on a crystal-blue quality. And the sun had a way of hitting your eye at a perfect slant to remind you that the greens of summer were giving way to the fiery reds, oranges, and golds that would paint autumn's landscape in Nature's last hurrah of the year.

The fall equinox was a fine time to be married—again—he chuckled as he knotted the tie Glenna's mother had bought him. Though today he'd be wearing his blue suit, he had another new shirt and jacket, also courtesy of the Morrisseys.

Did they find him a bit shabby after all? Glenna had said not. 'Twas only their way of showing affection, and perhaps a bit of a nod to how little he had brought with him from Ireland.

"Are you ready, lad? We've got a bit of a drive ahead of us and we don't want to keep your bride waiting."

Rory's brother, Craig, poked his head in the doorway to the bedroom which groom and bride were sharing at Glenna's parents' house in New Jersey. She had left half an hour earlier with her parents so they would have time to get her mother comfortably situated at the church.

"Ready and eager to get to the *céilí* afterwards at Fibonacci's," answered Rory with a slightly weary grin. "I've not minded the idea of a second wedding in the States so Glenna's family can attend. But after a week of my wife, her mother, her sister, and her friend Debbie clucking around me like a flock of hens, I'm more than ready to declare myself a well-married man and get on with life."

"Come on, then, and we'll see you to the finish," laughed Craig.

The ceremony was to be performed by the elderly parish priest who had baptized Glenna and her sister and then, a few years later, served their First Holy Communion at the family church in New Jersey. As the reception would be held at Fibonacci's, he had gained permission to perform the service at a sister church on Long Island.

The priest's shock of white hair reminded Rory of Father Crispin, who had sent his blessing and best wishes from the monastery and the dairy farm. One of the younger dairymen had even composed a poem which he said was inspired by the bovine ladies whose moist brown eyes had seemed to droop when he'd told them their favorite attendant was living in the States and probably wouldn't be back.

Glenna and Rory had suggested a small wedding, but, of course, that was not to be. Not with all of the bride's parents' friends, a bevy of Irish cousins, and dozens of her pals from Broadway.

Best of all, Aunt Finn had flown in yesterday in the company of Mary, her young lady-in-waiting. Dennis and Noreen had invited them to stay at their home, but the elder lady had graciously declined in favor of luxury accommodations at one of Manhattan's most famous hotels.

"My dear Charlie and I stayed at the Plaza on our last trip to New York," she explained. "I'll probably spend a good deal of time being driven back and forth to Long Island, but this is important to me."

Glenna had snickered to Rory her suspicion that Aunt Finn also wanted to expand Mary's horizons before the girl saddled herself with a local Galway man whose prospects the matriarch considered beneath her niece's potential. Mary had caught the bridal bouquet in Ireland. Aunt Finn had kept a keen eye on her ever since.

Rory was a bit restive until he and his groomsmen, Craig and Kevin, took their places in front of the exquisite altar and gazed out at the eager faces of those who cherished his Glenna.

'Twas good to be back in church. He should not have been surprised at the sensation. His soul remained a reverent one. The monk in him would always be aware of that.

When Mendelssohn's "Wedding March" boomed out from the

grand pipe organ and Glenna appeared in the doorway on her father's arm, Rory felt his heart swell to near bursting. Could a man love so much and not lift right off to heaven? He vowed to always remember this moment.

"I will not fail you, *a ghrá*," he whispered to his bride as her father relinquished his daughter's hand into the care of the man he was already proud to call "son."

The couple turned to the priest and the ceremony began.

An hour later they were zipping through side streets—courtesy of Craig's ability to drive on the right—on their way to Fibonacci's where Róisín and an army of helpers had prepared a massive feast of hot and cold hors d'oeuvres, desserts, and a special punch that sparkled like one of Saint Germain's golden elixirs.

As their guests preceded them into the coffee shop, which had been closed for the event, Lucky met the bride and groom at the door. "Come with me," he said conspiratorially. He whisked them through the bookstore and up the stairs to the ballroom.

During the previous week they had paid a visit to Fibonacci's, where they had met their hosts along with several of the Friends of Ancient Wisdom. They knew about the bookstore and coffee shop. However, they were not aware of the ballroom or its spiritual significance.

They were intrigued to observe that an altar had been set up at the front of the room. Waiting for them were several of the people they had met last week. They were soon joined by Róisín, Debbie, Craig, Kevin, and Sarah—without the stroller.

"Where are the babies?" asked Glenna.

"Being spoiled by a dozen relatives," said Sarah with a twinkling smile. "Thank you for inviting everybody to the reception. Nobody understands the value of hospitality like an Irish family."

When Glenna had learned that Sarah's and Kevin's families were in New York for the babies' christening the previous morning, she had encouraged them to attend the *céilí*.

"I've never been to one," she explained, "but Rory says it will be like a barn dance with food. Lucky and Róisín are excited beyond words to play host, so please come." She was delighted when they all accepted.

Lucky signaled that he was ready to begin whatever was about to happen next.

"Glenna and Rory, please take your places here facing the altar. Saint Germain has requested that a brief ritual be performed to seal your marriage vows and to officially induct you into our community of Friends of Ancient Wisdom."

"I had no idea, did you?" whispered Rory to Glenna. She shook her head and turned her attention to Lucky, who was lighting the tapers on two enormous spiral candelabra that stood tall as a man on either side of the altar.

"Please follow along with the other celebrants. I believe you will find this ceremony familiar."

Surprisingly, they did. They joined Lucky and the others as they sounded the OM. The vibration in the room began to accelerate as the chant flowed naturally into a number of mantras that were as familiar on their tongues as a rosary.

Bride and groom both had beautiful voices, yet, in this moment, each sensed that they had never sung or chanted with such profound emotion. The ballroom resounded as if filled by angelic choirs, and the burnished gold disc behind the altar glowed like the sun itself.

When their devotions reached a maximum intensity, rays of brilliant white and gold and violet light flashed out from the center of the sun disc. Saint Germain stood before them in the full, radiant splendor of his ascended-master presence.

The room fell silent as he began to speak.

My dear friends, your devotion and courage have called me here today to offer you my blessing and, henceforth, my protection. Rory and Glenna, please kneel in reverence of *An Síoraí*, the Eternal One, in whose name I speak to you today.

You have done well to make your way to these shores. For

here your mission as twin flames does truly begin. Much labor lies before you, and much joy as you discover the opportunities that have awaited your arrival at this rung on the ladder of your souls' advancement.

Receive, then, my blessing. Listen for my words of instruction as they will come to you, often from surprising sources. For I am with you always, whether or not you see me with your outer sight. Be stalwart, beloveds, and we will succeed in the work we share.

Having so said, Saint Germain removed from his hand his magnificent ring of amethyst set in gold with rubies and diamonds. While intoning words and syllables that were given only to an ascended master to pronounce, he pressed this powerful crystalline focus first into their crown chakras, then to the third eye.

He concluded with prolonged contact on their heart chakras. After several minutes, he returned the ring to his finger and spoke once more.

Rise, my son and daughter. Please accept this benediction and the spiritual wedding gifts I have prepared for you. You have earned them and will retain them according to your attunement with my love, which I freely share with you on this glorious day.

Bowing to the bride and groom and with a smile that would illumine the darkest night, the Master dissolved his light body and disappeared from sight. The radiance in the room faded and the Friends of Ancient Wisdom gathered around Glenna and Rory in heartfelt expressions of congratulation.

"Now, my dears," called out a beaming Róisín. "I believe there's a grand *céilí* going on downstairs that's missing its guests of honor."

Thirty-Eight

E njoy your meal," said Róisín as the bridal party and friends made their way downstairs and gathered at the tables reserved for them. "My helpers have saved you plenty, and we'll delay the speeches until everybody has had their fill."

While they were eating, they were highly entertained by some of Glenna's Broadway friends who performed an impromptu version of *Riverdance*. Everyone was impressed with their enthusiasm and with the authenticity of at least a few of their steps.

If anyone had asked Glenna, she would have firmly declared that Fibonacci's coffee shop was more than half again the size it had been when she and Rory were here last week. Of course, some of the normal seating had been recommissioned to create long tables set along a side wall to hold the mountains of food, while chairs and smaller tables were placed around the perimeter of the room to accommodate a generous dance floor.

Even so, Glenna could not have imagined there would be space for the three-piece Irish band (provided by some distant cousins) playing vigorously in the far corner as well as the hundred or more guests, many of whom were gaily dancing jigs, reels, and polkas.

Some magic in this place, of which she was becoming increasingly aware, had surely pushed back the walls to their present position. No doubt the coffee shop would return to its normal size at midnight.

Glenna was strolling among the revelers now, greeting this one and that. Exchanging more hugs than she had received in her entire life. And catching snippets of conversation.

In the back of her mind a recollection was percolating that needed

some contemplation before she gave it voice. At the moment she want‑
ed to savor the tender sense of community that enfolded her like a soft
blanket. She cast her eyes and ears around the room and celebrated her
good fortune in the clusters of loved ones who had gathered to wish her
and her husband well in their new lives together.

She sought out Sarah who was watching the dancing, one hand never
leaving the handle of the stroller that held her babies.

"Your twins are gorgeous," commented Glenna. Sarah's blissful
expression sparked a surprising flutter in her own body. Mothers and
babies. Would she ever join that club? A possibility she had never con‑
sidered flickered for a moment. Maybe someday.

She looked more closely at the perfectly matched pair who gazed up
at her from their stroller. "Their eyes are violet. Are yours or Kevin's?"
She peered into her friend's hazel eyes.

"Off and on," admitted Sarah, "depending on what we're doing. I
think the twins' are going to stay this color. I hope so."

Glenna gently rested her hand on Sarah's arm. "I can never thank
you enough. Who knew that a letter your muse imagined years ago
would spark such an adventure."

"You're very welcome, and really the thanks go to Saint Germain.
He's the one who prepared us, just as he's preparing you and Rory for
whatever mission he'll send you on."

"Be that as it may," said Glenna squeezing Sarah's arm for emphasis,
"we will always be in your debt. For your service to us in this life and for
our ancient friendship that I pray we can fully enjoy now with our two
men together."

Sarah laid her hand atop her friend's and whispered. "Oh, I second
your prayer, my dear Gormlaith." Then she brightened. "And now I want
to hear about Glenna the actress. Did you love playing Portia? I was so
happy you got that opportunity."

"I did. Very much. There was such depth and humor in her. She
taught me a lot. I've got the Bard in my bones now, though I'm not sure
how that will work out being back in New York."

Sarah's gaze took on a faraway quality as if she were looking into the past. "I'm remembering what an accomplished bardess you were in ancient Ireland. Don't worry. Whatever you need of Gormlaith will come back to you—for transformation and for higher levels of consciousness."

She patted Glenna's hand and looked across the room at her husband. "That's what Kevin and I are discovering about our own past lives, especially as druids. There's plenty of human error in each of us that's ripe for transmutation, and even more good karma for mastery that's waiting to be reclaimed."

"I'll remember that," said Glenna. She felt her own memories kindle and sighed as some were more pleasant than others.

"You have no idea how grateful Kevin and I are that you and Rory pulled through," said Sarah, her face beaming. She kissed Glenna on the cheek and pulled tissues from her pocket for both of them.

Glenna was still dabbing her eyes when she heard her mother's voice. "May I join you?" Noreen was inquiring of Aunt Finn. The *grande dame* was currently holding court with a group of young actors and actresses who were absorbed in the stories she was telling them about her past theatrical triumphs in London and Dublin.

"Of course, my dear, wheel on in here beside me." Aunt Finn bent her head to hear what Glenna's mother had to say. Her voice was slightly hoarse, yet still reminded Finola of the woman's daughter.

Noreen spoke softly. "I want to thank you for loving my Glenna."

"That is easily done. You have a beautiful daughter, as I'm sure you know."

"I do, and it's a pleasure to see her thriving. I can tell by the sweet looks between you that a special affection has developed in your time together. My girl deserves all the love a mother can give her." Noreen felt her throat clutch.

"And she feels yours profoundly, *a chara.*" Aunt Finn laid her elegant hand on the pale one that rested on the arm of her wheel chair. "Glenna has told me so more than once. Never fear. Your daughter is grateful for everything you've given her."

"Thank you. To hear that from your lips means the world to me."

"Kerry, Kaitlyn, be careful with the babies. They're fragile." Ivy's twins were kneeling on the floor next to the stroller that cradled their infant cousins. Four little faces held each other in rapt attention.

"I'm sorry, Sarah. They've been chattering for days about spending time with Gareth and Naimh. I hope you don't mind."

"Of course not," said Sarah. She wasn't ready to tell her sister-in-law that the twins had told their aunt all about the babies she would finally bring into this world.

"Don't worry, Mommy," said Kaitlyn, in her most grown-up voice, as if she were speaking to a child rather than to the woman who had given her life. "We're telling them about the Rose Lady. Of course, they already know her. We're only reminding them."

Kerry had a question. "Aunt Sewah, do you think the Rose Lady will visit us here when we move to New York?"

"You're moving to New York?" Sarah's eyes went wide in astonishment.

"Probably," admitted Ivy. "I wasn't going to tell you yet, but these two have already made up their minds that they must live close to their cousins. I think they're working some kind of secret alchemy. The way all the pieces are falling into place is miraculous." Who are these children? she wondered to herself, as she often did, several times a day.

Sarah's face brightened. "Tell me about your plans. I thought Brian's business was going strong in New Bedford. I never expected you would leave, but we'd be thrilled to have you live closer."

"Would you, really?" asked Ivy. "I'd like that, too. Actually, we've been looking at the house down the street from you."

"I know that house," said Sarah thoughtfully. "It's roomy inside, but the yard is much smaller than what you have now. What if you have more children?"

"We're, uh, taking steps to ensure that doesn't happen," said Ivy. She felt her face turn several shades of pink. She and Sarah were still finding their way to the intimacy of sisters. Here was another step.

"These two are plenty. We can handle them and the business and each other, but not more. We'd love to be your neighbors, if you wouldn't mind."

"We'd love it. If you lived close, we could share baby-sitting duties, and you could give me pointers on surviving the first year with twins."

Ivy laughed. "Trust me, you'll never want to see another poopy diaper or get up for another 2:00 a.m. feeding. But then you do kind of miss their infant innocence when they start telling you how to run your life."

The heads of two young mothers bent down to check on their children. Kerry and Kaitlyn were talking away to their baby cousins, who seemed to understand every word.

"We'll know in a week or so if we're actually moving. Our partner, Hank, is more than able to handle business in the Boston area. Brian wants to expand into the New York market and to do that, we need to be here. He's already hunting for a building."

Sarah looked around the room. "It's a shame you can't buy the block Fibonacci's inhabits, but it's not available. Too many complications to explain, but I'm sure something will work out."

"I expect that's what Kevin and Brian are discussing right now," said Ivy, cocking her head in the direction of the brothers-in-law who were deep in conversation with Rory. Glenna eased over to hear what they were saying.

"I could really use your help with the bookstore," Kevin was telling Rory. "Lucky is talking about retiring in a year or two. We've got excellent employees, but I need a full-time manager on site. The businesses are doing well, so your salary would be more than sufficient. I'll be glad to sponsor you for a green card, if that would persuade you."

"I'm your man," said Rory without hesitation. "Did I hear you saying something about starting a school? I'm not credentialed in the States, but I am a decent history teacher."

"That's right. Sarah told me," said Kevin. His face lit up as he warmed to his long-held vision. "I'm thinking of an academy where students of all ages, even adults, can come for tutoring or simply to follow their interests. Brian, if you do expand your business to New York, would you be interested in teaching a computer class or two?"

"At some point, sure. Once I get the family settled. You say these buildings aren't available even though some of them are empty?"

"Unfortunately. At the moment, I'm not even sure if we'll be able to keep Fibonacci's here. I was trying to get a historical landmark designation, but so far that process is not looking good."

"Keep me posted. Maybe there's an opportunity for all of us."

Glenna was pleased to see that some of the young people Sarah identified as Kevin's philosophy study group had stopped by. The one called Noah was here with a date. Valerie and Finn were talking to Aunt Finn and laughing that they had the same name. A young woman named Jenny was trying to draw her fellow student into conversation.

"Why so glum, Rudy? Don't you like the party? This Irish music is fantastic."

"Yeah, the music's fine. I've got something on my mind, that's all. And, no, I don't want to talk about it."

"Okay, okay," said Jenny holding up her hands in surrender. "Just don't let your whatever-it-is spoil a good time. I'm going to find somebody who will dance with me."

"Glenna, there you are!" Her agent, Mel, wove through the crowd to speak to her. He gave her a big kiss on the cheek and hooked his arm in hers to guide her to a couple of free chairs.

"Come sit with me a minute. We need to talk about your auditions. I've put off the casting agents for are long as I can. They understand you've been getting married, but they have production schedules. You're in demand, but they won't wait forever."

"I know, Mel. Could you hold them off until Tuesday? I can give you an answer then. I need to talk to Rory and the folks here at Fibonacci's. The truth is, I'm not sure I want to go back to Broadway."

She put her hand on his shoulder when he started to object.

"Hear me out, my dear friend. You have some idea of what Rory and I went through in Ireland, though not all. What I can tell you is that the experience changed me. I no longer see myself singing and dancing my way into the hearts of millions. I'd like to do more Shakespeare, but not much else. I'm sorry to disappoint you."

"Of course, I'm disappointed. But not entirely surprised. You have a different look about you these days. I don't think your current head shots come close to capturing the lightness of being I see in those blue eyes. Call me on Tuesday and we'll talk. Don't worry. You have to follow your heart. I do understand that."

"Cake time!" called Róisín from the back of the room. She was wheeling in a gorgeous pink extravaganza of a wedding cake, parting the sea of guests with her cart.

"Rory! Glenna! Come do the honors. Gather 'round, everybody!"

"Speeches first!" called Craig as he made his way to the head table where the bridal party was gathering. He laughed as he waved a fist full of papers. "I've got mine. I've been saving these stories for years. Watch out, brother, you're about to be exposed for the rascal you are!"

Lucky stepped up to act as master of ceremonies. "Wait your turn, Craig. I believe the father of the bride goes first. Dennis? No? Oh, I see. Kevin, you're standing in for Glenna's dad?"

"Daddy, I didn't know you were such a weeper," whispered Glenna to her father and gave him a hug. He merely nodded and wiped his eyes on a damp handkerchief. The bridal party decided to be seated. Cake cutting would have to wait.

"I am honored to speak for the bride's family, who have approved this message," said Kevin with a broad smile. "Rory and Glenna, you may recall this blessing as one that was given at a wedding many centuries ago. At that time, I was grateful to receive it and did my best to live the remainder of my days according to its inspiration. I hope you will accept these thoughts as still true today."

The purpose of life is to be Love,
to embody its unity as unspeakable joy,
to flower in Earth's garden as a hundred blooms
that have no other purpose than to nourish bees
and perfume the world with their fragrance.

Imagine putting down roots,
drinking in pure air, reaching for the sun,

being washed by morning showers,
while basking in *An Síoraí's* great presence
that simply is the essence of being
that holds us all together.

He raised his glass of elixir punch. "Blessings to you both. A toast to the bride and groom."

"The bride and groom!" echoed the guests with a hearty cheer.

"Now you may speak, Craig," said Lucky, "and don't keep us here all night, lad."

"Well, now, I do have a few things to say," said Craig. He held up a scroll and let it unfurl several feet into the center of the room. Laughter erupted and Rory looked more than a little worried.

"Just pulling your leg, brother." He then proceeded to regale the crowd with the wit of a stand-up comedian till tears were rolling down a hundred pairs of cheeks."

Mel took note. He'd have to contact that young Irishman to see if he had more material.

"Rory, your brother's a hard act to follow," said Lucky when Craig finally took his seat, "but 'tis your turn to toast your bride."

Still chuckling and shaking his head in disbelief, Rory stood and cleared his throat. "I can only say to you and to her that I have waited for this woman longer than you can imagine. She has already stood by me through some very thick weather and thin chances. Glenna, you are my heart, my joy, the twin of my soul, the very essence of my life. I will love you till the end of time."

He raised his glass, "To my Glenna."

"To Glenna!" cheered the crowd.

"And now I believe the bride has something to add." Lucky invited her to stand.

Rory took his seat, a puzzled look on his face. Glenna rose to her feet, radiant as a sunbeam in her ethereal blue dress.

"Thank you all so much for this incredible celebration and for joining us in this very special gathering of friends. I'm sure that many of you here know just how unique a place is Fibonacci's. Since earlier today I have felt its magic reminding me of a tune I had forgotten.

"Rory, my love, I believe you will remember this song. If you do, will you sing it with me?"

He raised his eyes to hers, a question furrowing his brow. Then he knew. She had remembered the song from his dream. The song he had been certain she was singing the day he found her in the mist on Mount Brandon. He stood and, taking both her hands in his, joined his voice with hers as they had not sung together in several hundred years.

Come dance with me!
Spin 'round and 'round
where time turns into timelessness
and forever spirals on Life's great wheel.

Male and female are we now,
flame and water, water and flame.
You are the spark; I am the tinder.

I'll be the sun, you be the moon,
for we are souls that sail to sea
across the ocean of *An Síoraí*.

What a lively dance is this:
spinning into luminous realms,
weaving garlands 'round our shoulders
opening our hearts to playful spirits
who come to puncture pompous displays,
and carry us off on clouds of laughter,
singing songs only fairies know.

Come dance with me in Life's sweet play!
Your smile's been tucked away too long.

Rory kissed his wife to the loudest cheers yet. "And now, *a ghrá*, I believe we're meant to cut this mighty cake."

Epilogue

Debbie was sitting by herself at a small table, finishing her piece of wedding cake. The party was winding down. The musicians were packing up, and Róisín's army of helpers was in the process of putting away food and drink and restoring Fibonacci's to order so they could open for business on the morrow.

Glenna and Rory had departed a few minutes earlier. They were sharing Aunt Finn's town car back to the Plaza Hotel where she was treating them to a night in the honeymoon suite.

To Debbie's complete astonishment, she had caught Glenna's bouquet into which she was now staring as if it were a crystal ball. The heavenly scents of peach and ivory roses had her wondering if she would ever be as happy as her friend Glenna and her handsome Irish husband.

"What are the flowers telling you, my dear?" F. M. Bellamarre seated himself in the chair opposite her. She had not heard him approach and no one else in the room seemed aware of his presence.

"We were discussing irony," answered Debbie. How like her dear Master to appear when she needed someone to talk to.

"How is that?" he asked.

"I've just declined Craig's offer of marriage."

"He is a good man. He would make a fine husband."

"He would. Just not for me," said Debbie with conviction. "I like Craig very much as a friend. He's a great storyteller and I love that he's so Irish. And yet, we're not . . ." she hesitated.

"You are not equally yoked," completed F. M.

"That's my feeling, yes. We share interests in outer activities."

"But not inner ones," added F. M.

"Exactly. I don't go around talking about my inner experiences, but

I would like to share them with a life partner."

"And so you should," agreed F. M. "You and Craig have been good friends in the past, but your *dharmas*, your life work, are not the same. He is merely the prelude."

"The prelude to what?" asked Debbie.

"To the real match. You see, my dear, it often happens that as an advanced soul, such as yours, begins to awaken to the vibrations of her twin flame, others will tune in to the powerful resonance that exists between those souls, even if they have not met in this life. Those others will believe that love is for them."

"I haven't been thinking about my twin flame—whoever he might be," said Debbie. "But I can definitely see that being involved in both of his brother's weddings has given Craig an idea for himself."

"You have the right of it, my gifted seer. And don't worry. Even now I believe Craig's perfect mate has her sights set on her distant cousin. She was just waiting for him to stop looking at you."

Debbie thought a minute and then laughed out loud when she caught the image F. M. was holding in his mind.

"Mary? Aunt Finn's lady-in-waiting?"

"The very one. Those family connections are strong and they are perfect for each other. Besides, Aunt Finn will approve and will call Craig back to Ireland so she'll have a strong lad as well as an efficient lass to mind her in her final years—which are many yet."

"I might say that's a miracle, except that with you behind the scenes, my dear Master, I know all is well in order. So, to return to what you were saying about preludes—do you think my twin flame is approaching, as if I were a sort of homing beacon?"

"We shall see. I must tell you that there is considerable opposition from the brothers of shadow who do not desire your reunion. But when you succeed—as I know you will—the power of illumination you can bring to the planet will be a remarkable accomplishment and a blessing to all."

"Then I need to be praying for *An Síoraí's* will, don't I?" said Debbie.

"You do, my dear daughter. I will not reveal more to you tonight, though I would ask you a question."

"Of course," said Debbie solemnly.

"What do you observe about the marriage of Lucky and Róisín?"

Debbie looked over at the pair of them, working together, hand in glove, returning their business to readiness for Sunday's early morning customers.

"They are a wonderful team."

"They are. Do you know why? They are not twin flames. So what is unique about them?"

Debbie allowed her gaze to rest gently on her friends and let their soul vibration touch her heart.

"They are utterly unselfish," she said at last. "Everything they do with and for each other is one hundred percent selfless."

"Precisely," said F. M. with a pleased nod. "Remember their example when challenges come to you and your twin—as they must—and you will experience love and, by the grace of *An Síoraí*, the Eternal One, marriage in a very high form."

"That is a wonderful thought," said Debbie. Then she added with a grin, "Can you give me any clues about this mystery twin?"

"You will know him when you see him, though he may not recognize you at first. He's a bit blind at the moment, but he will come around—if you mind your expectations about who or what to expect. This gift has a difficult wrapping which you are more than able to unravel."

"Now you do have me concerned," said Debbie.

"You are well prepared, my daughter. Only remember what I have taught you. Your heart knows the way and would lead you well, even if you were not each day regaining more of Dearbhla's ancient skills as a very fine seer."

F. M. took both of her hands in his and focused his luminous violet eyes on her light green ones.

"Good night, my dear. Rest well and be prepared for adventures that will soon appear on the horizon. We have much work to accomplish together, you and I and our closest friends. I would have you ready to respond."

Read the story that sparked the
Twin Flames of Éire Trilogy,
and learn where the path of reunion began
for Sarah and Kevin and their Friends of Ancient Wisdom.

Sometimes to move forward
you have to go back...

Sarah and Kevin recognized their connection as twin flames within minutes of meeting at a party that neither had wanted to attend.

They soon vowed to stay together forever. Yet, seven years later they are on the verge of losing each other—and not for the first time. For as they discover through dreams and visions, their shared embodiments were often scarred by painful separations.

Will Sarah and Kevin find a way to reconcile past and present to escape a future neither of them wants?

Only going back in time will tell.

Don't miss these exciting sequels to *The Weaving* in the *Twin Flames of Éire Trilogy*

The Ancients and The Call - Sarah and Kevin believe they resolved all of their differences last summer in the luminous atmosphere of Éire. But that experience was only the beginning of their mission on behalf of twin flames. Now they know that love can be lost unless they return to Ireland and merge with their ancient druid selves, Alana and Ah-Lahn.

The Water and The Flame - Broadway actress Glenna and Irish monk Rory are worlds apart. The chances of their meeting and realizing they are twin flames are slim. Until the magic of Éire and the support of their Friends of Ancient Wisdom sends them on a voyage of self-discovery and overcoming malevolent forces they never could have imagined.

The Mystics and The Mystery - The path of reunion for twin flames has never been more perilous than for seers Debbie and Jeremy. Must she surrender her visions of the love they shared in the past for the sake of his soul? Or will he summon his inner strength to join her and other mystics to combat the ancient forces that have opposed them?

Turn the page for a preview of The Mystics and The Mystery— the exciting conclusion to the Twin Flames of Éire Trilogy

Debbie was one of the last guests to leave Glenna and Rory's wedding reception that had been held at Fibonacci's coffee shop on Long Island, New York. Their grand Irish *céilí* had been a glorious celebration, shared among family and colleagues and members of the spiritual community known as Friends of Ancient Wisdom.

She'd felt guilty about not helping the owners, Lucky and Róisín, clean up. But by the time she and her spiritual master and teacher, F. M. Bellamarre, had concluded their conversation, the work was done.

"Go on home, lass," Róisín had urged, her green eyes sparkling with motherly affection. "I can see that F. M. gave you plenty to think about."

"He certainly did," agreed Debbie, who had been embodied as Róisín's granddaughter and fellow seer in first-century Ireland.

"Thanks for understanding. I'll catch up with you in a day or two. My sister is expecting a large shipment of herbs at her store on Monday, so I'd best be there to help her stock the shelves."

Debbie was pensive as she drove the few blocks from the coffee shop to her sister Cyndi's health food store, called Conroy's To Your Health. She parked in the spot reserved for her behind the building, let herself in, and climbed the narrow stairs to her one-bedroom apartment above the shop where she lived simply and rent-free.

Not quite ready to retire for the night, she made herself a cup of tea from the relaxing blend she had created for the store and sat in the upholstered easy chair she considered an essential luxury. She wanted to meditate, but her thoughts were still on the Master's comments that her twin flame could be in the process of making his way to her.

Who is he? she wondered. F. M. had said she would recognize him, though he would likely not remember her. At least not for a while.

"He's a bit blind at the moment," were the Master's exact words.

Debbie was tempted to go searching on the inner for clues to the identity of her beloved, but she already knew her seer's sight would be closed on the matter.

Instead of probing where she ought not, she settled her awareness in her heart and visualized a beam of pure light and love radiating out to her soul's other half, wherever he might be in the universe.

She did not expect her love to make contact, so she was surprised when she felt a flash of acknowledgment. An image began kindling in her heart—and a vision of an ancient past life appeared as clearly as if the scene had happened only yesterday.

A strange wind was blowing through Egypt and it had nothing to do with the desert breezes that signaled the beginning of The River's life-giving flood season. This wind was sinister in a way that young Meke had never felt. At least, never so strongly as now.

She was not comforted by her mother's attempt at lightheartedness or her father's determination to distract her with the games of strategy they had played together since she was very small.

There was danger in the capital and she was aware that all of her sisters knew it. With her being the youngest of Pharaoh's daughters, they sought to protect her.

But Meke had always been an observant child. She'd learned that from her grandmother, the Dowager Queen Mother. The one who had died suddenly more than two years ago. The one who had told Meke she thought the priests who practiced the dark arts had poisoned her.

Is that what had happened? If so, who was next? Her father? Her mother? Meke knew they had enemies among the priests of the hidden god, Amun. The ones whose temples her father had closed in favor of the Sun God, Aten.

Since the loss of her grandmother, her dearest friend and closest confidante, Meke had felt lost. And now she was very afraid. She couldn't identify exactly what or whom she feared. Only that she could feel an enemy lurking, unseen, preparing to strike without warning.

Had her parents been warned? They were certainly making their own preparations, though for what, Meke couldn't be sure. Again, no one was talking to her.

"I am old enough to be included. My older sisters were already mothers by my age of fifteen," she complained to Mau-Ba, her grandmother's gorgeous black panther.

Meke had been taking care of the silky feline, who had stopped eating when her mistress died. The granddaughter had coaxed Mau-Ba back to life, though she could tell the animal's will to extend her own advanced years had not fully returned.

It was only a matter of time before the beautiful creature slipped away from this life. But Meke had vowed to give her love and the best of care for as long as she remained.

Somehow, telling her troubles to the regal panther encouraged Meke in her resolve to be included in matters of concern to Pharaoh's family. She sought out her mother and asked the questions of the elegant Queen that had kept her youthful mind awake at night.

"Mother, what is going on? Why are there whisperings behind pillars? Why are people leaving the palace and not returning? Are we going to leave? Should I be packing?"

"Oh, my perceptive daughter. You are my brightest seer. I should have known we could not shield you." Meke's mother could not hide the concern in her cool grey eyes.

"Yes, my girl, danger is upon us. The forces that oppose us have grown bolder since the death of your grandmother. The Dowager Queen retained enormous power, even at her age. Now that she is gone, a vacuum of influence and persuasion has been created with no one to fill it."

"Are you afraid, Mother?" Meke searched her mother's refined features. Truly, she was the most beautiful woman who had ever lived. The sculptors and artisans had all said so for many years.

"I will not give in to fear, but our world is shifting, Meke, and plans must be made. Your father will not abandon his work here, and I will not leave his side. Your older sisters and their husbands are committed to staying. But, my dearest daughter, you must go."

Meke shuddered. Hadn't she always known her fate was to leave the glittering world of Egypt that her grandfather and great-grandfather had created?

Ever since she was a small child, she'd had dreams of herself sailing on a ship—out across The Great Sea into whose vast reaches The River emptied its blue waters in the delta that spread like a giant fan.

She wanted to burst into tears. But she was Pharaoh's daughter. She would prove her maturity and her worth. She straightened her spine and focused her unusual light green eyes on her mother's face.

"When must I go, Mother?"

"We do not know, my daughter. Perhaps weeks or months yet. Be brave and learn your lessons well. You will need all of your skills and knowledge in days to come. And, yes, you should pack a bag, just in case the time arrives sooner than we expect."

"Who will escort me if you or my father or my sisters cannot?"

"That remains to be arranged, my girl. Do not fret about these things. Your father will ensure your safe passage. You know you are his treasure. He grieves to know you must leave our side, though it is for the best."

"Thank you, Mother, I am content," said Meke as she departed from the Queen's presence.

But, of course, she was not content. Who would go with her? Would *he* be the one? She breathed a prayer to Aten that her friend, the soldier Jarahnaten, might be her escort.

He was ten years her senior, a strapping young man with a muscular physique that glistened in the desert sunlight as he stood guard at the palace.

Jarahnaten also had a tender heart. It was he who helped her bring Mau-Ba around. He had a way with animals as well as with people. They had become fast friends and soon discovered they had more than a love of animals in common.

He seemed to know much about palace intrigues. He listened to what was said and was observant of people's actions. Sometimes others gossiped to him. But mostly, he just knew.

"You see things, don't you, Jarahnaten," Meke ventured one day. She focused her luminous green eyes on his dark brown ones, willing him to admit what she suspected. "You see into the next world like I do. I can tell. Your aura changes. Does mine, when I am seeing?"

"It does, my bright friend. But do not share our secret. There are spies everywhere. You must do your best to be invisible."

"Oh, yes, I know how to do that," said Meke proudly. "Grand-mother taught me."

"Good, then see that you practice. You may soon need that skill."

A shiver went up Meke's spine and she suddenly did not want this handsome soldier to leave her side. "Will you keep me safe, Jarahnaten?" she asked urgently.

"I will," he promised. "To the best of my ability, I will protect you." He prayed to Aten that his best would be enough.

Glossary & Pronunciation Guide

Letters ch (written phonetically as chk or hk) are pronounced as in loch

Names	**Pronunciation**	**Meaning**
Ah-Lahn	ah-LAHN	*Var.* Alan, noble, rock
Alana	ah-LAN-ah	Dear child
Arán Bán	rahn BAHN	White bread
Ciara	KEER-uh	Lovely dark features
Cormac	KOHR-mak	Son of the charioteer
Cróga	KRO-guh	Brave, hardy
Dearbhla	DAR-vla	Daughter of the poet
Finola	fih-NO-la	White shoulders
Gareth	GEHR-eth	Gentle, watchful
Gormlaith	GOORM-luh	Blue princess
Laoise	LEE-shuh	Radiant girl
Naimh	NEE-av	Luster, sheen
Óengus	O-en-gus	Singular strength
Riordan	REER-duhn	Royal poet
Róisín	roh-SHEEN	Little Rose
Saoirse	SER-shuh	Freedom, liberty

Place Names	**Pronunciation**	**Meaning**
Éire	AY-(rhe)	Ireland
Inis Cealtra	IN-ish KALL-truh	Holy Island
Lough Derg	LOCHK-derg	Largest lake on Shannon
Lough Gur	LOCHK-gur	Lake in County Limerick

Endearments	**Pronunciation**	**Meaning**
A chairde	a-CHKAR-dyeh	My friends
A chara	a-CHKAR-uh	O friend, my friend
A chara dhílis	a-CHKAR-uh YEE-lish	My faithful friend
A ghrá	a-GHRAH	My love
A pháistí	a-FAHSH-tee	My children
Buachaill cróga	BOOCKH-uhl KRO-guh	Brave boy
Mo chroí	mu-CHKREE	My heart
Mo mhuirnín	mu-WOOR-neen	My darling

Terms	**Pronunciation**	**Meaning**
An Síoraí	un SHEE-uh-ree	The Eternal One
Bealtaine	bee-YOWL-tin-eh	Spring fire festival
Ceann-druí	KYAHN-dree	Chief Druid
Garda	GAHR-deh	Police
Lughnasa	LOO-nuh-suh	Fall harvest festival
Seanchaí	SHAN-uh-chkee	Storyteller

Phrases with Pronunciation and Translation

Beir bua	bed-BOOA	Best of luck to you, literally: to be victorious
Céad míle fáilte	cayd-MEE-luh-FAL-tyuh	A hundred thousand welcomes
Ceart go leor	KERT-guh-lore	Okay
Céilí	KAY-lee	A uniquely Irish word for a big social gathering
Comhghairdeas	coe-VORE-dis	Congratulations!
Go hálainn	guh-HAH-luhn	Beautiful (or great!)
Go raibh maith agat	GUH-ruh-MAH-haht	Thank you
Go raibh míle maith agat	GUH-ruh-MEE-luh-MAH-hah-gut	Thank you very much
Le gach dea-ghuí	leh-GACKH-duh-GHEE	With all good wishes
Oíche mhaith	EE-uh-wah	Good night
Paisean	PA-shun	Passion
Sean nós	SHA-nohs	Old style, traditional Irish *a capella* singing
Seisiún	SEH-shoon	Session (gathering of trad. Irish musicians)

Slán	SLAWN	Good-bye
Slán abhaile	SLAWN-a-WILE-eh	May you go safely home
Slainte	SLAWN-ti (as in pin)	Health, to your health
Tá fáilte romhat	tah-FAHL-tyuh-ROOT	You're welcome
Tá tú go hálainn	TAH-too-guh-HAH-luhn	You are beautiful
Tá tú go maith	TAH-too-guh-MAH	You're good (you're fine)
Teach na beannachta	TACHK nuh BAN-achk-teh	House of blessing

About the Ancients

Many spiritual traditions have their own words and definitions for the manifestations of the Divine that mystics have been observing and experiencing for centuries. The following denote specific aspects of divinity as they are understood by the characters in the *Twin Flames of Éire Trilogy*.

An Síoraí, the Eternal One
> Higher Self, I AM Presence, The Magic Presence
> Individualized manifestation of the I AM THAT I AM
> Soul's unique God-identity, God Self, Divine Monad
> The soul's spiritual origin, source of one's divine plan
> Spiritual Home to which the soul longs to return

Because *An Síoraí*, the Eternal One, abides in Spirit, the human mind requires a mediator to bridge the communication gap between Spirit and Matter. This "translator" is referred to as the True Self.

True Self
> Higher Mind, Christ Self, Buddha Self, Real Self
> Source of intuition, the still small voice
> Inner guide, voice of inner wisdom

The True Self can be thought of as a personal, wise inner counselor who operates through the Higher Mind and communicates with both the Higher Self in Spirit and the human mind, which functions through the brain and does not have direct access to the I AM Presence.

In order to commune with *An Síoraí*, the Eternal One, the soul strives to become one with the True Self through various disciplines and practices designed to increase awareness of the Divine and dissolve limits of human consciousness.

Goddesses & Gods
> Cosmic beings who can hold the consciousness of a certain divine quality, such as God of Freedom, God Harmony, Goddess of Liberty, Goddess of Light, or God of Gold.

Adepts, Ascended Masters & the Great White Brotherhood

Adepts are men and women from every culture who have answered the call of *An Síoraí*, the Eternal One, passing many profound initiations, and bonding with their True Self. Some remain in embodiment for a time and others ascend, depending upon their calling.

Ascended masters are adepts who have balanced their karma, fulfilled their divine plan, and reunited with their Higher Self.

The Great White Brotherhood is a universal body of adepts and ascended masters who, like Saint Germain, have dedicated their attainment to the liberation of souls from the bonds of the lesser self.

"White" refers to the pure white light surrounding their forms. Certain devotees of the highest spiritual truth are also members of the Brotherhood, which is also very much a Sisterhood.

Ascended Master Saint Germain

After making his ascension in the year 1684, Saint Germain was granted a dispensation by the Great Law to once again take on a physical body so he might guide the monarchies of Europe in their necessary transition to more democratic systems of government.

Widely known as the "Wonderman of Europe," he appeared for decades as a man in his early forties, dazzling those whom he wished to assist with his diplomatic skills, alchemical feats, incomparable wisdom, boundless grace, and loving-kindness.

Despite his monumental efforts, stubborn monarchists failed to heed his warnings, and many fell in the horrific reign of terror during the French Revolution. Finally, after Napoleon's betrayal in the early nineteenth century, Saint Germain declared that he would not be seen for a hundred years.

In the twentieth century, the Master once again contacted embodied individuals, this time empowering them as his hands and feet in the physical, and as his messengers to deliver his spiritual teachings.

The *Twin Flames of Éire Trilogy* novels are the author's musings of what might transpire, should Saint Germain gain a new dispensation to appear in a physical form suitable for face-to-face communion with his friends of ancient wisdom.

Acknowledgements

Every life is a journey through many planes of existence, both seen and unseen. Every person, place, or event we encounter on that journey is a teacher. Their lessons may bring us exquisite joy. Or they may challenge us to the very core of our beliefs about ourselves and others.

All are equally valuable because they form the warp and woof of the tapestry we weave that becomes the fabric of the life we create.

Gratitude for life's ups and downs allows us to observe the threads that belong to our partnership with the spirit of An Síoraí, the Eternal One, that lives in the deepest part of us. And, if we are wise, we will also acknowledge the many threads that others have woven into this miraculous creation we could not have fashioned alone.

I am blessed with colleagues Paula Kennedy Kehoe, James Bennett, and Theresa McNicholas who share my passion for publishing.

Special thanks to my dear friends Dónall Ó Héalaí and his father, Dr. Pádraig Ó Héalaí, for their priceless assistance with the Gaelic terms that speak to the beauty of the ancient Irish culture that inspired *The Twin Flames of Éire Trilogy.*

I have done my best to make faithful use of their suggestions. Any errors in spelling, usage, or pronunciation are mine alone.

These novels reach far back in time and point to a future still that is still unfolding, which gives me the opportunity to gather several millennia of thanks and send them out to countless teachers and mentors for all the lessons, including more than a few dark nights.

The story of twin flames belongs to all of us. Thank you, Mother, for letting me tell one small part of it. And to my beloved Stephen, whether together or apart, I live in you as you live in me. Thank you for helping me finally understand what that means.

Cheryl Lafferty Eckl has played many roles since she began her career as a singer/actress in musical theatre. Award-winning author, mystical poet, professional development trainer, life coach, inspirational speaker, and retreat facilitator.

These days, her favorite role is *seanchaí*—Irish for storyteller.

If you ask, she'll tell you that it's her love of Ireland—its people, language, land, and culture—that continues to inspire characters and stories in thrilling novels that follow the trials and triumphs of twin flames who sometimes struggle and very often succeed in unlocking Love's mystery.

Learn more about Cheryl's books, videos and audios
at www.CherylEckl.com.